'You're in a position to become better acquainted with Lord Camberline, but your involvement will be strictly limited to social engagements and nothing else,' Bart insisted.

Her astonishment gave way to a sideways teasing smile. 'You mean I won't be able to point a pistol at other people or you?'

'You can point a pistol at me any time you like.' He enjoyed this saucy Moira, and was elated by her tacit agreement. It meant they didn't have to part just ~~~~

'I can't sin~~~~ ~~~~d discuss her~~~~

'You can if~~~~ ~~~~ith her. There's ~~~~ ~~~~on tonight at the Royal Academy and Lord Camberline and his mother will be there.'

'If they suspect anything, what shall I say?' she asked.

'You'll have to come up with something.'

'Oh, well, if it's as easy as that I should have no trouble!' She laughed.

He winked at her. 'Welcome to the world of intrigue.'

Author Note

Writing *Courting Danger with Mr Dyer* was a new
challenge for me. Some of my previous stories have
had elements of intrigue in the plot, but intrigue wasn't
as critical to those stories as it is to this one. It was fun
to write the story not only from Bart's perspective as
a member of the espionage community, but also from
Moira's position as an outsider. Her innocence where
plots and treason are concerned was kind of like mine
when I began my research. I didn't realise how much
cloak-and-dagger work was going on during this time
period.

In order to craft the treason plot that Bart and Moira
work to uncover I did a great deal of research on
spying and plots in and around the Regency period.
William Wickham and Mr Flint—two men I mention
in the story—are real people who helped pioneer
early British espionage and the British Secret Service.
It was Mr Wickham's involvement in the London
Corresponding Society's plot to assassinate the
Prime Minister in 1793 that inspired the plot in
Courting Danger with Mr Dyer. I also reached a little
farther back into history to research the Gunpowder
Plot and Guy Fawkes. Not having grown up with the
Bonfire Night tradition, it was fun to learn about all
the key players involved and how it was eventually
uncovered and thwarted.

I hope you enjoy following Bart and Moira through
the danger and excitement of saving Britain and
falling in love!

COURTING DANGER
WITH MR DYER

Georgie Lee

Published in Great Britain 2017
by Mills & Boon, an imprint of HarperCollins*Publishers*
1 London Bridge Street, London, SE1 9GF

© 2017 Georgie Reinstein

ISBN: 978-0-263-92606-4

Printed and bound in Spain
by CPI, Barcelona

A lifelong history buff, **Georgie Lee** hasn't given up hope that she will one day inherit a title and a manor house. Until then she fulfils her dreams of lords, ladies and a Season in London through her stories. When not writing, she can be found reading non-fiction history or watching any film with a costume and an accent. Please visit georgie-lee.com to learn more about Georgie and her books.

Books by Georgie Lee

Mills & Boon Historical Romance

The Business of Marriage

A Debt Paid in Marriage
A Too Convenient Marriage
The Secret Marriage Pact

The Governess Tales

The Cinderella Governess

Scandal and Disgrace

Rescued from Ruin
Miss Marianne's Disgrace
Courting Danger with Mr Dyer

Stand-Alone Novels

Engagement of Convenience
The Courtesan's Book of Secrets
The Captain's Frozen Dream

Visit the Author Profile page at millsandboon.co.uk.

To my family, who are always so supportive.

Chapter One

London—1813

'You must do it.' Bartholomew Dyer banged Frederick Chambers, Fifth Earl of Fallworth, hard against the wall, trying to knock the fight back into him. The unprovoked swing the Earl had taken at Bart gave him hope it could be done. 'We need you.'

'I can't, don't you understand?' Freddy growled, fingers biting into Bart's forearms. 'I've given enough. I won't give any more.'

'Let go of him.' The lady behind him punctuated her command by cocking a pistol hammer.

Damn. Bart cursed under his breath. She'd just made the weapon more dangerous. If she wasn't competent with it, the ball would tear through him and the Earl under his elbow.

Bart took his arm off Lord Fallworth's chest and stepped back.

'Moira, it's not what you think,' Lord Fallworth choked as he leaned away from the wall and tried to wave his sister off.

Bart ground his teeth at the mention of Lady Rexford and the way it made his neck, and something much lower down, tense. A maid or the elderly aunt would have been preferable to Lord Fallworth's sister, and his one-time fiancée, having stumbled in on them. The young Dowager Countess of Rexford was as stunning as she was a complication Bart didn't need.

'Then what is it?' She kept the pistol pointed at Bart's chest and her beautiful green eyes fixed on his.

She'd changed since he'd last seen her five years ago when she'd been a young lady new to London and he an ex-soldier beginning his career as a barrister. The innocent, uncertain tilt of her head was gone, replaced by a confidence he imagined widowhood and the deaths of her father and sister-in-law must have given her. It made her sharp cheekbones set in an oval face and framed by blonde hair more striking and more tempting. He knew better than to fall for it. He had no desire to hear again from her family how he wasn't good enough for her or to have his official duties curtailed by her incorrect reading of this situation.

Bart bent into a bow. 'Good evening, Lady Rexford. It's a pleasure to see you again.'

'I can't say the same, Mr Dyer. If you weren't one of the most celebrated barristers in England with as many magistrates in awe of you as the public, I'd put a ball through you and end your scourge on this house.'

He opened his arms to increase the size of her target. 'Why not take the chance?'

She frowned at his defiance, the disapproving yet intriguing downturn of her mouth tempered by the still-raised weapon. 'Since I have no desire to be hanged for murder, I demand you leave at once and never return.'

Any other day her order would have been charming. This morning it was merely irritating. 'Your aunt used to make the same request and it didn't work.'

'I'd like to think I'm a touch more persuasive.' She nodded at the still-raised pistol.

He admired her desire to protect her brother, even if it was woefully misguided. However, what had brought him here in defiance of her

widowed aunt's dictates was far more important than his or anyone else's life.

'Moira, it's all right. Leave us be, we have
business to discuss.' Lord Fallworth took up
his drink and drained it.

'What business? Which gaming hell to
visit?' she challenged. 'Don't think Aunt Agatha didn't write to me about what you got up
to with Mr Dyer when you were in London
two years ago. I won't have you ruining yourself again a mere week after we've returned
to town.'

Bart suppressed a growl of irritation. If
Lady Rexford knew the real motives behind
those nights out, she'd lower the pistol, throw
her arms around his neck and thank him for
his service to their country.

'Freddy, I won't leave you to the influences
of a man like this.' Lady Rexford waved her
free hand at Bart. 'Not with you already so
vulnerable since Helena's—'

'You needn't say it.' Lord Fallworth snatched
up the brandy decanter and refilled his glass.

Bart opened his mouth to tell Lady Rexford
to step out of things she didn't understand,
then closed it again. With her brother slipping
into a liquor-induced fog, his suitability for this

mission waned while Lady Rexford's possible involvement played on him like a hunch. She stood straight, one foot in front of the other to make her gown drape across her shapely thigh. The firm set of her full lips beneath eyes as focused as a fox's made him take more notice of her than the pistol or her reluctant brother. No one would suspect a woman. Bart knew better. 'You're friends with Lady Camberline?'

A crease of confusion appeared between her shapely eyebrows. 'Not friends so much as acquaintances. We're both patrons of the Lady's Lying-In Hospital.'

'But you know her well enough to call on her and to receive invitations?'

'No, Bart, don't do it,' Lord Fallworth warned.

Lady Rexford glanced back and forth between Bart and her brother. 'I do.'

'Are you attending her ball tonight?'

'Yes, but what does that have to do with anything?'

'I said don't do it.' Lord Fallworth banged his glass down on the table, making the brandy slosh over the sides.

Bart ignored the glowering Earl. 'I need your help to—'

'No, not her.' Lord Fallworth grabbed Bart by the lapels and gave him a shake. 'I lost my wife to plotting scoundrels. I won't lose a sister, too.'

If Lord Fallworth were any other man Bart would drop him like a sack of flour, but the other man had sacrificed a great deal by helping Bart two years ago. Until today, Bart hadn't realised how much it'd changed his friend.

'What are you talking about, Freddy?' Lady Rexford asked in a shaky voice. 'What scoundrels?'

Bart exchanged a concerned look with Lord Fallworth. His sister didn't know the truth about Lady Fallworth's death, but then few people did. This wasn't the moment to enlighten her.

'Nothing,' Lord Fallworth answered in a voice to convince no one. 'I misspoke.'

Lord Fallworth eyed Bart with unease as he let go of him and shifted back. Bart studied him, aware of the pain he was causing his old friend. He would leave him in peace if he could, but this time, there was too much at stake. 'If I don't uncover their plans soon, the Government, the King could be brought down and Napoleon installed on the throne.'

'What are you two talking about?' Lady Rexford demanded.

'Let me tell her and allow her to decide,' Bart asked the other man in the same measured tone he normally used when delivering bad news to a client.

Lord Fallworth retrieved his drink, his signet ring clanking against the glass. Then he slumped down into his chair, the promising fight he'd shown when he'd lashed out at Bart gone. 'Go ahead then, tell her.'

'Tell me what?' Lady Rexford lowered the hammer with impressive and surprising skill. Anyone else would have slammed it down and set the damned thing off. It was another mark in her favour.

Bartholomew took a deep breath. What he was about to reveal could place his entire mission in jeopardy if she whispered it around the wrong tea table, but with Freddy unable to assist him, Lady Rexford might be his only chance. She'd proven herself discreet in the matter of their debacle of an engagement, making sure no one outside of her family and his had learned of it. He was certain he could count on her prudence again.

Bart turned to her with the same deference he showed when approaching the bench. 'I'm not just a barrister, Lady Rexford, but a stipendiary magistrate given power by the Alien Office to root out traitors working to undermine our country. I have a number of men under me, one of whom used to be your brother. The many nights I came here to collect him two years ago, the ones your aunt wrote to you about, weren't to waste money at cards but to uncover a plot by Lord McCreery working on behalf of the Scottish Corresponding Society to assassinate the Prime Minister. We spent nights drinking and gambling with many of the men involved with the society in order to learn the details of the plot. Alcohol is a great opener of mouths. It makes people forget themselves.' He cocked one suggestive eyebrow at her. The full lips he'd savoured five years ago drew tight at his reference to their past and the time they'd spent on Lady Greenwood's balcony in each other's arms. Bart ignored the appealing blush sweeping her cheeks and continued. 'Thanks to your brother's help, we stopped the plot, but now there is another. A group called the Rouge Noir, a collection of London aristocrats with ties to Napoleon, is actively working to undermine the Crown and install the Emperor on the throne.'

'You expect me to believe titled gentlemen are plotting to bring down the Government?'

She crossed her arms, the gun dangling beneath one elbow as she stared at him in disbelief, as sceptical as he'd been when Charles Flint had first approached him on William Wickham and the Alien Office's behalf. Even after his work uncovering fraud in order to protect his clients, and his time as a captain with the English army in Austria, the story had been hard for him to swallow. It must sound preposterous to a lady who'd been sequestered on a country estate for the last few years.

'I know you despise those of our class, but I didn't think you'd sink so low as to accuse them of treason.'

Bart narrowed his eyes at her, struggling to remain as collected as when he was arguing a case. She'd struck a nerve, one of the few people in a long time to do so. 'I may not like a great swathe of the nobility, but I swore to protect them. I won't see any of my countrymen, not the poor or the rich, trampled under Napoleon's boots.'

'It's true, Moira,' Freddy concurred. During

their interrogation of the Scottish Corresponding Society conspirators, there'd been whispers
of the Rouge Noir but never anything solid,
until recently.

She turned her shock on her brother. 'It can't
be.'

'It is,' Bart insisted. 'The Government is
weak, with no strong prime minister and a
handful of colourless men running things. The
King is mad and his son a worthless dandy. If
the Rouge Noir can wipe them out it will bring
this country to its knees, allowing Napoleon
to sweep in and restore order through tyranny.
I and my network of informers were able to
ferret out a number of lesser members of the
Rouge Noir some time ago and we thought
we'd disrupted the group enough to stop them.
Then, last week, a courier was caught in Dover
with a message for Napoleon telling him to
prepare for the coming of the Rouge Noir. I believe something is going to happen and soon,
but I don't know what and I don't know where
but I must find out. I suspect some in Lady
Camberline's circle to be involved, but I have
no way to get close to them without drawing
suspicion.'

'If you think Freddy will help you, you're

wrong.' She crossed her arms and stepped between Bart and Lord Fallworth, as if protecting her brother. 'He isn't well enough to have any part in your scheme.'

'I'm not asking him to have a part in it. I'm asking you.'

Moira dropped her arms to her sides. This wasn't real. It couldn't be, but the hard angles of Mr Dyer's chiselled face and the steeliness of his dark eyes told her it was. 'Me?'

'Lady Rexford, I need you, England needs you,' Mr Dyer pleaded. This was the first time they'd spoken since the morning five years ago when she'd called off their engagement with fumbling words about her duty to her father and upholding the Fallworth reputation. He hadn't taken it well, railing at her about the misguided priorities of the aristocracy and her failure to stand up for what she wanted. She'd tried to make him understand her father's concerns for her and her future, but he'd refused to listen. They'd parted with no small amount of bitterness on each side, and when Aunt Agatha's frantic letters about Freddy had begun to arrive, Moira had thought she'd avoided a bad mistake. Yet all along Bart had been fighting for something more worthy than bragging rights about a card win. 'You can get close to Lady Camberline and many of those in her circle, especially the ones I suspect.'

'You're Baron Denning's fifth son, so why not use your own connections?' she protested, unsure how to answer him. Surely she was not so important to the security of the Government.

'My work as a barrister and my father's railing against it—' the lines at the corners of Bart's brown eyes tightened, then relaxed '—have prejudiced too many against me and his rank isn't high enough to garner the notice of a dower marchioness and her marquess son. However, you can use your familiarity with the Camberlines to gather information on suspects.'

'Who might kill me if they discover what I'm doing.' She knew little about plots and schemes, but she'd read enough stories about them in the newspapers to understand what happened to those who dabbled in intrigue.

'If you choose to help me, I promise to do all I can to protect you, but I'll be honest and say there are no guarantees.' He shot Freddy an apologetic look to make her brother sink deeper into his chair, the darkness of the last two years shadowing him again.

Moira wanted to throw her arms around her brother and comfort him the way she had when, still in mourning for her own husband, she'd come to Fallworth Manor to help take care of Freddy and Nicholas, her nephew, and usher them through the darkest time of their lives after Helena's death. Now Mr Dyer was asking her to place herself in danger and risk having her steadying influence on Freddy and Nicholas ripped from them, leaving them to flounder as they had when Helena had been killed by a cutpurse. 'I can't help you.'

'Do you understand what's at stake? My parents and brothers will all be sacrificed to Rouge Noir's great vision of Britain and so will you, Lord Fallworth and your nephew if they succeed. With your help, we can stop them.'

'I do understand what's at stake, Mr Dyer, but while you ask me to risk my life for king and country there's a little boy who sleeps without his mother.' She tossed the pistol on the table besides her and it hit the wood with a rattle. 'I can't abandon them any more than you can leave this Rouge Noir to hurt England. My reason may not be as gallant as war or spies, but it's a good one.'

He straightened a touch, his stoic expression revealing nothing of his thoughts. With his impressive height and piercing eyes beneath dark brown hair cut short, he was an imposing man and clearly used to getting what he wanted. She braced herself for more arguments, expecting him to continue pressing her the way her family did whenever she resisted their plans for her. To her amazement, he didn't.

'You're wrong, Lady Rexford, I do understand your importance to your family and I appreciate all you've done for Lord Fallworth in his grief,' he offered in the deep voice she'd once heard in her dreams before the wedding bells had silenced it. 'You're right, your place is here with your loved ones. My apologies to you both. If you give me your word you won't repeat to anyone what we've discussed, I'll leave you be.'

Moira's shoulders settled at his admission and the reverent compliment in his words. He hadn't been so accepting of her refusal five years ago, but the situation had been so poorly handled by her aunt, and her, she couldn't blame him for the way he'd reacted. He was nothing but a gentleman today and she must meet his honour with her own. 'I promise not to say anything to anyone.'

'Thank you.' He bowed and, without another word, left.

She should have been happy to see the back of him, but she wasn't. In his eyes had been the night at Lady Greenwood's ball when, for the first time since before her mother's death when she was fourteen, she'd acted recklessly and free of constraints. She wished she could have held on to the young woman who'd briefly blossomed under Bart's admiration, but marriage to Lord Rexford had made it impossible.

Parting with Bart was for the best, she told herself as she had so many times before. She fingered the cold wooden handle of her father's duelling pistol on the table beside her, pointing the barrel away from her. Her father had viewed marriage to Lord Rexford as a way to ensure she would be taken care of after his death and she'd gone along with it in an effort to ease his anxiety so he could die without worry. Instead of a young and robust husband, she'd wedded an old man whose failure to give her children had ensured almost everything he had went to his nephew at his death. There'd been no reason for her father to think things would not work out as he, and even Moira, had thought they would.

Freddy heaved a weary sigh and pushed himself out of the chair.

'Perhaps you should go upstairs and rest,' she suggested, not liking how haggard he appeared this morning. It'd been a long time since he'd looked this low and she feared the events of this morning had ruined all the progress he'd made in the last few months.

'No, I must speak with Miss Kent about Nicholas's clothes and the Falkirk party.'

'I can speak with her if you'd like and remind her to be mindful of the cost of having the clothes made up.'

He reached out and clasped her hand and gave it a squeeze. 'That's very thoughtful of you, but I think it's time I took more of a role in my son's care.'

'Of course.' She covered his hand with hers, encouraged by his willingness to handle matters. Perhaps it meant the dark times were finally fading and he wouldn't be as dependent on her as he had been before. The thought heartened and troubled her.

Nicholas's laughter followed by the high

voice of his young nurse echoed through the house. The sound of it seemed to brighten Freddy even more and he let go of Moira.

'I'll speak to her now.'

Moira followed her brother out of the study and into the hall, glad to see him walking with his head up, at last thrilled to greet his son instead of displaying the uninterest in him, his estate and everything he'd shown after Helena's death. Even before their father's passing, Fallworth Manor had been in some straits due to a number of bad harvests. Freddy ignoring it all after Helena's death had made matters worse. It'd taken a great deal of hard work by Moira over the last two years to make it finally turn a profit instead of sinking deeper into debt. However, there was still a long way to go before any of them could live comfortably on the income.

They reached the entrance hall, met by the drumming of small footsteps down the back hall and the dark hair of her nephew as he rushed to meet them.

'Here's my sweet angel.' Moira knelt down and held out her arms.

'Aunt Mara.' Nicholas threw himself against her and wrapped his chubby arms around her neck.

She rose, holding the squirming three-year-old who smelled of milk and wet dirt. 'How is my little love today?'

His deep green eyes widened with excitement. 'Birdy day.'

'You saw a bird today?'

He slipped two chubby fingers into his mouth and nodded.

'Nicholas and I just returned from the park,' Miss Kent, the young nurse, explained when she approached. Only eighteen with a round face and petite figure, she was the youngest daughter of a baronet who lived near them in Surrey. With few prospects in the country, she'd come to Moira to offer her services and had proven an excellent choice for Nicholas's nurse. 'We took some old bread to feed the ducks.'

Freddy took Nicholas from Moira and held him firm against his chest. 'Perhaps Cook can give you a few more crusts and you can feed the birds in the garden.' His suggestion made Nicholas clap with delight. Freddy smiled at the boy and then Miss Kent, who blushed and stared at the floor. 'Miss Kent, if you'll come with me and Nicholas to the nursery, we can discuss Nicholas's new clothes and the Falkirk party.'

'Of course, my lord.' She dipped a curtsy to Moira then started upstairs after Freddy, who carried Nicholas, asking more questions about the park and what he'd seen.

Moira brushed little dusty fingerprints from her skirt, trying to ignore the twinge of jealousy in her chest. She loved the boy as much as she did her brother, but no matter how much she took care of Nicholas, he was not hers. She had no child to comfort her in her widowhood. It was the largest regret of the many she carried from her marriage.

'You spoil Nicholas,' Aunt Agatha remarked, entering the hall from the sitting room. She wore a copper-coloured morning dress which followed the curve of her ample and well-concealed bosom before flaring out to drape her stout form. Tight curls pinned to the sides of her head were touched with grey and further decorated by a turban of yellow silk pressed down over her coiffure.

'I can't help it.' Moira attempted to straighten the rather lopsided arrangement of lilies in a vase on a side table.

'Some day, you'll have your own to spoil.

After all, I don't see why you shouldn't. Some gentlemen prefer a lady of, shall we say *experience.*'

'Aunt Agatha!' She wasn't sure what astonished her more, Aunt Agatha's bluntness or how little experience Moira had garnered with Walter before his heart troubles had taken him. Intimate relations were the one aspect of marrying again she did not look forward to. She'd never cared for the deed the few times Walter had bothered her, but she'd done her duty as a wife, praying each time it would result in a child. She stilled her hands on the lilies. This sacrifice had been the most bitter because it'd been for nothing.

'It's true. After all, with your husband's estate and the bulk of his wealth having gone to his nephew, gentlemen won't pursue you for your fortune,' Aunt Agatha proclaimed and Moira snapped a brown lily off its wilting stem and laid it on the table, biting back a few choice words. Her aunt's candidness was growing more vexing with each passing year. 'Besides, with Freddy ready to face society again, I don't expect him to remain unmarried for long and then you will be nothing but the widowed aunt, and we can't have that. But let's not fret about it now. We have the whole Season to worry about it.'

Having dropped her truth, and careless of the craters it left, Aunt Agatha patted Moira's arm, then headed down the hallway.

Moira stared at the blue willows painted on the vase, the reality she'd suspected since leaving the country revealing itself a little too loudly for her liking. If Freddy did remarry, his new wife would become the mistress of Fallworth Manor and Nicholas's care would become her responsibility, and not Moira's. Should Moira fail to take this Season, she might find herself without purpose at Fall-worth, with no real place and nothing but endless and lonely days to fill. Having Aunt Agatha state it with her usual bluntness didn't help ease her concerns. Neither did seeing Mr Dyer again.

She frowned at the memory of Mr Dyer rather than the tilting flower arrangement. When she'd crept along the hallway, her heart racing while she'd carried the weapon after hearing the raised voices downstairs, she'd never imagined it would be Mr Dyer she'd meet. Moira's cheeks reddened at the memory of her aunt, in this very hall, laying out to him in blunt terms how his lack of station made him an unsuitable suitor. During her aunt's tirade, Moira had stood by, unable to meet Mr Dyer's eyes. With her father's health failing, she hadn't been willing to cause him more grief or to throw the house into further turmoil by defying him or her aunt.

Except her father was gone now and Mr Dyer had returned. The flicker of life which had been dormant for so long flared inside her, growing brighter at the thought of him.

He didn't come here to court me. She walked back to the study to retrieve the pistol and return it to its box, trying to put the encounter, and his proposal, out of her head, but she couldn't. What he'd told her, like his confession about his work, had changed everything she'd come to believe about him since their failed engagement.

In the study, Moira slid the pistol off the table and turned it over in her hands, admiring the fine scrollwork on the metal. Even after she'd treated him like a common thief, he'd had enough confidence in her to believe she could assist him with something as important as saving England.

I wonder if I could help him? It wasn't her

habit to deny anyone seeking her assistance, but she couldn't involve herself in something like this. She'd returned to London to re-enter the world, not to entangle herself in the affairs of state, but if Mr Dyer was right, then even innocent diversions had the potential to embroil her in a great deal of danger.

No, I can't get involved. Her place was here with her family, not out pursuing traitors. Turning on her heel, she made for upstairs. Helping Mr Dyer was a ludicrous idea and one she could not shake.

Chapter Two

'Bart, I didn't think I'd see you in Rotten Row today.' Richard, Bart's eldest brother, the heir and the only Dyer son who could do no wrong in their father's eyes, laughed as he manoeuvred his horse beside Bart's. 'I didn't think you one for the fashionable hour.'

'I'm not, but I ride here from time to time to meet with clients.' Court business didn't bring him here tonight. He sat on his mount off to one side of the crowded Row and watched the merry parade of titled men and ladies to see who was meeting with whom and the connections they revealed. With the Rouge Noir planning something, the members might be working to recruit more converts or make arrangements with one another. Rotten Row was a good place to do both. So far, he'd seen nothing but an overabundance of velvet and horse droppings.

'Mother said she hasn't heard from you about coming to their soirée the night after tomorrow,' Richard chastised, his horse shifting position. It blocked Bart's view of the Row at the same moment the Comte de Troyen entered in his red phaeton, his pretty, brown-haired daughter, Marie, on the seat beside him. The French *émigré* enjoyed the top place on Bart's list of suspicious people. The Frenchman had been observed meeting with the young Marquess of Camberline more than once over the last few days in parks or on street corners when they thought no one was watching. Bart's men had noticed, but none of them had been able to get close enough to hear what the two men discussed.

'Mother hasn't heard because I haven't responded.' Bart clicked his horse to one side to watch the Comte as his carriage paused. A man approached the Comte's conveyance, a beggar to all assembled, one of the many who lingered by the gates in search of a penny, but Bart wasn't fooled. The man's quality breeches beneath his dirty coat betrayed his disguise.

These two were meeting about something and Bart needed to find out what.

'Mother will be disappointed if you aren't there,' Richard pressed.

'And Father will be disappointed if I am.' Bart's father's concern for his sons decreased the further down the line they were from inheriting the title. It was a wonder his father even knew the names of his last two progeny. 'He doesn't want to pollute his drawing room with a mere barrister.'

Bart watched as the Comte slipped the beggar a piece of paper Bart would bet his horse was a note. He needed to discover who it was for and what it contained.

'Father doesn't disapprove of what you do, but he would prefer it if your cases were not so well known,' Richard continued, trying like their mother often did to mediate between father and son.

'If Father wants me to have quieter cases, he should tell his aristocratic friends to stop trying to swindle widows out of their inheritances. Now, if you'll excuse me.' Bart kicked his horse into a trot and rode over to one of the benches lining the row. The man sitting on it and reading a newspaper looked up over the top of the print at Bart. 'Follow the beggar walking away from the Comte de Troyen's carriage, the one with the stained coat and fine breeches. See where he goes and who he might meet with. Get a look at the letter the Comte gave him if you can.'

'Yes, sir.' Joseph, one of Bart's best men, folded up the newspaper in his fine hands. He was the kind of man blessed with the ability to blend in and deal easily with the merchants he sometimes impressed or the dockworkers he might drink with. Joseph tucked the paper under one arm and made for the beggar, following him at a discreet distance as he left the gates of the park and blended into the crowd in the road.

The Comte manoeuvred his phaeton into the endless stream of riders and conveyances. He drove at a leisurely pace, casually offering waves and greetings to many of the people he passed. Bart wasn't among those. They'd never been formally introduced and he couldn't simply approach him or his daughter and strike up a conversation. The most he could do was follow him and see who else he spoke with. Bart raised his feet a touch, ready to tap his horse into a walk and get closer to the Comte, when a female voice stilled his boots in the stirrups.

'Mr Dyer, I didn't think you one for Rotten Row.'

Bart shifted in his saddle to watch Lady Rexford bring her piebald mount up beside his with the admirable skill of a woman accustomed to riding. She wore a deep blue velvet habit, the skirt of which draped her curving legs where they arched over the pommel before flaring out to cover the saddle and the back of her horse. Across the front of the bodice, gold cord in a military style broke the severity of the blue and drew his attention to the swell of her pert breasts and the hollow of her neck visible above the collar. A short top hat set at an angle over her blonde hair cast a shadow across her nose and cheeks, but it didn't dampen the twinkle in her eyes. The sight of her startled Bart as much as her smile. It was a radical change from the way she'd greeted him this morning. 'You and my brother are of the same opinion.'

'I'm not usually one for it either, but I'm here in London to re-enter society and so here I am.' She opened her arms to the mash of people around them.

'Here you are. To what do I owe the pleasure of your company?' She'd been eager to
see him gone this morning and yet she'd approached him voluntarily now. She wanted
something, he was sure of it. It was too much
to hope she'd changed her mind, but Bart was
an optimistic man.

'I wish to ask you something, an idea I've
been considering since you left us this morning.' She nudged her horse closer to Bart's.
Over the smell of the grass and the sweat of
horses, he caught a hint of her lilac perfume.
With it came the memory of her in his arms
at Lady Greenwood's ball, her lips as sweet as
her voice and the small peals of laughter he'd
drawn from her with jokes and flattery. Her
laughter and grace had been a relief after the
difficulties of war and the endless haranguing
by his father about his decision to become a
barrister. Then the aunt had ended everything
and Lady Rexford had allowed it.

Bart adjusted his grip on the reins, this fact
as difficult to ignore as her while she watched
him from atop her horse. The height of her an-
imal brought her closer to him, allowing him
to study the pretty face which had not been
marred in the slightest by widowhood.

'It's about Freddy,' she clarified.

Bart nodded. 'I'm sorry. I hadn't realised until this morning how much he'd changed.'

'Few have. We stayed in the country because Aunt Agatha was afraid people might talk of madness if they saw how dark Freddy's grief was for Helena and she was determined to keep it a secret. It was the same way with my father after my mother died. She feared people would think madness ran in our family and it would prevent Freddy or me from making suitable matches.'

He ignored the uncharitable thought of how unsuitable her match to Lord Rexford had been and nodded his understanding of the danger of allowing people to believe madness ran in a family. He'd once defended a widow from losing her inherited lands to Lord Hartmore, her late husband's brother, when he'd tried to brand her a lunatic just because her father had been afflicted with madness.

'Like Father, Freddy was so deeply entrenched in his grief,' she continued, 'he lost interest in everything after she died, his estate, his son, but he's finally coming around.'

'With a great deal of your help, I'm sure.'

'Yes.'

'I'm glad to hear it. He deserves your care and concern.' Bart flicked a speck of dirt off his thigh, conscious of how much he'd failed his friend who'd done a great deal to help stop the assassination plot. On the battlefield, he'd excelled at keeping his soldiers safe and in court he was victorious when defending the weak against those attempting to twist the law to their advantage. When it came to those closer to him, despite his best efforts, he sometimes fell short. 'He deserves happiness instead of misery.'

'What did Freddy mean when he said he'd lost Helena to plotting scoundrels?' she asked with startling candidness. He was usually the one asking direct questions.

'Your brother didn't tell you after I left?'

'I didn't ask. Almost any mention of Helena sends him spiralling into a black mood. I'd like you to tell me.'

'I'm not sure you'd believe me if I did.'

She eyed the other riders with a suspicion similar to his. 'Before this morning I wouldn't have, but a great deal has changed since then.'

'It hasn't changed. You've simply become aware of it.'

She turned to him. 'And I'd like to know the rest.'

Bart pulled his reins through his gloved hands before at last answering. 'Your sister-in-law was not shot in her carriage by a random thief in St Giles. She was murdered by a member of the Scottish Corresponding Society.' Lady Rexford's full lips parted as if she intended to deny what he'd told her, but she didn't. 'Freddy was their intended target. He was supposed to be with her in the carriage that night.'

'But he was sick, so she went to the theatre without him,' Lady Rexford whispered.

'The man who attacked the carriage had orders to kill whoever was inside. He didn't know who she was and it made no difference to him. He did what he was paid to do, but he was paid through informants. When we pressed him—'

'You caught the scoundrel?'

'I have a number of connections in the underworld. It's how I'm able to win so many cases against fraud. Unlike other barristers, I'm not afraid to get my hands dirty. The murderer was hanged soon afterward. Freddy was there when he dropped.'

Except his death hadn't brought Lady Fallworth back. Nothing could.

Lady Rexford traced the stitching on her glove with her finger. 'Thank you for telling me. It explains a great deal about Freddy's grief.'

'He blames himself.' *When he should blame me. I could have done more and I should have done more to protect her.* He was glad Moira had turned down his request for help. He couldn't fail her the way he'd failed Lady Fallworth. He'd been a fool to even ask, but with precious few leads he'd grasped at any chance to learn more about the Rouge Noir and their plans before it was too late.

'He does.'

Moira continued to trace the lacing on her glove with her finger, so many things about the last two years finally making sense. While Aunt Agatha had always written to Moira wringing her hands over Mr Dyer and Freddy's friendship, Helena's letters had never mentioned any concern about Freddy's late nights out. Then, when she'd been murdered, Freddy's grief had been so intense it used to make her ashamed of the shallowness of hers for her deceased husband. Walter had been amiable and pleasant enough, but she'd never possessed the depth of feeling for him that Freddy had held for Helena.

'It's why the Rouge Noir must be stopped before they can ruin any more lives.' Mr Dyer watched the endless parade of people riding by, the hardness in his eyes startling. 'These noble traitors hate the country giving them their very lives, incomes, titles and influence and are plotting to bring it down with a ruthlessness and glee to make you sick. They haven't seen the starving people in France, the wounded and dead in Germany and Austria, the suffering, disease, and misery Napoleon's army leaves in its wake. All they have are their ideas from afar, their so-called noble ideals and the disgusting willingness to see them carried out. I intend to make sure they don't succeed.'

Moira studied everyone around them, wondering who among them were as evil as Mr Dyer claimed. They all seemed so innocent, going about their day, caring for almost nothing except dresses and society, scandals and balls. Even the shallowest among them didn't deserve to have their security and livelihoods ripped from them. She remembered the tales her grandmother used to tell her of France dur-

ing the early days of the revolution and how
everything solid they'd built their lives on had
been pulled down, leaving them with nothing. Moira would listen, wide-eyed, at the dinner table while she spoke, trying to imagine
what it would be like to have everything torn
from her and replaced with fear. If Mr Dyer
was right and the Rouge Noir wasn't stopped,
Moira might find out.

She adjusted the collar of her riding habit
against a brisk breeze, but it wasn't the fear
of the Rouge Noir making her shiver, but an
awareness of Mr Dyer beside her. His strong
presence overshadowed everything, including
her reason, as she'd discovered when she'd allowed him to lead her behind the topiary on
Lady Greenwood's portico. He'd taken her in
his arms and kissed her before pulling back
and smiling like the devil, as if he'd known
before she did she would agree to his kiss and
his proposal. The thrill of it had been as intense as this morning when she'd faced him
with the pistol. If things had been different and
she hadn't given in to the pressure from Aunt
Agatha and her father, she wondered where
she and Mr Dyer might be now.

She lowered her hand and adjusted her skirt

over the saddle. It didn't matter. Things were as they were and she could not make the past any different. It was the present she needed to concern herself with, the one which had become very uncertain in the space of only a few hours.

Then something across the park jerked Mr Dyer's attention away from her. She followed the line of his gaze to see Aunt Agatha being driven in the open-topped landau towards them. Mr Dyer's horse danced with his rider's agitation before he brought him firmly under control.

'Moira, I'm pleased to see you here,' Aunt Agatha observed, eyeing Mr Dyer as if he were a pickpocket. 'Although I'm not as enamoured of your chosen company.'

Mr Dyer's horse snorted.

'Mr Dyer, you remember my aunt, Lady Treadway.' Moira made the introduction, trying to keep the ice between them from hardening further.

'I do.' His response was glacial.

'I'd like to say it's a pleasure to see you again, Mr Dyer, but after our last conversation, I'd expected you to think twice about approaching Lady Rexford.'

'Remind me of our conversation, Lady

Treadway,' Mr Dyer urged with a smile as sharp as broken glass. 'After all, it has been some time since we last spoke.' Bart remembered exactly what she'd said to him, but he wanted to make her repeat it. He wasn't about to leave without a fight or be shooed off like some kicked dog because the Dowager scowled at him.

Lady Treadway shifted her shawl on her shoulders, more reluctant this time to speak so boldly to him. 'As you know, my niece is a countess, the daughter of an earl, the sister of an earl. Her prospects are quite high.'

'Aunt Agatha!' Lady Rexford exclaimed, trying to stop her aunt, but she was as determined to put Bart in his place today as she'd been five years ago.

'It's true, my dear. I'm only looking out for you.'

'And once again you've deemed me unsuitable.' It was all Bart could do to sit in the saddle with dignity as he stared down at the small woman dressed in purple and lace, her bearing as stiff as a female workhouse warden. There was no longer a promise between him and Lady Rexford, but it didn't mean he'd allow anyone to dictate anything to him. What

Lady Rexford allowed others to dictate to her was her own affair.

'My niece is a very generous young woman. I don't want her friendliness to be mistaken for an invitation.'

'Aunt Agatha, you have entirely misread the situation and Mr Dyer,' Lady Rexford protested, to her credit. It was more than she'd dared to say to her aunt the last time they'd been in a similar situation.

'No, she's read me exactly as she wishes to.' Bart leaned over in his saddle, the horse's height combined with his allowing him to tower over the diminutive woman. The aunt didn't back down, but straightened, meeting his hard look with an even more determined one. For a brief moment he admired the little force in silk. Despite her snobbery, she truly had her niece's best interest at heart and he begrudgingly admired her for it. 'Did you wake up this morning, madam, with the express intent of insulting me?'

This made her back down and she looked away, fiddling with the handle of her unopened umbrella. 'I don't mean to insult you, merely to remind you of the facts of the matter which, as a barrister, I'm sure you can appreciate.'

'Yes, I do.' He turned hard eyes on Lady Rexford, wishing she possessed as much strength of spirit as her aunt. It might have changed a number of things about the past five years. 'Good afternoon, Lady Rexford.'

'Mr Dyer, wait,' Moira called after him, but he dug his heels into the flanks of his horse and bolted off down Rotten Row.

'Let him go, my dear, it is for the best,' Aunt Agatha declared as if the topic was finished and it was most certainly not.

'Why did you insult him?' Moira demanded. 'There was nothing taking place between us except conversation.'

'It always begins with conversation.' Aunt Agatha sniffed in the superior way which annoyed Moira.

'And it ends with me being pressured to marry a man twice my age, one I didn't love and who was incapable of giving me any of the things I wanted.'

Aunt Agatha's pale skin went pink near her greying hair. What Moira said wasn't a secret, but it'd never been openly acknowledged either, not by her or any of the people who'd insisted she marry Lord Rexford. Her horse tossed its head and Moira tugged the reins, wishing she could control her emotions as easily as she did her mount, but ever since this morning, the many thoughts and feelings she'd done her best to bury and forget had been rising up, refusing to be ignored.

'We did what we thought best for you, Moira,' Aunt Agatha answered at last without apology.

'I know, but perhaps it's time for me to make such decisions for myself.'

'Not if it means entangling yourself with Mr Dyer again. He might be a very successful barrister, but he is still a barrister and can offer you and the family name nothing.'

'Lord Rexford was an earl and what did he offer us?' Moira pointed out.

'I'm not going to discuss this with you if you're going to be deliberately obtuse about the difference between Lord Rexford and Mr Dyer,' Aunt Agatha huffed before waving one gloved hand at her driver. 'Drive me to Lady Windfall's carriage. I'd like to speak with her.'

Before Aunt Agatha could set off, Moira turned her horse around and cantered down Rotten Row, gripping the reins so tight she thought they would split the seams of her gloves. How dare Aunt Agatha question her judgement or talk to her like some senseless schoolgirl. She, more than Aunt Agatha, recognised the difference between the two men for she'd been forced into intimate relations with one while forsaking the more virile of the two. Everything Lord Rexford had promised her she might have enjoyed with Mr Dyer: a home, family and security. Instead, she'd wed a title and prestige and it'd proven as hollow as her late husband's chest.

Moira adjusted herself in the saddle, pushing back the encroaching sadness and regret, refusing to allow it to dominate her. Despite what Aunt Agatha believed about her judgement, she would choose her own husband this time, assuming any man worth having stepped forward to offer her his hand and heart.

She slowed her mount, remaining at the outer edges of the crush as the traffic in the Row increased. Young ladies in fashionable habits sat upright in their saddles in the middle of the path, their grooms following at a discreet pace. The bold ones flashed the available gentleman tempting looks to entice them to turn their horses and join them. The more timid ones relied on their mothers to summon

the young men to them. Moira possessed neither the boldness nor the necessary guardian
to assist her and she failed to catch anyone but
old Lord Mortley's notice, much to the displeasure of his wife who rode in the carriage
beside him.

The steady clop of her horse's hooves punctuated her heavy mood. She'd come to London
to marry again. It'd seemed like a Herculean
task before they'd journeyed to town. Being
here as a widow without a fortune or lands
trying to compete with all the glittering young
ladies with large dowries made it even more
so. Despite what Aunt Agatha believed, Moira
wasn't sure experience would gain her a match
worth making.

Lord Camberline passed her on his fine
stallion, oblivious to the inviting smiles of the
young ladies and their mamas. Moira turned
in her saddle, watching him continue down the
row before stopping to speak with the Comte
de Troyen and his daughter, Marie. His presence reminded her of the other trouble vexing
her today.

Even if she did find a man who could make
her happy, the stability of her home and happiness might be at risk. Mr Dyer believed some-

thing would happen soon and if it did, where would she and her family go? France wasn't open to them and travelling to Germany was too perilous. There was always America, but it was so far from everything she cherished and loved, the same things she might lose if the Rouge Noir succeeded.

She clutched her reins tight. *They can't be allowed to succeed.*

Napoleon's domination of the European ports and his interrupting of trade were already making things in England worse. The restrictions added to the food shortages from the bad crops, inciting the workers in the north to revolt even more against the factory owners who were fighting a shrinking market to sell their goods and pay the very people turning against them and their new machines. The turmoil in the countryside would be nothing to the havoc Napoleon and his soldiers would wreak if the Rouge Noir destroyed the Government and brought the Emperor here. The thought of her safe world being torn apart scared her more than spending a lifetime without a husband and children of her own.

I won't see the Fallworth lands torn from

Freddy or little Nicholas left with nothing while French soldiers swarm over the country.

She'd do what she could to help bring down the wicked people who wanted to destroy them and rob everyone of their freedom the way Napoleon had pillaged and robbed so many people in Europe of theirs, the way her family had stolen hers when they'd insisted she marry Walter. She would have a life of her own and with it a future. She would help Mr Dyer.

Chapter Three

Moira stood near the back of the line of mamas watching their daughters whirl about the Dowager Marchioness of Camberline's impressive ballroom. A grand, arched ceiling presided over the rectangular space, at one end of which, in a balcony, the musicians played. At the other end, guests traversed the curving staircase to join the festivities or paused on the single landing to look over the crush. Tall windows punctuated the long run of the opposite wall and all of them were open to let in the cool night air. Camberline House in Mayfair was one of the last houses still surrounded by an extensive garden and land. There was some distance between it and its nearest neighbour and the stately trees and rolling lawn beyond the windows, illuminated by torches, gave

Moira and the other guests the impression of being in the country.

A few days ago, Moira had eagerly looked forward to tonight. Once here, the thrill of it lost its allure. Freddy was in the gaming room while Aunt Agatha was off enjoying refreshments with her friends. Moira, being a widow, didn't need a chaperon and so she'd been abandoned to face the crush alone. Growing up, she'd never spent much time in London, and after marriage and widowhood, she'd continued to avoid town. It left her with no friends here her age and no social circles beyond those her aunt had dragged her into, including as a patroness of the Lying-in Hospital. Those people she did know were from her parents' or grandparents' era and she was hesitant to approach them. She'd spent her marriage surrounded by an old husband and his aged friends. She was a young woman and she longed to spend time with people her age. Moira played with the string of her fan, trying to catch the eyes of those around her, but with all their acquaintances already set, no one was interested in forming a new one with her.

Moira sighed. It'd been like this during her very brief and awkward Season, making her isolation even more severe. It seemed as if things had changed, but they hadn't. Aunt Agatha still railed against Mr Dyer while Moira continued to stand alone in ballrooms.

'Good evening, Lady Rexford, I'm so pleased you accepted my invitation,' an elegant voice with a hint of a French accent greeted Moira, breaking the solitude surrounding her.

Moira turned to find the Dowager Marchioness of Camberline beside her, the woman as stately as a Gainsborough in her swathes of mauve silk and black netting. With her grey eyes above a thin nose, she'd turned a number of heads in London after she'd fled the Reign of Terror. Once here, she'd enjoyed her pick of suitors, settling on the much older Marquess of Camberline and the fine fortune and title he'd offered her. Despite a son who'd just reached his majority and being a widow, she was still a stunning woman with little grey in her dark hair. It should have been a relief to at last have someone to speak to, but something about the stately woman placed Moira on edge. 'I have fond memories of your grandparents dancing at Lady Elmsworth's parties after I came over from France. Your grandmother was one of the few who refused to wear the red ribbon around her neck. A number of people considered her eccentric because of it, but she adapted so well to England, unlike many others. Good evening, Lady Rexford.'

Her strange reminiscence shared, the Dowager Marchioness swept off to join Lord Moreau, Lord Lefevre and the young lady beside him holding his arm. The woman, who Moira didn't recognise, was about Moira's height with blonde hair and a gown cut much lower than even the current fashion favoured.

Lady Camberline tolerating the bold young lady surprised Moira, but not her abrupt departure from Moira. Lady Camberline had been similarly terse with her time and words when she'd extended the ball invitation to Moira and Aunt Agatha while they'd been here for the patroness meeting two days ago. She was surprised the other woman had deigned to notice her tonight, but perhaps Moira was not as easily overlooked as she'd believed.

Moira cast about in search of a familiar face or a friendly invitation by another guest to indulge in conversation. Neither was forthcoming, but she didn't mind as much as before. In truth, it was Mr Dyer's presence she eagerly sought instead of anyone else's. In the few

short hours since they'd parted, she'd thought
of little except him and his request. Not even
the dilemma of which woefully out-of-fashion
gown to wear, or the worry of re-entering society after having been gone for so long, had
been enough to banish the memory of his stern
eyes on hers and the pointed tone of his voice.
It seemed, despite the importance he'd placed
on tonight, he hadn't managed to secure an invitation. It ruined her chance of offering her
assistance. Let Aunt Agatha disapprove of an
acquaintance with him, it wasn't up to her to
decide who Moira did or did not consort with.

Then, at the top of the staircase, Mr Dyer
entered the ballroom. He wore a sedate coat of
black, a white shirt and cravat and the required
fawn-coloured breeches. The darkness of his
coat emphasised the seriousness of his expression and captivated Moira. She shouldn't be
this taken with his appearance, but she couldn't
help it. Thankfully, there was no one about to
notice her reaction and condemn it. She didn't
need others adding their doubts to hers and
making her waver in her resolve.

While the footman was busy listening to
the names of an older couple waiting to descend, Mr Dyer slipped around behind him

and down the short staircase. At the landing, he stopped to take in the room with the same seriousness as the moment before he'd galloped away from Aunt Agatha. He scanned the guests like a hawk does a field in search of prey, making Moira wonder who he saw and what he suspected, but she couldn't tear her attention away from him long enough to follow his gaze.

Sensing her watching him, he turned to face her. She didn't look away, but smiled as if he were a welcome visitor in her house. A scowl crossed his face, especially when she began to thread her way through the guests towards him. Her heart beat as fast as an out-of-control carriage the entire time she moved, afraid he'd stride away from her as quickly as he'd ridden off this afternoon. She wouldn't blame him if he cut her, but it didn't make the possible slight, and the disappointment it would bring, any easier to endure. She craved another taste of the hint of adventure he'd offered her this morning and at the same time recognised how silly she was for pursuing it. This was real treason with potential consequences, not some scintillating crime story in the papers. Still, she didn't stop, but approached him with confidence, refusing to question or alter her decision.

He didn't bolt off in the other direction, but moved down the stairs, one firm hand on the railing, watching her the entire time until he was at the bottom and she was before him.

'Mr Dyer, I'm glad to see you tonight.' He didn't smell of cologne or shaving soap, but the more potent scent of sweat and leather, the same one which had enveloped her during their misguided and brief engagement. Her husband had never smelled this raw, not even in the midst of his exertions. She snapped open her fan and waved it in front of her face, more to revive rather than to cool herself.

'Are you?' Mr Dyer challenged, his self-assurance nearly shaking hers.

'I am.' She adjusted one of her diamond earrings, turning to watch the crowd instead of him, but keenly aware of him beside her. 'I've given a great deal of thought to what you and I discussed this morning, and this afternoon, and I've decided to offer my assistance by making whatever necessary introductions you need tonight. I may not know very many people here, but I know a few.'

She traced the heavy necklace pulling at

the back of her neck while she waited for his response.

He didn't smile in grateful relief, but eyed her with a strange curiosity which made her shift in her slippers. 'What brought about this change of heart?'

She pitied the people he'd interrogated in the past. He was being kind to her and already she felt herself shrinking. 'I've had more time to consider the situation and I realised you were right. This is larger than me or Freddy. I love England and I won't see her, and with it Freddy and Nicholas's legacies, destroyed.'

Five years ago there might have been more to her offer, but whatever intimacy they'd enjoyed had been snapped like a frayed rope pulled too hard. It couldn't be knotted together again and she shouldn't wish it to be. He had his duties and she had hers. Helping him was the only place where they intersected.

Bart noticed how Moira's fingers trembled while she adjusted her necklace, the play of her fingers so near the swell of her firm breasts as startling as her offer to help him. After Rotten Row, he'd written her off, intending to come here and find some way to manage things

himself. He hadn't expected her to change her
mind and he should accept her help, but he hesitated. Her offer was sincere, but he doubted
the veracity of Lady Rexford's sudden change
of heart. She'd do him no good if she crumpled every time the aunt opened her mouth and
he had more important business here tonight
then fending off disapproving relations. If he
wanted to do that he'd attend his parents' soirée. 'Won't your aunt object?'

'Yes, but it and so many other things are not
her decision but mine.' She settled her shoulders with admirable seriousness, the movement
making the diamonds sparkle.

Her defiance revealed a strength of will he
hadn't witnessed in her before, one he hoped
she continued to develop. He sensed her happiness relied on her doing so. It shouldn't matter to him if it did, but by volunteering to help
him she was coming under his protection and
he was never one to give up on any person in
his service, and he needed her. With none of
his former clients in attendance, she was, at the
moment, the best person to help him. 'Thank
you, Moira.'

She started at his use of her given name.
He hadn't intended to be informal with her,

but it'd slipped out, her name as natural on his tongue tonight as when he'd proposed to her. He flexed his hands at his sides, refusing to dig up the past. It had no bearing on the present situation.

'You're welcome, Bart.' She adjusted a comb in the tangle of blonde curls arranged high above her neck. 'Now, who would you like to meet?'

'The Comte de Troyen.' Bart nodded at a dark-haired man with a long face and the longer nose of the Hapsburgs standing by the window with Prince Frederick. 'He came over during the Peace of Amiens and is good friends with the Prince.'

'You think he's one of them?'

Her arm brushed Bart's when she shifted on her feet to get a better view of the Frenchman. The charge arching between them was unmistakable. He didn't flinch, but it threatened to rock him off balance as hard as when Mr Flint had first told him of the plot. He drew on the steadfastness of purpose he used in the court to keep opposing counsel from rattling him to put aside his personal feelings and focus on the Comte.

'His friendship with His Highness gives him

ease of access to sensitive information and he has the strongest connection to France.'

'Most of the people here have deep connections to France.' Moira levelled her fan at a group of elderly men and women chatting near the dance floor. 'Mr de Rue's father was the Chevalier de Rue. Lady Mortley's father was the Comte de Boulogne. Lady Wortley's parents were the Duc and Duchesse d'Oiseau. All of these people had aristocratic parents or grandparents who fled to England after the revolution and married their children to earls and dukes.'

'What about Lord Camberline's grandparents?'

'They weren't lucky enough to escape and were guillotined in France, but not before they spirited Lady Camberline to England to be raised by Lady Elmsworth. She was an old goat of a countess who used to give me the chills whenever Mother had her in for tea.'

Bart studied the clutch of ageing aristocrats. He rarely spent time in society or paid much mind to who did what unless it was pertinent to one of his trials or investigations. It left him at a loss and he didn't like being without information. It was the reason he'd first approached

Lord Fallworth and why he was grateful, if not surprised, to have his sister beside him, the creaminess of her smooth skin heightened by the candlelight. 'Those are connections but they're older ones, before Napoleon came to power. The Comte was in France until the Peace of Amiens and when Napoleon restored many of the old aristocrats' titles and lands, the Comte de Troyen's were returned to him as well, and no one knows why.'

'Maybe Napoleon was trying to lure the Comte back to France to help bridge the gulf between the old guard and the new regime. I understand the Comte was an accomplished French statesman at one time. It's how he survived the Reign of Terror.' She touched her fan to her delicate chin. 'It seems to me neither his title nor lands are much good to him in England. With the blockade, not even letters can get through, much less any payments.'

'Given what I've seen of smugglers, it isn't difficult to slip things through the blockade. If I knew why Napoleon restored his lands, it might answer a great deal to either his innocence or guilt, but the Comte is adept at keeping his business to himself, making him one of the more difficult men for me to investigate.

The members of the Rouge Noir are a cautious lot.' They didn't gamble or drink to excess, making learning much of anything, including the identity of its members, difficult.

'I can't guide you on how to investigate his circumstances, but I can arrange the introduction. My father, and my husband, were well acquainted with Prince Frederick, making him one of the few people here I know. Follow me.' In a flutter of dark blue silk, she made for the pair of men.

Bart followed, noting the sway of her dress around her hips and the tempting view of the smooth skin of her shoulders and neck beneath her high coiffure. He appreciated her assistance, but not the reminder of her connection to the Prince. He'd been disgusted when he'd learned she'd married Lord Rexford, a man thirty years older than her and in ill health. He understood personal sacrifice, his career had seen a bevy of it, but he couldn't comprehend surrendering legally and in body to another person just because her father had wished it. He'd never allowed his father, or anyone above him in rank, to dictate his future, much to his father's continued dismay.

They approached Prince Frederick and the

Comte de Troyen, and Bart buried any distaste he experienced for either man. It was a skill he'd honed during his many trials when he'd faced down some of the worst men to see justice done by pummelling them with arguments and evidence instead of his fists. He could be as polite and engaging when the time called for it as he could be ruthless and unforgiving when it involved rooting out enemies of the Crown.

'Your Highness, it's been too long since I've seen you.' Moira held out her hand to Prince Frederick.

'Lady Rexford, my condolences on your husband.'

Prince Frederick bowed over her hand. He was balding and it added to the sloped forehead sliding into a long and pointed nose. The two small eyes fixed on either side of it focused more on her chest and the generous swell of her breasts above her bodice than her lively smile. Bart had to fight the urge to step in between her and the lecherous royal. It wasn't his place to act as her chaperon.

'Lord Rexford and your father were a great help to me in securing funding from the House of Lords for munitions during the War of the

First Coalition and you're too young to be a widow.'

'Thank you.'

Bart noticed how Moira gritted her teeth at the mention of her loss, and the brief flash of pity in Prince Frederick's eyes, but her charming smile didn't fade. It appeared, like him, she'd developed a talent for hiding her thoughts.

'He always spoke well of his days with you and I think he regretted giving up the service. I'm very sorry to hear what happened to you, losing your post as Commander in Chief of the Army. They were wrong to let a man of your talent go. Thankfully, they came to their senses and called you back.'

'Bloody fools, but they haven't got a brain in their heads, not between the lot of them and no real leadership,' Prince Frederick blustered, the veins along the sides of his nose turning a deeper red. 'How we manage to get anything done on the Continent is amazing. Why, one lethal fever among a few too many in the Government and the entire country would plunge into complete chaos.'

'*Mon ami*, surely it can't be so dreadful,' the Comte de Troyen exclaimed as he laid his hand over his cravat. He was tall and lithe, a bit thick in the middle from age, but the man who'd cut a swathe through society ten years ago was still evident in his aquiline nose, air of divine superiority and attire. He wore more brocade than was fashionable and a black wig.

Prince Frederick tipped the rest of his champagne into his mouth. 'It's worse than you think. If we didn't have Wellington leading the army, we'd be done for.'

Bart tried not to groan at hearing Prince Frederick bluster on about the weaknesses of the Government in front of the Comte. If he was this loose with his words while mostly sober at a ball, Bart could just imagine what secrets he let slip when he was drunk at private parties. The Comte or any other traitor wouldn't have to work hard to garner secrets for Napoleon from Prince Frederick.

Moira looked back and forth between Prince Frederick and the Comte, silently soliciting an introduction.

'Oh, forgive me, what with the scandal and all I've quite forgotten my manners,' Prince Frederick mumbled. 'Lady Rexford, may I introduce the Comte de Troyen. You were probably too young to remember when he was the toast of London.'

'I might have been young, but I could never forget the dashing Comte. You're even more handsome than either the pictures in the paper portrayed you, or my grandmother used to say.'

'And you, my dear lady, are *trés magnifique.*' The Frenchman admired her with too much interest, making Bart's back stiffen. 'And so was your *chère grandmère*. So many wonderful times in Paris we had. It's a shame the Revolution ended it all.'

'My grandmother always used to say so, too.' She matched the sombreness of the Comte's voice, allowing his regret and hers to hang in the air a moment. Bart marvelled at her skill in gaining the man's trust. Some of his younger agents had yet to master such delicate persuasions. Then, after the moment passed, she motioned to Bart. 'Your Highness, may I introduce Mr Dyer?'

'Yes, the accomplished barrister. I've heard a great deal about you.' Prince Frederick introduced Bart to the Comte. 'Monsieur le Comte, if you're ever in any legal trouble, this is the man to have at your side. If he'd been able to represent me in my awful affair over the sale of commissions, I might not have had to resign as Commander in Chief of the Army. But in the end I was exonerated.'

'The truth is always the most powerful defence,' Bart remarked and the Comte shifted in his silver-buckled shoes. It made Bart wonder what about the mention of the truth had made the Comte go white beneath his wig. It increased his suspicions about the man. 'The discovery of which I strive to achieve in all my trials.'

'I'll certainly keep you in mind, Mr Dyer, but I live such a quiet life, I see no chance of troubles.' The Comte returned his attention to Moira. 'Might I have the pleasure of this next dance, Lady Rexford?'

Bart wanted to tell her to refuse because he wanted the Comte to remain here and not sneak away, but he was in no position to do so. He tried to catch Moira's eye and silently dissuade her, but he failed and she held out her hand to the Comte.

'Yes, you may.'

While the Comte led her away, she looked back over her shoulder at Bart and threw him a conspiratorial wink. He realised she was now in a better position than he was to gather intelligence on the Comte. Although Bart didn't want her anywhere near the man and danger, he was forced to stifle an answering smile, amazed once again at this brave new Moira. With any luck, she could pry some useful information out of the Frenchman while they danced, but he prayed she remained subtle with her enquiries. He didn't want the Comte, or anyone else who might be connected to the Rouge Noir suspecting her of more nefarious motives.

'If you'll excuse me, Mr Dyer. I must speak with Lord Palmer.' Prince Frederick strode away, having nothing further to discuss with Bart. It didn't matter. It was the Comte and Moira who commanded all his attention.

A thrill tripped up Moira's spine as she took the Comte's hand and the musicians began the allemande. It wasn't the Frenchman who inspired her, but the hint of danger in dancing with him. Bart watched from the edge of the dance floor. Despite not looking at him, she was more aware of Bart than the Comte holding her hand for the turn. It took a great deal of effort to remember the steps and to charm the Frenchman.

'Why have I not seen you in London before tonight?' The Comte circled her with admirable elegance.

'Mourning and family obligations have kept me in the country.'

'My deepest sympathies. I, too, have suffered. My wife passed and I must see to my daughter's marriage and welfare.' He motioned to where a young lady with his nose and eyes conversed with the tall and dashing Marquess of Camberline, much it seemed to the Dowager Marchioness of Camberline's disapproval. Lady Camberline marched up to her son and drew him away from the crestfallen and chastised young lady. Moira pitied the girl, knowing all too well what it was like to have a disapproving parent dictate a young woman's affections.

The Marquess didn't stay long with his mother, making for a door at the back of the room after offering her a curt remark which made the Dowager's lips purse.

'I'm sorry to be so rude, Lady Rexford, but I must end our dance early,' the Comte apologised, bringing them to a halt in the middle of a chasse. 'There is someone I must speak with. Please excuse me.' With a shallow bow, he hurried away in the direction of the Marquess, leaving her to stand alone in the centre of the whirling couples.

Aware of the many people watching her, Moira gathered up all the self-possession she could muster and strode back into the anonymity of the crowd. She was making for the far wall near where the chaperons stood bored and ignored when Bart appeared beside her.

'Where's he going?'

'I don't know.' She nodded in the direction of the tall door on the far side of the ballroom. 'But I believe it's wherever Lord Camberline is headed.'

Without a parting word, Bart dashed off into the crowd, working to keep sight of the Comte before leaving the ballroom in pursuit of him.

Moira remained where she was, wishing she could follow him instead of being forced to remain here. Without him to chat with or to force her to interact with others, she was alone and ignored once more. She picked at her fan, wondering what she should do next when Aunt Agatha approached her.

'Given the crush at this ball, I'm surprised to find you standing by yourself. You should make more of an effort to meet people, especially gentleman who are apt to overlook you in favour of younger and wealthier ladies.'

Despite the sting in the remark, Moira thanked providence it was her solitude and not her time with Bart her aunt had noticed. He was the one man Aunt Agatha didn't want her to speak with and Moira didn't relish another argument about him.

A group of women strode past them, jostling Aunt Agatha when they passed because of the crowd.

'Lady Camberline should better manage her guest list. I've never seen such a crush, but I suppose one can't expect much from a French aristocrat, no matter how long she's been in England.' Aunt Agatha frowned as she was forced to step aside for another group of passing people. She'd been prejudiced against the many titled French people who'd come to London after the Revolution for a long time, never really losing her dislike of them even when her brother had married Moira's mother. She could remember the Christmas dinners when her grandparents sat on one side of the table and Aunt Agatha the other, wincing each time they spoke French to one another. It hadn't mattered to Aunt Agatha if they'd almost lost their lives to the guillotine. Aunt Agatha detested the French nobility. 'Well, you might as well join me and my friends. There's no point in being a wallflower.'

'I might as well.' Heaven knew when Bart would return or if he needed her any longer. Spying Freddy leading young Miss Filner on to the dance floor, she realised people not needing her was fast becoming an all-too-familiar pattern in her life.

Bart followed the Comte de Troyen at a discreet distance through the refreshment room, past the one reserved for gambling and down the long hallway leading to the back of the house. The number of guests thinned as they walked and Bart dropped further and further behind the Comte to avoid being noticed. The Comte paused at a juncture where the main hallway was crossed by another one. Bart stepped back into the narrow alcove of a closed door and pressed himself deep into the shadows, not daring to move.

After a long breath, Bart leaned forward, but the Comte was gone. Bart hurried to the juncture, the thick rug muffling the fall of his shoes. He hazarded a look down one side and then the other. In the centre of the right hall-way, the Comte stood with Lord Camberline, less regal and more irritated than he'd been in the ballroom. Bart leaned back against the wall, near the corner to listen to their heated exchange.

'Don't think I'll allow you to renege now, not with so much at stake,' the Frenchman insisted, showing no deference to the young man's superior rank.

'I won't renege,' the Marquess answered, as agitated as the Comte. 'But it's been more diffi-cult than you realise to put everything in place.'

'I think you're stalling for time, to avoid doing what we agreed must be done.'

'I want this as much as you do. It will change everything and I want it changed. I'll send word when all is ready. I promise, it will be soon.'

'It better be or you'll regret it,' the Comte threatened.

The Comte's shoes thudded against the car-pet as he stalked away from Lord Camber-line. Bart dashed down the hall and into the first room he found. He left the door cracked open slightly, hiding behind it while the Comte passed by, muttering to himself in French. Whatever he and the Marquess were embroiled in, the Comte held power over the younger man and he wasn't going to let him get cold feet. Bart would make sure the young man's feet froze solid before he let him compromise himself or the country.

Bart waited in the empty room to give the Marquess time to pass, his eyes adjusting to the moonlight falling in through the windows along the far wall. Above the scent of wood oil, he caught another familiar and more deadly scent.

Gunpowder.

If this were a masculine room he wouldn't be concerned. Stored hunting rifles improperly cleaned by a footman might leave a lingering scent, but the gilded chairs and comfortable sofa set before a delicate writing table near the windows told him this was a lady's domain. The scent of gunpowder shouldn't be here.

Bart made his way around the room, searching for the source of the scent. He found it near the writing table. He pulled open the drawers on the left side and rifled through them, but there was nothing inside except blank papers, pens and extra ink. He closed the last one and moved to search the right-hand drawers when his foot came down on something. It was a small envelope and it grated like it held fine gravel. He picked it up and carefully opened the envelope to examine the substance inside. It was gunpowder, but a redder and more pungent variety than any he'd encountered before. The colour and smell of it concerned him as deeply as the conversation he'd overheard. He tucked the envelope in his coat pocket, then peered cautiously through the cracked door to make sure the hallway was empty before he left the room.

He retraced his steps, the people and conversation growing thicker as he approached the gaming room. He moved past them and into the ballroom, intending to return to Moira. She might know something about Lord Camberline and a way for one of them to get closer to the young lord and learn more.

He stepped into the crowded ballroom, searching for her light hair, the elegant line of her jaw and the captivating eyes that had met his across a ballroom similar to this one five years ago, making him forget the need to be cautious about young ladies of higher rank. She'd accepted his invitation to dance without the snide condescension of other ladies in search of more lucrative elder sons of lords. They'd wanted nothing to do with a fifth son who earned his living from hard work, and he'd refused to endure their insolence. Moira hadn't cared about his rank or dismissed him because of it.

No, she'd left it to the aunt to do it for her.

He spied her across the room standing with her aunt and a number of other elderly ladies, irritated at the old slight and captivated by her present beauty. Whatever the aunt still thought of him, it was clear Moira didn't share her opinion or her aunt's enthusiasm for her present company. She appeared as bored by the gaggle of biddies as Bart was disappointed. He couldn't approach her while she was with them.

Damn.

Lord Camberline and the Comte were up to something and he was sure it had something to do with the gunpowder in his pocket. He needed to give the sample to Mr Flint and have his man, Mr Transom, examine it, and tell his superior what he'd overheard in the hallway. Maybe Mr Flint had received some more intelligence to help them make sense of it. It meant leaving the ball and Moira early, but he'd find a way to meet her again tomorrow and explain everything without the aunt interrupting them. He was sure Moira would understand his abrupt departure. He hoped she did because he needed her. She'd shown him tonight how she could charm men like the Comte with an ease none of his other agents could match and she was already an acquaintance of the Camberlines. It gave her access to them and their house, one he could not otherwise obtain. In light of what he'd overheard and what he'd found, it was a critical connection he had to take advantage of.

He reached into his pocket and rubbed the envelope with the gunpowder between his thumb and forefinger. The granules grated beneath the paper and his fingertips. He didn't want Moira involved in this or in harm's way, but her help might prove crucial to stopping the Rouge Noir. If he could keep her work to chatting to titled men and women at parties, asking the right questions or simply listening, she should be safe. He would do all he could to ensure it and not fail her or England as he'd failed Lady Fallworth.

Chapter Four

'A woman? Have you gone mad, Dyer? This is no work for a woman and a lady in particular.' Mr Flint's ruddy nose turned a shade darker. They sat in his office in Whitehall. The dark desk he occupied matched the rich tones of the panelled walls punctuated by two windows separated by a painting of the Battle of Marathon.

'Lady Rexford is in an even better position than her brother to get close to people like the Comte and Lord Camberline. No one will suspect a woman of eavesdropping. If they did, then men wouldn't say half of what they do to their mistresses.'

'That's how we got most of what we did out of Italy, through Mrs Hamilton,' Mr Flint mumbled reflectively as he rubbed the fleshy roundness of his chin. He'd started his career

in France under William Wickham and the
Alien Office, recruiting spies and support-
ing the Royalists. He'd risen with the man
as they'd sought intelligence first during the
French Revolution and now against Napoleon.
'Being a widow with no children is unfortu-
nate for her, but to her advantage and ours in
this matter. She has no dependants to put at
risk, enjoys freedom of movement and is more
appealing to gentlemen.'

Including Bart. He'd thought as much about
her last night as he had the sample of gunpowder and everything he'd seen and heard at the
ball. He cursed the distraction. This was no
time to lose his head, not with the fate of the
Crown at stake. 'What about the gunpowder
I gave you?'

'Mr Transom is examining it and will re-
port to you soon.' Mr Flint removed his spectacles and cleaned them with his handkerchief.
'Any more information on the man who met
the Comte de Troyen in Rotten Row?'

'Joshua is still investigating him. Given
what I overhead last night, I'll tell him to re-
double his efforts.'

'In the meantime, you should pay a visit to
gaol. Mr Marks, one of Jacques Dubois's un-

derlings, was arrested last night for getting into a brawl down by the docks.'

'Not like one of Mr Dubois's men to be careless and get arrested.' Mr Dubois was a well-known smuggler and arms procurer who was as good at getting many in the Admiralty their French wine as he was at acquiring weapons for the war effort. His deliveries of munitions meant the Government looked the other way when it came to his smuggling activities. Until this point, he'd never been suspected of treason. 'He could be the one slipping notes and money between Napoleon and the Rouge Noir,' Bart suggested.

'Only one way to find out.'

Bart rose and made for the door. 'After a night of risking gaol fever, Mr Marks should be willing to tell me a little about his employer's less savoury connections.'

Moira reviewed the dinner menu, but was forced to read over the selection more than once before it stuck. It was difficult to concentrate on fish and chicken when all she could think about was Bart. When she'd agreed to help him and they'd walked together to meet Prince Frederick and the Comte de Troyen, she'd moved with purpose through the ball-room, a wallflower no more. Her purpose had come from Bart and his desire, shared by her, to help their country. It'd been more thrilling than anything else she'd experienced in recent memory.

And I gained nothing for my efforts.

She tapped her pen against the menu. If her help had assisted him in any way, he hadn't informed her. He hadn't even had the decency to send a note thanking her for her assistance or explaining his abrupt departure and failure to return.

Footsteps behind her made her turn. Freddy entered the sitting room. He appeared better today, the despair surrounding him after Bart's visit yesterday having dissipated. However, there was a seriousness about him that made Moira grip the back of her chair as she turned to face him. He always appeared like this whenever he was about to ask her for something she wasn't going to like.

'I understand Mr Dyer was at the ball last night.' Freddy picked up a German glass dish on the table beside him and turned it over to inspect the bottom. 'A friend of mine saw you speaking with him.'

Moira tightened her grip on the chair. 'Once Aunt Agatha abandoned me for her friends, and you left me for the cards, there were few other people I was well enough acquainted with to speak to.'

'Surely there must have been someone else.'

Moira rolled her eyes, not interested in travelling where this conversation was leading. 'Don't tell me you're going to be like Aunt Agatha and start railing against him, too?'

'I am.' Freddy set the dish back on the table. 'Bart and I were very good friends once, but I have to insist that you have no further dealing with him. You don't realise how dangerous it is to our welfare.'

'I do. He told me what happened with Helena.' She rose and laid her hands on his shoulders. His muscles tightened beneath her palms. 'Please don't fret, Freddy. All he did was ask me to introduce him to Prince Frederick and the Comte de Troyen and I did. There was nothing more to it. I never even saw him after we met the gentlemen.'

'If that's all there was to it, then promise me you won't become involved with or see him again.' Freddy took her hands off his shoulders and clasped them in his, pleading with her in the oddly gentle way everyone always did whenever they asked her to make sacrifices for them.

She peered up at her brother, troubled by his anxiety. She should agree, set his mind at ease, take the easy path and avoid the conflict rumbling just beneath his request, but something in her rebelled. This was too much like five years ago when her father and Aunt Agatha had demanded the same thing. 'I can't do that, Freddy. I respect Mr Dyer and his work too much to cut him.'

Freddy let go of her and stepped back, a rare anger flashing in his green eyes. 'Does he mean so much to you that you're willing to risk your relationship with Nicholas to see him?'

Moira drew back in shock. 'How can you threaten such a thing after everything I've done for him and you?'

Freddy had the decency to redden with shame. 'Of course I appreciate all you've done. Nicholas, and I, and Fallworth Manor couldn't have survived without you. It's why I'm asking this of you.'

She was about to answer him when the faint clearing of a gentle voice made them face the sitting-room doorway.

Miss Kent stood at the threshold, a paper-wrapped bundle in her fine hands, her cheeks brushed with the flush of a recent walk. 'Lord Fallworth, I have the clothes I collected from the tailor for Nicholas. Would you like to come to the nursery and see them? It's time for me to wake him from his nap.'

Freddy lit up at the sight of her and it made Moira more uneasy than his interest in her and Bart. *Surely it's because of Nicholas and nothing more*, but the feeling it wasn't was difficult to set aside.

'Yes, I'd like that. Go up and wake him. I'll join you both shortly.'

The pretty nurse curtsied, then left. Freddy turned back to Moira, his elation from the interruption gone. 'I'm not trying to be stern with you, Moira, but I have to think of Nicholas. He was too young to grieve for Helena, but not for you. I won't have him suffer the way I did.'

'How much will he and all of us suffer if the Rouge Noir succeeds?' she challenged.

He frowned, not appreciating being trapped by her logic. 'Such affairs are not our concern. Leave them to Bart and others to manage, otherwise, I'll do what I must to protect my son.'

He turned on his boot heel and strode out of the room, leaving Moira alone with his threat.

She wrapped her arms around her waist to fend off the worry engulfing her. If she didn't heed his request, Freddy might take Nicholas away from her. She loved the boy and didn't want to be parted from him, but she chafed at being placed in this situation again. She'd given Bart up five years ago and gained very little in return for her sacrifice. She wouldn't allow it to happen again, especially not with Freddy likely to remarry this Season. Moira's place in Nicholas's life would be supplanted by his new stepmother no matter what Moira decided to do today.

She walked to the window to take in the street outside, struggling against her rising frustration. With Freddy making it clear she was not as valuable to him as she'd believed, it was nice to think someone still needed her, even if it was only for a short time. Except she wasn't sure Bart did need her. After all, he'd done nothing to make her believe he would require further assistance from her.

Then why didn't I simply agree to Freddy's request? Because, until she heard otherwise from Bart, there was still hope. She'd come to

London to gain a new life for herself, and if she allowed others to dictate who she should and should not see then she'd never claim the independence she craved.

'I'm here to see the man they brought in last night. I need to talk to him.' Bart stood before the desk of the rotund gaol warden.

He didn't look up from the large mug of cheap ale he poured himself, but continued to fill the pewter until he was satisfied, then set the jug down with a thud. 'That might be hard. He died last night. Gaol fever.'

'Then I want to see the body.' He never trusted anything until he confirmed it, not the information his men brought him, or even Moira's rejection of him five years ago as the aunt had related it until he'd spoken to Moira in private in the square near her house. It'd been a painful conversation.

The warden smacked his thick lips together as he eyed Bart. Then, with an as-you-wish shrug, he left the room, motioning for Bart to follow. They passed numerous stinking and dark cells crammed with people. Bart didn't flinch. He'd been here too many times be-fore to speak with possible witnesses and informants to be horrified by the dirty hands reaching out to beg a penny off him. The warden led him to the end of the block of cells and down a flight of rickety stairs to the cold stone cellar. Two bodies were laid out on tables beneath stained sheets. The smell in here wasn't much worse than the one engulfing the cells upstairs.

'Here he is.' The warden flicked back an old sheet to reveal the ashen face of Mr Marks. 'He'll be chucked in the pauper's pit this afternoon unless you want him. No one else does.'

'I don't want a dead man.' Bart yanked the sheet off, revealing the stab wound in the man's stomach. 'Gaol fever?'

The warden shrugged. 'Easier than bringing in the constable, especially for scum like this.'

'Any idea which other prisoner did this?'

'Yeah, him.' He pointed to the man on the table beside him.

Bart flicked back the sheet. The second man had a similar wound. 'A right epidemic.'

The warden threw out his hands. 'You know how it is in here at night.'

He did. Leaving a man here to face it often opened his mouth or jogged his memory when

Bart returned the next day. 'Any idea who did the second man in?'

'Can't say. Lot of people coming and going yesterday on account of it being wages day. You can look at the register if you'd like.'

'Yes.' They returned to the warden's office at the front of the gaol and a half-hour later one name stood out among the many. 'What did this Mr Roth look like?'

He'd heard the man's name in connection with Mr Dubois before.

The warden shrugged, his dirty coat rising and falling with his thick shoulders. 'Like all the rest.'

Bart slammed the register shut, making the fat man flinch. 'I pay you for better information than this. Either provide it or I'll haul you before the magistrate for miscarriage of justice.'

The fat man blanched, scratched his head, then his stomach and spoke. 'I remember him, he was thin, with a long scar on his left cheek.'

Bart stood and tossed a coin at the warden. 'Send word if he returns or if you hear anything of interest.'

He strode outside into the street, past women bringing their incarcerated husbands food, and inhaled the slightly cleaner air. Bart would bet his carriage Mr Roth had been sent by Mr Dubois to make sure Mr Marks didn't say anything to anyone about Mr Dubois's business. Bart would instruct his men to talk to their informers about finding Mr Roth and for news on Mr Dubois's activities. They might learn more about Mr Roth, but Mr Dubois kept everything close to his chest. However, if one of Mr Dubois's men had been foolish enough to get arrested, and another dumb enough to sign his real name and be noticed, there might be others careless enough to talk while drunk or when bribed.

In the meantime, he needed to discover if there was a connection between Lord Camberline, the Comte de Troyen and the Rouge Noir. The two men were definitely up to something, but he had no idea what and he needed to find out. There was only one person who could help him. Moira.

Bart hailed a hack and gave the driver directions to Lord Fallworth's residence. Once inside the mouldy vehicle, with the streets of London passing outside the window, he wondered what kind of welcome he'd receive from her today. She wasn't likely to point a gun at him or banish him from the house, but it didn't mean the aunt or Freddy wouldn't do it for her. Visiting her was the only way to find out.

'Lady Rexford, a note arrived for you,' the butler announced.

Moira looked up from her book. After her discussion with Freddy, she'd retreated to her room to try to gather her thoughts, but they'd been as scattered as the light through the crystals hanging from the nearby candleholder. Freddy's request has rankled with her through each chapter of her book, even though there'd been little reason to silently debate the matter of whether or not to continue an acquaintance with Bart. She still hadn't heard from him, indicating her interest in maintaining a friendship with him was greater than his interest in her and all her fretting was for nothing. 'Who's it from?'

'I don't know. A boy delivered it and is waiting downstairs for an answer.'

She snapped the book closed, took the mysterious note and read it.

Meet me in the square.
BD

She folded the paper and slipped it between the pages of her book, trying to control her excitement. It seemed she wasn't as forgettable as she'd believed and it made the unsettled debate between obeying Freddy and making her own decision more acute. Freddy was right, there was a great deal at stake if she meddled in the Rouge Noir affair, but so far Bart had asked very little of her in that regard, and what Freddy and Aunt Agatha didn't know couldn't hurt them. Besides, she was a widow with the freedom to do as she saw fit, and at the moment, she saw fit to meet Bart.

She went to her desk and jotted a quick note to Bart saying she would meet him, then handed it to the butler. 'Give this to the boy.'

'Yes, my lady.'

Moira summoned the lady's maid, the one she shared with Aunt Agatha to avoid the expense of two, and changed out of her morning dress and into a walking dress of dark purple embroidered with yellow flowers. The maid set a matching purple bonnet over her curls and Moira frowned at herself in the mirror. She was tired of dressing like an old matron and living a half-life. She only hoped the risk she was taking in meeting Bart was worth it.

Thankfully, no one noticed her leaving, preventing her from having to lie to either Aunt Agatha or Freddy about where she was going.

Outside, the air was crisp and the bright sun glistened off the leaves of the trees planted along the pavement, but the beauty of the day didn't ease the knots in her stomach. The last time she and Bart had met like this, she'd been twenty and she'd stolen out of the house near dusk to meet Bart in the same square. In the encroaching darkness, she'd tried to make him understand why Aunt Agatha had said what she had to him and why she must obey her father. He hadn't understood and she hadn't blamed him, but that was years ago when she and Bart were different people. Aunt Agatha might have railed at him last night as if nothing had changed, but it had.

She glanced behind her towards their town house. She couldn't see it from here because of the curve of the street. She hoped Freddy didn't end his time with Miss Kent and then decide to take a ride. If he did, and he saw her with Bart, she would become very familiar with consequences. She twisted her reticule string around her finger as she approached the square, wondering if she should return home and forget Bart, but she couldn't, she never had. Many times, after her marriage, when she'd sat alone at Allwick Hall surrounded by nothing but old portraits while her husband had secluded himself in his library with his tonics and fossils, she'd thought of Bart and cursed her weakness. She never wanted to be the Moira who sat alone with regrets again, but this time it seemed they might haunt her no matter what she decided to do.

She stopped at the iron gate set in the fence surrounding the square. Bart stood a short distance away with his back to her, his light coat smooth across his wide shoulders, his feet in their dark boots planted firmly on the cobblestone path beneath the trees. She wrapped one gloved hand around a cold finial, hesitant to approach him. Five years ago, they hadn't known one another long enough for her to risk her relationship with her father to be with him. The truth was, they still didn't, but seeing the man he'd become told her so much about who he was. In court, he argued on behalf of innocent people against those who sought to deceive them. In Austria, he'd defended England and then returned home to do more of the same. He wasn't a frail old man, but a robust one who fought for what he believed in, except he hadn't believed in her enough to fight for her.

She let go of the gate, the old heartbreak washing over her. He'd let her go so quickly, making her question the depth of his regard back then and ever since. If he'd truly cared for her, surely he would have struggled to find a way for them to be together? Except she hadn't been willing to fight to stay with him either and it'd given him no reason to fight to hold on to her.

She pushed open the gate and strode forward, refusing to be guided by their past. This was about claiming a future for herself and she must remember it. 'Hello, Bart.'

He turned, the severe set of his lips softening into an appreciative smile as he took her in. It was a far cry from the glare he'd pinned on her five years ago and she adjusted the buttons of her spencer, her heart racing beneath the fine wool.

'Good afternoon, Moira. Thank you for meeting me. I wasn't sure you would.'

'I almost didn't,' she admitted. 'Aunt Agatha is no longer the only one insisting we have nothing more to do with one another.'

'Freddy?'

She nodded.

'I'm not surprised.' Bart laced his fingers behind his back. 'What I asked of you yesterday isn't suitable work for a lady.'

'What? Making a few introductions?' she scoffed, afraid of where his comments might be leading. 'It's hardly daring.'

'Perhaps, but I have no desire to come between you and your brother.'

Moira struggled to hold her smile, afraid Bart, in his attempt to do the right thing, would pull away from her and she didn't want him to go. Given Freddy and Aunt Agatha's objections, there could be nothing serious between them, but without him, who knew what gaping loneliness might consume her life.

'You won't. Aunt Agatha is too busy with her London friends and Freddy with Nicholas and his club to notice what I'm up to,' she lied, the guilt pricking her as much as her worry over being seen with him. 'I'd be happy to make more introductions if you need them.'

Bart admired her conviction and her new willingness to decide her own fate. How different she was from the woman he'd met in this square five years ago. He'd blamed her back then for being weak when he should have been sympathetic. He'd spent years standing firm against his father's attempts to dictate his life or tear him down. She'd fought the same war. He thought she'd lost it, but she hadn't. Her strength had been dampened by needy relatives, but it had burned beneath the surface, giving her what she needed to be strong while those around her fell apart.

Bart moved back the sides of his coat as he pressed his knuckles into his hips, fighting against his lingering reservations to bring her deeper into this game. With an attack imminent, he needed to employ every resource he could muster to uncover it. If she was willing to sneak out to meet him in defiance of her family, she might continue helping him in his quest to unmask the Rouge Noir. 'What I need from you is more than a few introductions.'

'More?' Excitement and nervousness mixed in her voice as it had when he'd suggested she join him on Lady Greenwood's very dark portico the night they'd met. It was as enticing as the sweet parting of her lips and almost distracted him from what he'd come here to do.

'Yes. I must discover if Lord Camberline is

involved with the Rouge Noir. You're in a position to become better acquainted with him
through his mother. Your involvement will
be strictly limited to social engagements and
nothing else.'

The part of him still mourning his role in
Lady Fallworth's death silently urged her to refuse, but the man who enjoyed staring at her as
the shadows from the overhead leaves caressed
her cheeks and the dappled light glinted in her
green eyes willed her not to. If she declined to
assist him, he would walk away from her for
good. He wouldn't come between her and her
family because, despite her flimsy protests to
the contrary, he recognised it was possible. He
hoped she didn't force him to give her up. He
and England both needed her.

Then, her astonishment turned to a sideways
teasing smile which lightened the heaviness in
his chest. 'You mean I won't be able to point a
pistol at other people or you?'

'You can point a pistol at me anytime you
like.' He enjoyed this saucy Moira and was
elated by her tacit agreement. It meant they
didn't have to part just yet. It shouldn't matter to
him if they did or didn't, but it very much did.

'Then I should have brought one and aimed

it at you for abandoning me like you did last night.'

'I apologise for leaving so abruptly, but I needed to find out where the Comte de Troyen was going.' He told her about the Comte and Lord Camberline's conversation but didn't mention the gunpowder. The less she knew, the better. He would not have another lady's death on his hands.

'Lord Camberline seems too young to be involved in something so nefarious.'

'His age means nothing. The young can be ideological and as brainless as a sack of rocks. I watched enough of them hang for spying or treason when I was in Austria to realise what troubles the strength of their ideals and the weakness of their life experiences can lead them into.'

'But I can't imagine him having any love for France. Lady Camberline's parents were guillotined there. If she hadn't been spirited out to England, she would have died, too. Surely she must have spoken against the evils of zealous idealists many times, the way my grandmother used to do with me.'

'Then perhaps her son is acting out of rebellion. He may have reached his majority, but

I understand his mother continues to control him and his money with an iron fist. You will have to find out which it is.'

'How? I can't simply call on a marchioness and discuss her private relationship with her son.'

'You can if you become better friends with her. There's a painting exhibition tonight at the Royal Academy and my sources tell me Lord Camberline and his mother will be there. It's an excellent opportunity for you to further your acquaintance with them. Can you attend?'

Moira touched one gloved finger to her lips while she considered his proposal, the gesture as innocent as it was enticing. He could almost recall the sweet taste of her and the pressure of her body against his when he'd held her in his arms long ago. It was a memory as tempting as it was dangerously distracting and a warning rose up in his mind as powerful as those he used to get before a French attack. There might be more risk in his working with Moira than gunshots or traitors.

'Neither Aunt Agatha or Freddy enjoy art, so it shouldn't be too difficult for me to attend without them.'

'Good, then I'll meet you at the gallery at

nine p.m., but we must be discreet.' He explained how they'd meet at the exhibition without being obvious. 'People won't be suspicious of us talking given my past friendship with your brother, but if we're seen too often together and someone begins to suspect I'm investigating the Rouge Noir, it could place you in danger.'

'And if they do suspect anything, what shall I say?'

It was clear subterfuge was not at all a part of her character. Sadly, it'd become second nature to his. 'You'll have to come up with something.'

'Oh, well, if it's as easy as that, I should have no trouble.' She laughed.

He winked at her, bringing an amused frown to her full lips. 'Welcome to the world of intrigue.'

Chapter Five

Bart watched Moira enter the Royal Academy.
She paused on the threshold to admire the tall
room with the paintings hung three and four
high on the walls. Her grey dress lined with
lace and covered by a sheer net of white muslin enhanced the whiteness of her smooth skin.
The colour of her dress was matched by the silver comb placed in her light hair, the one she
touched as she searched for a familiar face,
uncertainty marring her confidence. Unlike
the numerous other ladies filling the gallery,
she didn't enter on a man's arm or surrounded
by a clutch of family or friends. No one broke
from their circle of acquaintances to rush up
to her and draw her over to look at the mar-
vellous painting of the countryside or to share
gossip. It was as if her presence meant nothing to anyone, except Bart. He couldn't un-

derstand how, with her delicate manners and the grace of her movement, people could fail to miss her. He never had, not tonight or the first time he'd noticed the petite young woman standing alone by a pillar in Lady Greenwood's ballroom. He'd talked Richard into bringing him to the ball in the hopes he could use his brother's connections to gain clients. Moira was the only person he'd wooed that night, his efforts rewarded by her light laugh and charming smile.

Moira spied him at last and the hesitation of being here alone was banished by the smile spreading across her lips and lightening her pretty face. She wasn't as striking as some of the young ladies fresh to society, or elegant in the manner of the more matronly ones in their diamonds and feathered coiffures, but she was beautiful in a demure way, like a maiden from the country. She took a step forward to approach him before she remembered his instructions on how they should meet and turned to study the large painting to her right instead.

Bart strolled across the gallery towards her, stopping at various intervals to pretend to view some of the marble statues, but not even the voluptuous woman in the arms of a satyr could draw his attention away from Moira. She stood on the outside of a group of ladies admiring a painting of a family, her simple dress striking beside their more elaborate ones. Experience had given her innocence an edge of worldliness, making her familiar with grief and troubles. Yet somehow she'd remained unsullied by them and he regretted having to tarnish her with his plots and intrigues. However, if anyone could wade with him through the swamp and still come out on the other side with their goodness intact it was her.

At last, when the ladies moved on to the next painting, Bart stepped up beside her.

'Good evening, Lady Rexford.' He faced the painting instead of her and focused on the weight of the pistol hidden in his coat to help him stay fixed on uncovering the Rouge Noir instead of Moira's alluring perfume.

'Good evening, Mr Dyer. I'm surprised to see you here tonight,' she said a little too loudly, aware of the people around them. They had no interest in either her or Bart. His reputation as one of the most celebrated barristers in England garnered him a few looks once in a while, but most titled people simply nodded and passed by. They had no reason to speak with a barrister and a few others, like his father, did not take kindly to him prosecuting cases against others of their station. 'I didn't think you one for appreciating art.'

'I'm not, especially pieces having to do with domestic matters.' Bart nodded at the painting above them of a pretty woman with her husband. Their many children surrounded them on the columned steps in front of their ancestral home.

Moira stepped a bit closer to him and her upper arm brushed his, the pressure of it as distracting as the satin tone of her lowered voice. 'At one time you were a man for marriage.'

He cleared his throat. 'Events have since convinced me otherwise.'

The sparkle in her eyes dimmed. 'You have no desire for a son to train up to be a barrister?'

'My father hasn't exactly enamoured me of the idea of parenting offspring.' It would kill him to be as disappointing a father as he was a son or to bring a child into the world only to treat it the way his father treated him. He tapped his fingers against his thigh, agitation making it difficult to stand still. He could win the admiration of clients, judges and the law community, but when it came to his father he often seemed to come up short.

'Perhaps you simply haven't found the right woman to convince you otherwise,' she mused.

At one time it might have been her. She was the kind of woman who possessed the softness necessary to dull the sharp edges of a man like him. Unlike his mother, who'd allowed his father to run roughshod over her children, expressing her deep love in private but never openly demanding her husband treat them with even a fifth of the kindness she offered, Moira possessed the strength to make sure those she loved were treated well. 'If I haven't found the right woman it's because I've been doing a great many other things except looking.'

She touched one finger to her chin and fixed him with an impish smile. 'Perhaps when this danger is past we might find you some lovely women to make you change your mind.'

'The danger never passes, Moira. There's always more lurking in the background, and if not danger then someone in need of defending. My father may not think highly of how I earn my living, but I've made a great deal of difference in the lives of many people who appreciate my willingness to see justice done.'

She lowered her hand, making her reticule swing and brush her thigh. 'I appreciate what you do and it's very noble of you to do it.'

He reached beneath his coat to adjust the pistol. 'Then perhaps I should bring you to my parents' soirée tomorrow night and let you tell my father so.'

Moira laughed. 'If he refuses to listen to all the people in London who sing your praises, then I doubt he'll listen to me.'

'He doesn't listen to them because they're commoners, but you have the one thing he admires most—rank.' Bart stepped closer to Moira, aware of her bare upper arm so close to his wool-covered one. He wanted to trace the smooth skin with the back of his fingers and feel the warmth of her body against his. It was a dangerous and distracting temptation. He wasn't here to have yet another chance with Moira fail, but to get closer to Lord Camberline and, hopefully, the Rouge Noir. 'But enough of me and my domestic arrangements, we have other business tonight. Lord Camberline is here with his mother. They just entered the room and are quite taken with the Watteau.'

Moira glanced over one shoulder, her delicate chin above her almost bare shoulders. With her long neck exposed by her hair drawn up against it, she was as stunning as the painted wife on the wall before them.

Moira twisted the other way to snatch a peek at the room. 'The Comte de Troyen isn't here.'

'No, he isn't.' He glanced past her at mother and son. 'They're alone in front of the Watteau. It's a good time to approach them and see if you can get them to reveal anything.'

'How?'

'Flirt with Lord Camberline.'

Her pretty mouth dropped open. 'I can't do that! He's too young for me'

'He's a single man searching for a wife and you're a widow recently returned to society. No one would question you flirting with him.' Those words were harder for Bart to say than when he'd asked for her help yesterday morning. He didn't relish her turning her charm on any other man except him, especially one possibly involved in treason.

'I won't act like a ninny in front of a man who's barely reached his majority. I'm sure I can find another topic to entice them.'

'Try praising Napoleon and see how Lord Camberline reacts.'

She wrinkled her nose in disgust. 'I hate Napoleon.'

'Not tonight you don't.'

'It seems my impressions of a great many people are about to change.' She took hold of the back of her dress and, with a confident flick, flung the small train behind her. 'Wish me luck.'

She strode off across the gallery towards the Camberlines.

Bart admired her boldness. She might have hesitated when entering the gallery alone, but she didn't shrink from setting herself up in a position to catch the Marchioness's eye and begin the slow and steady process of working her way into their favour. He hoped whatever she said to Lady Camberline moved things on quickly. This afternoon, he'd visited Mr Fink, a talented forger in St Giles who produced fine documents for various clients both high and low born. After a generous payment had restored his memory, Mr Fink had told Bart about a recent shipping pass he'd done for Mr Dubois. Bart guessed it was in anticipation of an upcoming blockade run to France, and this, combined with Mr Roth's actions, suggested something was going to happen soon. Bart didn't have time to wait for the delicate sensi-bilities of societal etiquette to help Moira ob-tain entrée into Lord Camberline's circle. She needed to do it now.

Moira's heart pounded in her chest as she crossed the room. For all her pretence to cour-age, without Bart beside her she was nervous and she hoped it didn't show. Leaving the house to attend a society function had not been as difficult as Moira had feared. Freddy had been occupied in the sitting room with Nich-olas and Miss Kent, oblivious to them even being in London for the Season, and Aunt Ag-atha had made plans to dine quietly with her old friends. She'd been thrilled at Moira's de-cision to be seen more in society by attending the exhibit. Aunt Agatha and Freddy would have apoplectic fits if they discovered exactly what it was in society Moira was doing and with whom.

What am I going to do?

Her courage began to waver and she paused in the centre of the room to glance back at Bart. He stood sideways beside the painting, watch-ing her out of the corners of his eyes while pretending not to. Sensing her nervousness, he turned his head slightly and nodded his encouragement. In such a pose, he reminded her of one of the marble busts of a Roman emperor positioned on a pillar between the paintings. He was so sure of himself and unafraid to face any challenge. She couldn't say the same, but she would do her best to mimic him tonight.

Taking a deep breath, she offered him a little smile in thanks for his silent support and continued on to the Camberlines.

'Lady Camberline, it's a pleasure to see you here,' Moira greeted as she stepped up beside the Dowager Marchioness.

'I adore French art.' Lady Camberline nodded to Mr Watteau's *Soldiers on the March* hanging on the wall before them.

'So do I,' Moira lied, the words tripping over her conscience as they came out. She wasn't one for falsehoods and deceits and here she was embroiled in one. She much preferred English painters like Gainsborough over French ones, but what she was up to had little to do with artistic preferences. 'Nothing can compare to their depictions of the glories of France, especially those before the Revolution, the ones my grandmother used to describe. I've done what I can to encourage a love of France in my

nephew the way my grandmother did in me.'
She said a silent prayer for her grandmother
to forgive her for besmirching her memory.

'And have you succeeded?'

'In some ways…' Moira took a deep breath
before she spoke her next words '…but my
brother and I don't see eye to eye on Napoleon. He doesn't recognise the benefits the Emperor has brought to France and many other
countries.'

Moira studied Lord Camberline while she
spoke. He didn't seem as interested in the conversation as his mother and the only response
her comment solicited was the slight curl of
his lips in distaste. She wasn't sure if it was
distaste for her or her comments. The desire
to retreat back to the safety and anonymity of
Bart took hold of her before she fought it back.
She would not be frightened away from helping him, not by the disapproving Marquess or
her own doubts.

'And what benefits do you see?' Lady Camberline asked with a great deal of reserve.

Moira swallowed hard. She might very well
be putting the lady completely off her by air-
ing such false thoughts, but there was only
one way to discover it. 'His ability to govern

well. Think of the law and order he's brought to France. There are a number of countries in need of such forceful rule of law.'

'Indeed,' Lady Camberline murmured with, if Moira was not mistaken, an air of approval. 'Napoleon has turned France from a backward nation of rebels into a glorious empire. At present the north of England could benefit from a stern hand. But alas, we fight him instead of learning from him.'

'We do.' Hearing Lady Camberline praise Napoleon made it all too clear there were people who should know better who were enamoured of the Emperor. Whether or not Lady Camberline or her son was enthralled enough with the Corsican to act on their convictions remained to be seen. 'My grandmother would have been proud to see France returned to its former splendour.'

'I'm glad to hear, unlike so many children and grandchildren of *émigrés*, you have not forsaken your ancestry.' She slid her son a hard look he met with one of his own. If Moira didn't know better, she'd think he didn't share his mother's views, but she wasn't certain and it forced her to play on.

'Grandmother made sure I always appreciated the superior tastes and culture of her homeland.' Moira glanced back and forth from mother to son, none too subtle in her desire for an introduction.

Lady Camberline studied her as if weighing whether or not she should oblige. Then she raised her jewel-bedecked hand and levelled it at her son. 'Lady Rexford, may I introduce my son, Lord Camberline?'

'A pleasure to meet you, Lady Rexford.' The young man offered a shallow bow, his face emotionless as he eyed her. He was tall, with the same grey eyes and long nose as his mother. Some of the softness of youth still hung in his cheeks and she guessed in a year or two he would lose it and, if he wasn't already married by then, he would become an even grander catch for all the heiresses new to the marriage mart.

'It's been ages since I last spied you in society.' Moira tipped forward a touch while curtsying to offer the young man a better view of the tops of her breasts above her bodice, deciding to take Bart's advice to flirt, no matter how much of a fool she felt like for doing it.

Lord Camberline didn't appear to appreciate or welcome the generous view. His smile, which had never been wide or welcoming, faltered about the corners before vanishing. He bowed to her again and then to his mother. 'If you ladies will excuse me?'

'Where are you going?' Lady Camberline demanded with a terseness to make Moira's back straighten. The Dowager's words didn't have the same effect on her son. He scowled at her, drawing more of her silent ire.

'To view the other works and to leave you both to enjoy your love of all things *French*.' Lord Camberline strode off towards the door leading to the adjoining gallery. Moira hazarded a brief glance at Bart who watched Lord Camberline with the seriousness of a terrier rooting out its quarry. Then he strolled off as though he were simply moving on to the next exhibit and not deliberately following the young man.

'Please forgive my son for his lack of manners. He doesn't share my enthusiasm for my native land, despite the French governesses and nursemaids I hired to help instil it in him. He is also having a difficult time accepting his duties as the Marquess, especially where his need to wed is concerned.'

'He is set on someone?' Moira pressed casually, trying not to put her off by being impertinent whilst at the same time drawing her into a confidence.

'He thinks he's in love with a lady entirely inappropriate for a marquess.' Lady Camberline stuck her nose further in the air with indignity. 'Eventually, he will come around to my way of thinking and give up whatever romantic notions he holds about choosing his wife.'

She seemed so certain it made Moira's heart ache for both the young lord and whoever was the object of his heart.

'I'm sure, with your good guidance, he'll come to realise the betterment of his family name is more important than anything else,' Moira stated, almost choking on the words.

Her statement seemed to work on Lady Camberline as well as her admiration for France for the woman viewed Moira with new potential. 'Perhaps further conversation with you could help convince him of the wisdom of following my counsel instead of the fickleness of his heart?'

'I'm not well acquainted enough with your son to impart such wisdom.'

'That can be changed. You must come and

have tea with me tomorrow. I should love to speak further with someone who truly understands and appreciates the way of things, and the old days in France.'

'I'm afraid, in regards to France, I can only offer you my grandmother's memories,' Moira said with a smile, 'almost all of which were from the days before the Revolution had gutted it.'

'They will have to do.' Lady Camberline flicked a quick glance over Moira's shoulder, focusing on something or someone there before settling her attention back on Moira. 'Until tomorrow.'

With a shallow curtsy of dismissal, Lady Camberline swept off across the gallery and into the next room, joining Lord Moreau, Lord Lefevre and a young blonde woman Moira didn't recognise in front of another French painting.

Moira looked around for Bart, wondering if she should risk joining him to tell him about the discussion. Lady Camberline's openness about her son and the invitation to tea were promising. Perhaps in the privacy of her sitting room, the other woman might slip and reveal if her admiration for Napoleon had led to her or her son's involvement in the Rouge Noir. Moira laughed to herself. If Lady Camberline's son was involved in treason, she wouldn't be careless enough to tell it to a near stranger, but perhaps there were ways to subtly draw her out, ones Bart could suggest.

Moira approached the other room, searching for Bart, eager to gain some guidance on how to proceed with Lady Camberline. She spied him near the far corner and began to make her way towards him. Here, in public of all places, she was free to chat with him, to listen to his smooth yet forceful voice, to stare into his dark eyes and bask in his intense focus on her. It was broken by brief bouts of humour she longed to see more of, to watch it brighten his eyes and perhaps hear again the laugh she'd enjoyed five years ago.

Don't be silly. He isn't with you for amusement, but to seek out traitors.

She played with the cord on her reticule as she paused before yet another painting, wondering if she should approach him or if she should go home. For her own protection, they couldn't give those around them any hint the two of them were working together, but something in her longed to be a little bit reckless, like the night she'd slipped out of the house to join him at Vauxhall Gardens and enjoy a few stolen kisses in the shadows of the garden.

She touched her gloved fingers to her lips, the memory of his kisses as vivid as the colours in the paintings on the walls. It was dangerous to dwell on such temptations especially when Bart had made it clear he didn't share her desire for a home and family, but she couldn't help herself. Not one kiss from her husband had ever ignited her insides the way Bart's had and the old sensation gave her hope.

Stop it. What she was doing was foolish in so many ways, but especially where her emotions were concerned. She wanted a family and he wasn't the man to give it to her. The constant derision of his own had poisoned him against the notion of a wife and children. Besides, he'd asked for nothing more than her assistance with this Rouge Noir, and after Aunt Agatha's treatment of him yesterday, and Freddy's threat, he wasn't likely to have an interest in aligning himself with her in anything but a professional manner.

'Lady Rexford, how wonderful it is to see you in London,' Lady Windfall exclaimed as she joined Moira before a painting of a church near a pasture. The elderly woman had been an old friend of her husband's whom Moira had hosted a few times at Allwick Hall.

Moira exchange pleasantries with the woman, the entire time subtly watching Bart out of the corner of her eyes. She half-heartedly answered Lady Windfall's questions, all the while debating if she should approach Bart or continue with the exhibition and then go home and wait for him to send her word about their next meeting. He offered her no silent indication about what she should do, his attention focused on Lady Camberline and the red-headed man she spoke with. Judging by Bart's grim expression, something about the strange pair bothered him, but she couldn't see the man for he stood with his back to her.

Once the red-haired man was done speaking with Lady Camberline, he moved into the adjoining gallery with surprising alacrity. Bart followed the red-haired man, hurrying as fast as decorum allowed. She wondered what about the man had aroused his suspicions, except this time she wasn't about to wait for him to seek her out tomorrow and tell her. She'd find out tonight and then gain from him some advice on how to handle her tea with Lady Camberline.

'If you'll excuse me, Lady Windfall, there's something I must see to.' With a smile of apology, Moira dashed away from her sedate companion and across the gallery, moving as quickly and delicately as she could manage without drawing too much attention to herself. She made for the adjoining room which was more crowded than the first, forcing Moira to peer over the tops of turbans and curled ringlets to try to catch sight of Bart. At the far end she saw his wide shoulders disappear around the corner and she twisted her way through the gathered ladies, explaining to any she accidentally jostled that she was looking for the women's retiring room.

She reached the end of the hall and turned left. It led to a door slowly closing, indicating where Bart had gone. Taking a quick look around to make sure no one was watching, she slipped through it.

Chapter Six

The solid thud of Bart's feet on the concrete somewhere up ahead drew Moira forward into the semi-darkness of the hallway. The one or two lanterns hung along the length of it were turned down low and offered more shadows than light. She slowed her pace and ran her hand along the wall, struggling to see ahead and unsure about where she was going. She passed a dark bisecting hallway and on the other side considered returning to the gallery when a solid mass of man grabbed her from behind.

She let out a yelp.

'Moira?' Bart's voice hissed in her ear, the familiar scent of his shaving soap cutting through the darkness and her fear. One of his arms sat hard against her waist, the other stretched across her shoulders, keeping her tight against him. 'What are you doing here?'

He didn't let go of her, but continued to hold her close. She leaned against him, as thrilled by the firmness of his arms around her, and his wide chest against her back, as she'd been terrified when he'd grabbed her. She longed to tilt her head back, slide her hand over her head and along the back of his neck and draw his lips down to hers. She almost twisted to face him until she remembered herself and where they were.

'I was following you. I have news.'

'It can wait.' He let go of her and shifted away, denying her the pleasure of his strong embrace. 'Go back to the gallery.'

Before she could respond, the squeak of a door opening somewhere up ahead in the darkness set Bart into motion. Without a word, he bolted off down the corridor, leaving her alone in the darkness.

Moira considered returning to the gallery, but she wasn't about to stand by herself in the wide rooms wondering if he would come back while lamenting the way everyone around her, except the most aged of the lot, ignored her. She was tired of being overlooked and the excitement of the chase, and the desire to remain close to Bart, sent her racing after him.

She struggled to keep up with him as he rounded a corner and then shoved open the door leading to the outside.

Bart burst out of the building and stopped in the dark alley behind it. Reaching the end of the building, he plastered himself against the corner and peered around it to try to catch sight of the man and where he'd gone. Beyond this narrow alley was the main street in front of the Royal Academy. Bart surveyed the gathered carriages and people converged there, searching for the man, but there was no one except drivers huddled in groups smoking pipes and chatting. He had to find the man and corner him without getting shot. He'd seen the outline of the pistol beneath his jacket when he'd stepped away from Lady Camberline, but it didn't scare Bart off the chase. He touched his own pistol in the holder beneath his coat, hesitant to draw it. He couldn't rush down the middle of the busy street waving his weapon and draw the wrong kind of attention.

The whisper of silk beside him and the faint scent of lilacs caught his attention. Without looking, he knew Moira was with him. 'What are you doing here? I told you to go back to the gallery.'

'And I decided to ignore you.' Her breath was as rapid as his from having kept up with his pace. Her impertinence would have been charming if they were in a sitting room instead of an alley. 'Who are you chasing?'

Bart was about to tell her when a flash of red hair beneath a carriage lantern caught his attention. He took off after Mr Dubois, aware of the delicate fall of Moira's slippers echoing behind him. Focused on not letting Mr Dubois get away, he didn't insist Moira return. They raced down to the end of a street, Bart steadily gaining on the smuggler who was more winded than fast. He had to catch him. The armament procurer for the War Office didn't have the pedigree to rub elbows with peers, at least not in public. Few men here might know him and those that did might gladly purchase his questionably acquired munitions and French goods, but they weren't likely to acknowledge a connection to him at an art showing. Nor would a man like him openly approach a marchioness unless he'd had dealings with her before. Bart needed to know what they were and what he and Lady Camberline had been discussing.

Bart was sure it wasn't French wallpaper for her sitting room.

Bart turned a corner to the street where a group of men spilled out of a tavern. In the glow of the light coming from the tavern's windows, the skunk caught Bart's eye, his swarthy mouth turning down at the corners. He didn't wait for Bart, but took off in a fast walk through the assembly of drunken men. A few cursed at Mr Dubois's rough handling as he headed towards the street on the other side.

His pushing created an opening for Bart to follow. The scoundrel jogged around a corner, making for the wrought-iron fence of a private courtyard on the opposite side. Mr Dubois raced through the gate and the screech of the hinges carried over the rustle of rocks beneath Bart's shoes as he ran after him. He threw out his arms to catch the swinging gate, then hurried into the passageway leading to the dark courtyard just beyond it.

Mr Dubois turned a sharp corner. Bart did the same, then dug his heels into a hard stop, nearly hitting the end of a pistol. He knocked the weapon aside as it went off. Plaster and brick shattered behind him and Moira screamed. Bart turned to see her grab her neck and crumple to the ground. It was the distraction Mr Dubois needed to escape. He took off running in the opposite direction as Bart hurried back to Moira.

She knelt in a heap of silk on the corner, her hand pressed to her neck, blood staining her white glove.

Bart crouched next to her, his heart racing faster than when he'd been chasing the smuggler. He pulled her hand away from her neck, desperate to get a look at the wound.

'A piece of the brick hit me,' she answered in a shaky voice, sitting back in her beautiful dress in the wet and dirt of the street.

He examined the cut, relived to see it was more ugly than deep. He slipped a handkerchief out of his pocket and pressed it to the wound, anger tingeing his relief. 'Why did you follow me? I told you to stay behind.'

He bit back the rest of the sentence about her having given the man the opportunity to get away. She was not one of his trained men, but a woman he'd thrown into a strange and dangerous situation. She was already wounded enough because of him. She didn't need him making her feel guilty to add to the sting.

'I'm sorry I didn't listen,' she apologised,

her wide eyes glistening in the faint light from the lone street lamp overhead.

'It's all right.' He placed his arm around her shoulder and drew her against him, trying to ease her trembling, and the jolt of fear searing his insides. She'd narrowly missed sharing Lady Fallworth's fate. 'Come with me.'

He helped her to her feet, clasping her tight to him as he guided her away from the alley and back to the Royal Academy. She leaned hard against him as the lanterns illuminating the front of the Royal Academy came into view between the carriages.

'I can't go back in there, not like this,' she protested.

'We aren't going inside.' He turned her away from the main street and led her down a darker side one to where his conveyance stood waiting. He'd learned years ago not to muddle his vehicle in with the others, but to leave it out where he could make a hasty retreat. He waved for his driver to remain in his seat and then tugged open the door. 'Get in.'

'I can't leave with you,' Moira protested, staring into the interior of the carriage. 'What will my driver think when I don't return?'

Bart signalled for Tom, the boy sitting beside his driver, one of the few convicted pick-pockets he and his men had trained to serve the law instead of breaking it, to hop down. 'Find Lady Rexford's driver and tell him she's decided to go home with Lady... Moira, was there someone there tonight you're familiar with?'

'Almost no one,' she answered, the tremble in her voice made worse by the shame of her admittance. 'But I did speak with Lady Windfall who used to visit me and my husband in the country.'

Bart turned back to Tom. 'Tell the driver she's gone with Lady Windfall and to return home instead of waiting for her.'

'Yes, sir.' Tom dashed off to find the Fallworth driver and relay the message.

'I'm sure we needn't resort to such lies. I'm perfectly capable of going home in my own vehicle,' Moira protested as he handed her inside.

'No, I must see to your wound.' He climbed into the coach and settled in beside her. 'I'll take you home afterwards.'

He reached past her to draw the dark curtains over the windows and his knees bumped hers when the vehicle rocked into motion. Neither of them pulled away or made a move to place some distance between them, even while the space inside the vehicle seemed to shrink with their closeness. He turned up the carriage lantern and the orange light highlighted the blood staining her glove. 'Let me see it.'

She kept the handkerchief pressed to her neck, her skin paler than normal. 'You needn't bother. I told you it's only a scratch.'

'Let me see it.' He took her chin with his fingers and tilted it to the side as he removed her hand from her neck. The wound was straight and clean and not too deep, but the jarring contrast of the cut against her luminous skin made him want to hunt down Mr Dubois and pound him into the pavement. 'I'll clean it. It should heal well, although I can't promise there won't be a permanent mark.'

A shiver made her full breasts tighten along the edge of her gown. It was all Bart could do to control his reaction to her enticing curves. He shrugged out of his coat and draped it across her shoulders.

'No, I can't. I don't wish to stain it.' She tried to shift out from under the garment, concerned as always about others and never herself, but he wouldn't allow it.

'I insist.' His fingers brushed her shoulders

when he settled the wool firmly over them. She clutched the lapels and drew it closed, but not close enough to disturb her wound. He reached past her, aware of how near his arm came to her stomach as he opened a panel in the side of the carriage to reveal a hidden compartment. Inside sat two tumblers and a decanter of brandy. The sensation of her stomach against his forearm when he'd held her in the dark Royal Academy hallway increased the heat of her nearness. If he could clutch her against him again he would, but she was here to help him save the Crown, not to enjoy a fling. He sat back, his grip tight on the cold glass of the brandy decanter.

'You travel well stocked.' A touch of humour brought back the hint of blush the scare had drained from Moira's cheeks.

'It's to calm nervous clients on the way to court and to subdue less co-operative witnesses.' He tapped open another small panel behind him to reveal a selection of pistols and knives.

'It's that dangerous being a barrister?' She nodded at the pistol in the holster against his side.

'It is when you regularly extract information

from forgers and other lowlifes.' He splashed a bit of brandy on his handkerchief.

'And to think, so many look down on men in business. If they really knew how exciting it was, they might join you,' she teased with a lilting smile, the encounter with Mr Dubois failing to extinguish her spirit.

'I doubt it. The soft dandies don't have the stomach for it.' He pressed the brandy-moistened linen to the wound and she drew in a sharp breath. 'My apologies.'

'It's all right.' She winced again as he continued to clean the cut.

He wiped the soft skin in delicate circles to remove the trail of blood threatening to stain the lovely bodice of her dress, ignoring the clenching of his stomach at the memory of the gunshot and her collapsing in the street. When he'd stood with his soldiers against the French, he'd seen many men go down on either side of him. Their deaths had shaken him, but not the way Moira's near miss had. It was as if he'd been shot himself. It made it more acute the risks he was asking her to take by helping him and he debated not taking her home. If Mr Dubois had recognised her, she might be in as much danger as her sister-in-law had once been. He kept his concerns to himself, unwilling to alarm her. She'd had enough of a shock already. 'You handled the encounter much better than most ladies would.'

'I've nursed two men through illness and raised a small child. I'm no delicate flower.'

'I'm glad to hear it,' he said, even if the mention of her late husband made him as angry as what Mr Dubois had done to her.

'How am I going to explain this to Freddy or Aunt Agatha?' She folded her hands in her lap with a sigh. 'Between the smell of brandy and the blood, they'll think I've been in a pub fight.'

'In a way you have been.' Bart focused on the dark red wound, doing all he could to ignore the swell of her breasts as she took in a sharp breath when he ventured too close to the cut. 'Tell them you weren't paying attention on the way to Lady Windfall's conveyance and you walked into the sharp edge of a tail board.'

'Do you think they'll believe it?' The faint humour she'd shown before was gone, replaced by real concern.

'I'm sure they will.' Her eyes met his, her doubt as certain as his, despite his words. 'Why wouldn't they trust you?'

'Because I'm lying to them.'

Bart sat back, lowering the brandy and the filthy handkerchief, his guilt expanding. It wasn't only her life he'd put in danger through their alliance, but her future with her nephew. He had to count on Freddy's love and concern for her to imagine all might be well. His own experience with his father made it a difficult faith to extend. He stuffed the cork back in the bottle and returned it to the hidden compartment. 'I'm truly sorry for what happened tonight.'

She tugged off her bloodstained glove and wadded it into a ball. 'I'm the one who should apologise. If I'd just gone back to the gallery like you asked instead of following you I wouldn't have been hurt and the man wouldn't have escaped. Who was he?'

After what she'd been through, there was no reason not to tell her. 'Jacques Dubois, a notorious arms procurer and smuggler.'

'Oh, dear.' Moira touched her fingertips to her mouth, the glove having stopped her delicate skin from being stained. 'Do you think he saw me?'

He didn't need to warn her about the other consequences of tonight. She'd already guessed.

'I doubt it. It was dark and he isn't likely to be familiar with you. In the small chance he is, I'll assign a man to watch you and your house.'

'Won't it be suspicious to have a strange man following me?'

'My men are so good, no one in your family will notice. In the meantime, I must figure out why he was there and speaking with Lady Camberline. He doesn't have the pedigree to rub elbows so freely with the mother of a peer.'

'He's known Lady Camberline for a long time. His mother was a French *émigré* who became Lady Camberline's governess. His father was married to the governess,' Moira stated the same way his mother did whenever she relayed gossip he needed for a case.

'How do you know so much about Mr Dubois?'

'My governess was friends with Lord Camberline's governess. They used to talk during house parties in front of me and Freddy. She spoke excellent French, but she was not discreet. It's why Mama dismissed her when I was ten. I started asking too many questions and demanding explanations for things I shouldn't have known anything about.'

'Even if he is well known to Lady Camberline, a marchioness isn't likely to publicly flaunt a lowly connection, unless her son isn't the only one involved in the Rouge Noir. Like my recruiting you, few would suspect a woman of her reputation to be involved in treason.'

Moira snuggled deeper into his jacket and leaned into the corner of the carriage. Not even Bart's cedar scent permeating the wool could overpower the disappointment of him referring to her as someone in his service. The idea shouldn't trouble her, especially in light of Freddy's threat, but it stung more than her aching neck.

'After my discussion with her tonight, I wouldn't be surprised if she is somehow involved. She doesn't shy away from sharing her favourable opinion of Napoleon.' She relayed her brief interaction with the Camberlines, determined to be as professional as him in this matter. 'It's what I chased you down to tell you, that and she invited me to tea tomorrow.'

Bart rubbed his chin with his fingers. 'How did Lord Camberline react to the conversation?'

'He seemed uninterested in it, hostile even, and eager to be away from us.'

'Perhaps he doesn't like his mother openly

flaunting her opinions and placing them at risk by arousing suspicion.'

'Then you think she is involved?'

'I can't say, but the possibility makes your continued acquaintance with her valuable. After tonight, are you willing to keep the engagement with Lady Camberline or would you prefer it if we ended our arrangement? I'll understand if you want to.'

He was trying to let her go sooner, to sever the faint connection binding them. She should accept it, take the cut on her neck as a warning and stop risking her relationship with her loved ones over something so dangerous, but she couldn't. When he'd been seeing to her neck with the same tenderness he'd shown during their first kiss, his shoulder so close she could have laid her head on it, she was certain there'd been something more than professional interest in his concern for her. It'd touched her deeper than his fingertips on her shoulders and she was loath to lose it. 'No, I'll have tea with her tomorrow and see what else I can garner.'

'I appreciate your help.' Her importance to him, even if it didn't extend beyond his investigation, warmed her against the chill in the carriage. 'She must know something about what her son is up to, as I'm sure you know everything the people in your house are up to.'

Moira twisted the soiled glove around her finger, the satin stiff with dried blood. Yes, she knew exactly what was going on in her house. She'd seen the looks between Freddy and Miss Kent, noted the amount of time they'd spent together over the last couple of days. Moira couldn't blame Freddy for falling for the young woman, she was pretty and sweet, but her brother should know better than to trifle with her. Moira wasn't about to deny anyone in love their chance at happiness, no matter what their station, but she better than Freddy understood the challenges they'd face if he tried to make his son's nurse his wife. Aunt Agatha would find a way to separate them and Moira wasn't certain her brother could withstand such pressure and persuasion. If he couldn't, it might ruin Miss Kent's reputation and future expectations, and her faith in love. It wasn't an experience Moira wanted the girl to endure.

'Are you all right, Moira?' Bart asked. She examined him where he sat across the squabs, one of his long legs so close the fabric of her dress brushed his calves. She envied the silk, and his sure posture, wishing she possessed his confidence. Nothing seemed to rattle him, except her and what had almost happened tonight.

'I was thinking of a domestic matter, nothing as important as what you're dealing with.' She'd stopped him from catching his suspect, all because she hadn't wanted to be in a gallery alone.

'Of course it is, if it matters to you.'

She studied him, amazed once more at how ready he was to compliment her on the small things ruling her life. He could have railed at her for having defied him and causing him to lose Mr Dubois, but he didn't. Even yesterday, he hadn't demanded she help him, but simply requested it. When she'd refused him, he'd respected her decision instead of belittling her or trying to coerce her into doing his bidding the way her family did whenever she dared to defy them. 'You surprise me, Bart.'

'Good. I'd hate to be predictable.' He smiled with a wickedness to make her toes curl in her slippers.

'You certainly aren't.' Unlike her. She was very predictable, dependable and boring. 'I used to read about your cases when I was living in the country.'

He raised his eyebrows in surprise. 'Even with your aunt's letters railing against me?'

'Not so much after those, but certainly before. Your case against Lord Hartmore on behalf of his widowed sister-in-law was the talk of the countryside and enlivened many a winter gathering at our house.'

'Did you brag to your friends about having known me in London?'

'They were my husband's friends, not mine, and, no, I didn't tell anyone about you.' She tugged off the clean glove and laid it across her thighs. 'Our time together, however brief, was my secret to keep. It made me feel young when all the responsibilities of caring for a sick husband did their best to make me feel old. I'm sure it must sound silly to hear.'

'Not at all. After enduring war in France, and so many other things since coming home, I sometimes feel much older than my thirty years.'

'It's one of the reasons I love Nicholas. When I'm around him I feel a little of his excitement over the world and the innocence with which he approaches it.' She laid her hands over her stomach and the emptiness inside her. She craved a child of her own to cuddle and love as she did Nicholas, but there was none. During the first months of her marriage, the possibility had arisen and then quickly passed. The midwife had assured her it was normal and she would soon be with child again. She'd clung to the hope until it'd become apparent the lost chance would be her only one. With her husband's health failing, he hadn't possessed the energy to try for more. She'd disliked his attentions, but she'd been willing to endure them because they were the only means by which she could achieve her dreams of a baby. Her hope had been extinguished entirely once he'd passed, leaving her as hollow inside as the morning she'd miscarried. 'I don't think I remember a time when I was innocent, or without burdens and concerns.'

'What your family did to you was wrong, especially with your aunt capable of handling your family affairs.' He knew of her past because she'd told him about it during their whirlwind, and failed, engagement. 'She could have easily taken over the management of Fallworth Manor after your mother died instead of leaving it to you. And then when Freddie's wife was murdered, she once again foisted all the responsibility back on you, taking advantage of your generosity to avoid any real work herself.'

Moira fingered the soiled glove in her lap, his accusation against Aunt Agatha striking a chord she didn't wish to hear. It was one she sometimes heard inside her own head late at night after an especially trying day with Aunt Agatha. Bart saying it so bluntly out loud made it impossible to ignore. She loved her family and would do anything for them, but there were moments when she wasn't sure if all the things they'd done for her had really been in her best interest, or theirs. 'Perhaps, but if I hadn't taken over my mother's duties at the manor or helped with Freddy and Nicholas, who would have?'

'You refusing might have forced your father or aunt or brother to step up to their responsibilities.'

'Or driven them deeper into their mourning and cost us all our living. I couldn't allow that to happen, especially not with Nicholas's future so dependent on the estate. Freddy is grateful for everything I've done to help him.'

'Is he?'

'Of course.' Despite her insistence, his doubt made her shift in her seat, especially after her conversation with Freddy this morning, but she ignored it. Bart only saw things from the outside, he hadn't been there in Fallworth Manor for the last two years. 'I'm sure you'd have done the same for your family if they'd needed you.'

He crossed his arms over his chest. 'It would depend on who was involved. I'd lay down my life for my mother and brothers. Not for my father.'

'Bart, you can't be serious.' She understood what it was like to be frustrated by loved ones. Freddy and Aunt Agatha often annoyed her but even in their worst moments she couldn't be so heartless as to turn away from them.

'You mattered to your father, Moira. Mine barely noticed me or the three others above me. Once he had my two oldest brothers and the security of the line, the rest of us might as well have not existed. When Richard's wife gave him a son and heir to secure the succession beyond any doubt, even Stephen, the next youngest brother after Richard, discovered what it's like to be ignored like the rest of us except when Father wants to give one of his endless lectures about everything we do needing to bring honour to the family name.'

'What you do is honourable.'

'Not in his eyes. He'd rather I be a forgotten clergyman in some distant parish than involving myself with criminals and repeatedly landing my name, and by association his, in the newspapers.'

She could almost taste his bitterness and his pain. For all the good work he did on behalf of so many, he didn't deserve this, just as she didn't deserve Freddy's ire after everything she'd done for him. No, of course Freddy was thankful, he was just scared because of what had happened to Helena. It was why he'd threatened her like he had. 'Maybe your father is proud of you but doesn't know how to show it?'

He shook his head. 'I doubt it, but I suppose there's always hope.'

'We must believe in it, the alternative is too awful to consider.' Such as Freddy or Aunt Agatha not appreciating her as much as she'd always believed.

'And what do you hope for, Moira?'

She touched the sore wound on her neck. It was time to turn the conversation to more mundane subjects. The carriage wasn't large enough for this much emotion and she was too tired from the night's events to fend him off, but the desire to at last say her dreams aloud to someone who might listen and not scoff at her or offer compliments laced with insults like Aunt Agatha did was too tempting. 'I might be a widow, but I'm still a young woman who wants all the things other young women have: a home, a family, children of my own.' She didn't dare say love. Bart was too practical for romance and she'd embarrassed herself enough already by being so open with him.

Bart longed to slide across the squabs and sit beside Moira, to slip his hands around her waist and claim her lips, but he remained where he was. If he could give her all the things the far-off look in her eyes said she wanted, he would, but he wasn't a man for marriage and children. To take her into his arms would be to lead her into a lie. Deception was too much a part of his life already and he refused to deceive her. 'I'm sure you'll find a man worthy of your heart.'

'I hope so, but sometimes it's difficult to imagine, especially when I see all the other young ladies.' She picked at the embroidery on her dress. 'I don't have their daring, or their ability to flirt and make a spectacle out of my-self to catch a man's eye.'

'You may not make a spectacle of yourself, but you certainly have their daring and a cour-age worthy of any soldier on the battlefield.'

This brought a smile to her face, but it was one of embarrassment. She tilted her head down and looked up at him through her eye-lashes, innocent and alluring all at the same time. 'Now I see why they only allow male judges on the bench. No female judge could withstand your flattery.'

'Perhaps, but a man is as easy to flatter as a woman, one just has to do it a little differently.'

She leaned forward, her green eyes spar-kling with a wit he wished to see more of. 'And how does one flatter you, Bart?'

He leaned forward, resting his elbow on his thigh and bringing his face achingly close to hers. He could wipe the playful smirk off her lips with a kiss, taste again her sensual mouth and the heady excitement of desire he'd expe-rienced with her five years ago. Except he was no longer young and thoughtless and neither was she. He'd experienced the consequences of forgetting himself with her once before. He had no desire to repeat the mistake again, no matter how tempting it might be. There was a great deal more at stake this time than his heart. 'You can help me discover what the Camberlines are up to.'

Her smile faltered around the corners. This wasn't the answer she'd expected, but in the circumstances it was the best one he could give. She sat back with some of the same self-possession she'd shown when she'd walked away from him to meet Lady Camberline in the gallery, except this time there was a shadow of sadness and disappointment behind her eyes. Whatever possibility she saw in him was an illusion and he couldn't allow either of them to be fooled by it. 'Then I'll do my best to see what I can discover tomorrow.'

The slowing pace of the horses told Bart they'd reached her house. With a great deal of reluctance, he opened the door and stepped down when the carriage stopped. He wanted to climb back inside and tell his man to drive on, but he couldn't. Instead, he waited by the door with his hand outstretched, ready to take hers.

She slipped his coat off her shoulders and laid it carefully across the squabs, then placed her bare hand in his, gripping the firm flesh of his palm tightly as she stepped out of the carriage. Around the square, all the windows of the houses including hers were dark, indicating the late hour. He shouldn't have risked bringing her to the front door, but there was no alley to the mews and he wasn't about to leave her down the street to walk home alone.

His hand tightened around hers and they stood so close her breath brushed his neck above his cravat. The memory of them together like this five years ago, when, as she'd come home from dinner at one of her aunt's friend's houses, he'd slipped from around the carriage and stolen a kiss from her while the aunt had sauntered inside, rushed over him. Back then there'd been promise and potential in the furtive meeting of their lips. The only potential tonight was for disappointment. This wasn't a life for a lady, especially one like Moira. She was too good and caring, and he wanted to shield her from the ugliness of this work that had already marred him.

Bart opened his fingers and let her go. 'Meet me tomorrow at the Tyburn turnpike a half-hour before your tea with Lady Camberline and I'll advise you on how to proceed,' he instructed, focusing on why they were together and concerned about her safety. He wouldn't rest easy until she was in and out of the Camberline house without adding another wound to her enticing body.

Moira stared up at Bart. Despite his bravery and determination, there was a loneliness to him she could almost touch. He needed the love and care of a woman, and the joy of children, as much as Freddy had needed her and Nicholas's love both during and after his loss. Some day, perhaps, a woman would catch Bart's attention, one who could break through all of his reservations and prejudices about marriage and give him everything he needed. It wasn't up to her to foist on him something he was resolutely against. 'I'll be there.'

'Goodnight, Moira,' he offered in a deep voice barely above a whisper. It took hold of her the way he had when she'd been on the ground clutching at her neck and fearing the worst. He'd been a steady rock for her to cling to while she'd shivered with fear. She wanted to draw in more of his strength, to climb back in the carriage with him and let consequences and concerns be damned, but she didn't.

'Goodnight, Bart.' She gathered up her short train and slowly made her way to the front door. Before slipping inside, she turned to look at him. He remained by the side of the carriage, watching her with a look she couldn't read. She wasn't foolish enough to believe it was longing or anything more than a desire to see her safely home. She reluctantly stepped inside and closed the door on Bart. Home was the one place she didn't want to be. She wanted to be with him.

Chapter Seven

Moira descended the stairs and headed for the breakfast room, the late night with Bart setting hard in the small of her back. She'd crept into the house and up to bed tired from the excitement of the evening, and Bart, but she hadn't been able to sleep. She touched her neck, the wound hidden by the high collar of her morning dress, the faint memory of Bart's fingers on her skin while he'd seen to her still potent, as was their conversation. Once, he'd been eager to wed her and accept everything marriage entailed. Last night, he'd made it clear that whatever interest he'd held in a union with her was gone.

The sunrise hadn't brought Moira much more than a few hours of stolen sleep and she came downstairs in a fog of thoughts until the footman passing by with Freddy's travelling trunk cleared her haze. Moira paused at the bottom of the stairs, the flurry of activity looking a great deal like someone was leaving. Freddy's voice down the hallway drew her to the morning room and she stepped inside only to be stopped short by Aunt Agatha and Freddy's hard stares.

They know I was with Bart last night.

Fear slipped up her spine, but strangely, not regret.

Setting her shoulders, she strode into the room, refusing to confirm their suspicions or to be humbled like some wayward child. She ignored the food set out on the polished sideboard, beneath the matched paintings of her parents, and took her place at Freddy's right and across the round table from Aunt Agatha. 'I saw the footman carrying trunks. Is someone leaving this morning?'

Freddy and Aunt Agatha exchanged a conspiratorial glance, before Freddy sat back in his chair the way their father used to do whenever he gave his progeny dictates at the breakfast table. 'You didn't arrive home from Lady Windfall's until one o'clock in the morning.'

'What were you doing up at such an hour?'

Since Helena's death, Freddy seldom indulged in late nights. It meant something, or someone, had kept him awake. It increased her suspicions about her brother and the comely nurse.

'I had trouble sleeping.' Freddy fiddled with his knife. 'I was worried about you.'

She didn't believe his being up had anything to do with concern for her and she would have said so if Aunt Agatha hadn't spoken first.

'It's a good thing he did stay up. He saw you come home in Mr Dyer's carriage,' Aunt Agatha spat. 'How could you lie to us about where you were and who you were with, and with Mr Dyer of all people?'

'Would you prefer I insult him to his face like you did?' Moira shot back, making her aunt's mouth drop open in surprise. She'd never been one to cause problems, but to settle arguments and make sure all was right between them. It was a role she could not maintain today.

'We discussed the matter of Mr Dyer,' Freddy said in an even voice, trying to sooth the tension between her and Aunt Agatha. 'I thought you understood what I'd asked of you.'

'You weren't supposed to see him again,'

Aunt Agatha exclaimed, dousing the rising fire with lamp oil.

'It isn't your place to tell me what to do and who not to see. I don't chastise Freddy for his interest in Miss Kent.'

Aunt Agatha sucked in a sharp breath and Moira wasn't certain if it was because Moira had dared to air a family secret within the hearing of servants or if it was because she'd failed to notice the illicit liaison taking place under her nose. She turned her hard eyes on her nephew. 'Is that who had you up so late last night?'

'What I do with Miss Kent is my own business,' he snapped.

'And what I do with Mr Dyer is not yours,' Moira challenged in a soft and shaking voice. Let them rail at her. It might be scraping out the inside of her stomach, but it was necessary. She wouldn't allow them to separate her from Bart again.

With sad eyes, Freddy turned to her and dropped his voice, aware Aunt Agatha was still listening. 'You know the dangers involved in what you're doing.'

'I do.' Moira touched her neck. She'd been all too aware of them even before last night.

Now she must pay the price for her decision to ignore them.

'And you still wish to carry on with him.'

'I will, just as you'll continue to carry on with Miss Kent despite the risk to her reputation. Will you marry her if you get her with child?' He could do what he liked, but she had to ensure Miss Kent would be protected. She'd been entrusted to the family by her father and Moira didn't want to betray his trust.

'He can't marry a nurse. Think of the scandal,' Aunt Agatha screeched.

'Is he to leave her to ruin, then?' Moira pressed, stunned once again by her aunt's callousness.

'Enough of this.' Freddy folded his linen napkin and laid it down beside his plate with a deep sigh. 'Nicholas and I and Miss Kent are returning to the country this morning.'

'Freddy, how can you possibly think to take Miss Kent to the country after, well, after what Moira has suggested?' Aunt Agatha's voice rose with each word. 'Surely if Moira has imagined it, others have, too. Moira, as soon as we are home, you must do something about this.'

'I'd prefer it if Moira didn't come back with

us,' Freddy almost whispered, but the words were loud enough to hit Moira like a slap.

'What?'

He glanced at her before he focused again on his plate. 'I can't have you placing your desire for Mr Dyer over Nicholas's welfare.'

'You know very well that's not what this is about.'

'Isn't it?' he challenged.

Bart's hand in hers last night on the sidewalk, the tilt of his head and low voice made her doubt her comment as much as Freddy. 'No, and even if it were, how many times have I placed your needs over mine? How many times have I sacrificed to help you? Did I not come to you after Walter's death and do everything I could to support you and Nicholas? Can you not stand by my decision now? I would stand beside you and Miss Kent if you asked me to, as long as your intentions were honourable.'

Aunt Agatha let out a sharp squeak, but the siblings ignored her.

Freddy fidgeted with the end of the napkin dangling over the edge of the table, refusing to meet her eyes. 'It's not the same thing, Moira.'

'You know perfectly well that it is, and if

you'd allow me to explain, you'd see how the things you're worried about won't happen. I'm only going to—'

'I don't want to hear any more about it.' Freddy stopped playing with the napkin and raised his eyes to meet hers at last, his expression stony. 'You will regret this, Moira, maybe not today, but you will, as I learned the hard way.'

Freddy rose and strode into the hallway, calling to the footmen to hurry up with the packing so they could leave at once. He then called for Miss Kent, wanting to know if Nicholas was ready.

Moira's heart constricted. She understood his concerns, but he hadn't even bothered to listen to hers or to allow her to reassure him all would be well like the many times she had during those first days after Helena's death. After all she'd done for him, returning to Fallworth Manor two years ago wearing her weeks-old mourning dress, her paltry widow's portion in trunks in the cart along with the papers outlining the expected meagre payments each quarter, ready to help him and Nicholas, he'd cast her aside like some slatternly maid the moment she'd defied him.

Bart had been right. Freddy didn't appreciate every sacrifice she'd made for him and Nicholas.

Nicholas. He's taking him away from me. Tears stung her eyes, but she blinked them back. *How could he be so cruel?*

'I hope you're happy.' Aunt Agatha shoved back her chair and stood, the spite in her words drying Moira's tears. 'Look at all the trouble you've caused.'

'After everything I've done for this family, you sneer at me? What will you do in the country even supposing you keep Freddy from ruining Miss Kent? Run Fallworth Manor? You've never taken control before, not even when I was fourteen and mourning the passing of Mother and you were more than capable of stepping in. I have a difficult time imagining you'll accomplish it now with enough success to ensure it remains profitable.'

Aunt Agatha opened and closed her mouth, at a loss for words before she recovered herself. 'I'm sure Freddy is more than capable of assuming management of the estate.'

'If not, then your security will suffer along with his. Are you willing to take such a risk?'

'As willing as you are to stake your reputation and future on a man like Mr Dyer. Don't come crawling back to us when your good name is in tatters because of your association with him. He might be revered for his skill in the courtroom, but it doesn't extend beyond there.'

Aunt Agatha turned on her dainty feet and stormed out of the dining room. The footman remained by the door, pretending he'd heard nothing.

Moira's hands trembled where she clasped them tightly in her lap. She wanted to run after Aunt Agatha and Freddy and beg for their forgiveness, to apologise for causing trouble and secure once more her place of importance in their lives, but she forced herself to sit still. They were turning their backs on her, making it clear how unnecessary she was to them even though they'd relied on her so heavily before. If they didn't need her, then no one did. If she didn't have Fallworth Manor and all the people there, she had nothing.

No, Bart needed her, and for more important reasons than to ensure the silverware was polished.

Except it wouldn't last. At any moment he might catch the Rouge Noir and her assistance would no longer be necessary to him either. It would make all her sacrifices to help him meaningless, like Walter's death and his failure to give her a child had made her father's ambitions for the marriage, and her secure future, worthless in the end.

She unclenched her hands, rose and went to the sideboard, ignoring the painted faces of her parents watching her while she helped herself to breakfast. She could imagine what they'd have to say about this if they were here, but they weren't, and part of her was glad. She didn't want to endure anyone else criticising her decisions or trying to talk or force her out of making them.

She returned to the table and sat down, the emptiness of the room engulfing her. It would be like this tomorrow when it was only her here and no one else and then what would she do?

Exactly what I'm doing now.

She tucked into her breakfast, more hungry than she'd realised. If she could face a musket ball and not be destroyed then she could face this, even if she longed for the day when she no longer had to endure her troubles but could defy them and thrive.

* * *

'Any news on the man you were following who met with the Comte de Troyen in Rotten Row?' Bart asked Joseph from where he sat in a leather chair across from his solicitor partner, Mr Steed, in their Temple Bar office. Mr Steed knew about Bart's work for the Government, but had no place in it. His purpose was to serve their clients, especially those who came to them in search of protection against fraudsters, forgers and thieves.

'He isn't a beggar, but he isn't working for Mr Dubois either,' Joseph informed them from where he stood by the window. 'He's Lord Camberline's valet and he's been carrying a lot of message back and forth between his lordship and the Frenchman.'

'What's in those letters?'

'Can't say yet. The valet is one of the most faithful servants I've ever seen outside your employ and one of those teetotallers. I can't load him up with ale at the pub like I normally do and I've had my fill of the drinks at the chocolate house.' Joseph placed a hand over his stomach and stuck out his tongue to emphasise his distaste for the overly sweet beverage.

'I appreciate your sacrifices in the name of

service to the King,' Bart acknowledged with a smile.

'I suppose it's better than when you sent me into that brothel and I had to watch all those men meeting while ignoring everything else going on around me.'

'I'm sure you had a little fun there.'

'I'm not saying I didn't, but there are some things a man sees that he can't forget and they're almost as horrible as what I witnessed in war.' Joseph laughed, then sobered. 'To be honest, my gut says whatever the two men are using the valet to communicate, it doesn't have to do with France. Whenever I bring up the topic of France or Napoleon, the valet doesn't become shifty as you'd expect a guilty man to do.'

'Maybe he doesn't know what's in the messages he's passing between the men,' Steed suggested.

'It's a poor valet who doesn't know everything his master is up to.'

'Or a simpleton with a little too much admiration for his lord,' Bart mused.

'He's devoted to Lord Camberline, so it's possible. Also, he told me Lady Camberline is holding a dinner tomorrow night. He's upset

about it because he might have to act as a footman since many of the staff are sick. It isn't
the usual society dinner either, but one with a
lot of high-ranking guests, including the Prime
Minister.'

'The Camberlines aren't a political family.'
Steed stated exactly what Bart was thinking.
'Unless Lord Camberline, in the midst of preparing to take his seat in the House of Lords,
is building support and his mother is doing
what she can to help him.'

Bart rubbed his chin as he stared at the
scuffed toe of his boot. 'It's possible.'

'If Lady Rexford can secure an invitation
then you might find out. Even toffs have lim-
its as to how free they'll be in the presence of
servants, but they aren't so cautious around
woman of their class, especially attractive
ones,' Steed suggested.

The idea of Moira becoming even more embroiled in this affair knotted Bart's stomach,
but Steed was right. She was the best person
to find a way to attend and see what this political party entailed and if it had anything to
do with the plot.

'I'll speak to Lady Rexford and ask her to
secure an invitation. Joseph, pick a few men to

try to obtain positions with the Camberlines. I also need your best and most discreet man to keep an eye on Lady Rexford.' Bart told them about Mr Dubois and the incident in the alley, working hard to keep his personal feelings out of the tale. 'We can't make the same mistake with her as we did with Lady Fallworth.'

'Awful deal, that,' Joseph shook his head with regret. 'I'll put Mr Smith on it right away.'

'And keep on the valet. I want to know what Lord Camberline and the Comte are up to.'

'Yes, sir.' Joseph left Bart and Steed to see to his duties.

Bart crossed to the bookcase and the selection of liquor on top of it. He poured himself a healthy measure of brandy and took a hearty sip, the guilt he'd endured after Lady Fallworth's death burning his insides as much as the drink. He'd stepped back from spying in the months afterward and thrown himself into his barrister duties, trying to make up for his failings by helping others. It hadn't worked. He gripped the empty glass tightly, praying he wasn't making the same mistake with Moira. 'I shouldn't have dragged Lady Rexford into this.'

'With your men watching her, she's well

protected,' Steed reassured. 'What I wonder is, who's going to protect you?'

Bart took in the office with its dark wood desk and the leather furniture, and the bookcases and paintings of horses and hunting dogs adorning the walls. The masculine air of it contrasted sharply with what he remembered of the inside of Lady Rexford's feminine home. The difference was evident throughout his life. Every since he'd gone to war, there'd been nothing to ease the hardness growing inside him and he wondered how long it would be until it closed him off from anything of beauty and charm until he became as craggy as his old bachelor uncle. It didn't matter, nothing did except the task before him. 'I've dealt with worse men than the Rouge Noir.'

'I don't mean from pistols, but more womanly charms.'

Bart swirled the brandy in his glass, then drained it. Steed was coming closer to the truth than Bart cared to admit. He'd been there the first time Bart had been involved with Moira and beside him when he'd done a fair amount of cursing and drinking after it had all gone wrong. It was back before Bart had learned to master his thoughts and emotions thanks to his years of arguing before the bar. His lack of discipline had led him to rush into a relationship with Moira, but after coming close to death in France so many times, he'd wanted to enjoy life, especially with her.

He rubbed his forehead with his fingers, understanding Steed's concern. Here he was considering Moira and his own situation instead of focusing on this new information and what it meant to his investigation. She was here to help him bring down the Rouge Noir, not to change his past or his future. 'Unlike some of our clients who never learn when it comes to women, I know better.'

'Sure you do. What's the old saying? Pride goeth before a fall.'

'The pride these Rouge Noir members have in their ability to bring about Napoleon's reign in England is the only thing about to fall.' The clock on the wall above Steed chimed the time. 'I have to go. I have an appointment with Lady Rexford.'

'Take care, Bart, not just with her safety, but yours.'

Bart descended the stairs with Steed's warning ringing in his ears. He wasn't as confident in his control over his emotions as he'd led his partner to believe. More than once last night, when Moira had been so close to him he could have pressed his lips to hers, he'd been tempted to cross the imaginary boundary between them. Whatever had drawn them together five years ago still existed between them. It was incredibly difficult when they were alone together to ignore it, but he must. He refused to trifle with Moira, or place her in a situation where she had to choose between her family and him. He had enough troubles with his father to not wish the same kind of difficulties on her, but her ability to get close to the Camberlines was too essential to the investigation for him to stop meeting her.

Bart stopped in the middle of the pavement, his reasoning too much like the one he'd used to keep Freddy involved in the Scottish Corresponding Society plot. If he'd ended Freddy's involvement sooner, they wouldn't have discovered it and murdered his wife. If Bart pushed Moira into securing an invitation to the dinner party, and the Camberlines were involved in the Rouge Noir, it might place her in the same danger.

Bart walked faster, his need to protect England at odds with Moira's safety. This was his battle and he wouldn't sacrifice Moira to ensure he won, but it was a fight he couldn't lose either. The stakes were too high. He'd marched through the cities Napoleon's cannons had levelled and seen the villages wiped out by the typhoid Napoleon's army had carried with them. He'd endured the desperation in the survivors' eyes as they'd pleaded with him for help he couldn't give. He refused to see it mar the faces of his fellow countrymen, but he didn't want to ensure their safety at the risk of Moira's. This cause was greater than the two of them, but she wasn't a proper agent trained to deal in deception and capable of protecting herself. She was relying on him and he'd already let her down last night. He couldn't bear the thought of doing so again.

Up ahead, Tyburn turnpike came into view and he spied Moira across the street from the busy landmark. She stood in the shade of her carriage, watching the sea of people passing back and forth, and the carts and conveyances lumbering past. Bart almost ran to reach her and hear again the lightness of her voice and enjoy the warmth of her smile, but he forced himself to slow. The closer he drew, the more apparent her lack of peace became. She'd been a picture of contentment and beauty from a distance, but up close it was clear all was not well. She wasn't worried, but troubled in a deep way he understood. It was the same look his soldiers often wore after a fight when their best friends or their innocence had been sacrificed to the horrors of war.

'The wound looks better than it did last night,' Bart remarked when he reached her. Her dress didn't hide the ugly red mark and the sight of it infuriated Bart, increasing his desire to make the Rouge Noir suffer.

She touched her neck. 'None of my tea dresses have a high enough neckline to cover it. I hope your excuse about walking into the sharp edge of a carriage is convincing enough.'

Her smile faded, increasing the unease in her expression.

'What's wrong?' he asked.

'It seems this wound isn't the only one from last night I collected.' She explained about her row with Freddy and her aunt, and their leaving for the country.

'I'm sorry.' Bart bit back a few choice remarks about her brother. At one time he and Freddy had been close and he'd respected the Earl and his dedication to his country. It made hearing what his friend was doing to his sister worse and reignited Bart's internal battle between allowing her continued participation and his desire to remove her from it. The more embroiled with him and the investigation she became, the more she suffered. 'This isn't how I wanted things to be for you.'

'Don't be sorry. You were right. They didn't appreciate all I'd done for them as much as I'd believed.'

'Some time without you might help them realise how important you are.'

'Even if it doesn't, I'm glad I discovered it before they dragged me back to the country, insisting I care for them while neglecting myself and losing all hope of ever getting the things I want in life.' She offered him a wan smile, trying as always to remain positive, but he could see the hurt in her eyes. What was absent was defeat. 'Perhaps I should have done more to assert myself sooner instead of hiding away from the world at Fallworth Manor.'

She'd received a strong blow today, but she hadn't crumpled into a corner in self-pity. Instead, she remained strong and determined to carry on. He admired her spirit, sure this game wouldn't wreck her as it had Freddy, but would strengthen her like steel dipped in cold water before it is heated again. It was a test of spirit she didn't need to face, especially after everything she'd already been through in her life. 'You didn't hide. You stepped in when you were needed most, just as you've done with me, as you've always done. I admire your ability to look after those you care about. It isn't a trait everyone shares, or appreciates.'

Moira marvelled at his words. He was the first one to see her work on behalf of her family in such a light. She'd discovered this morning how much they took her for granted and it had cut her like the day she'd miscarried, but she refused to allow her pain to consume her. Whether this rift with Freddy would ever be healed remained to be seen, but Bart's admiration gave her hope. If he appreciated her efforts on behalf of everyone, then perhaps some day there would be another man who could, too, one she would spend the rest of her life with. It was a pity it couldn't be Bart. It might have been if she'd been a stronger person back then, but there was no point dwelling on the past, not from five years or even five hours ago. 'Thank you. Your compliments mean a great deal to me, as does my ability to help you. How do you think I should proceed with Lady Camberline today?'

His certainty in her changed to marked reservation and she sensed he was about to say something which, unlike the compliment, she didn't wish to hear. 'Do nothing at the tea today to try to gather more information or to work your way into a better acquaintance with the Marchioness. You can no longer be involved in this.'

Moira felt as if the pavement had been ripped out from under her. First Freddy and Aunt Agatha had turned their backs on her. Now Bart was pulling away. 'I thought you needed me.'

'I do, but the danger is too great and I promised to keep you safe.'

Moira crossed her arms over her chest, determined to be as stubborn as him. 'I don't want to be safe. I've been safe for years and dead inside. After so much grief and misery, to feel something other than hopelessness or sadness has given me a greater appreciation for life than anything I've experienced in years and I want more of it. Can't you understand?'

'I can. It's why I pursued you the way I did

five years ago. After the carnage and fear in France, it was a pleasure to live again.' His candidness caught them both off guard. He peered across the street, grinding his jaw at his slip, but Moira refused to turn away.

'Then don't deny me the same chance.' She took his hand, not caring who in a passing carriage or on the walk behind them saw it. His admittance revealed the depth of his regard for her, even if it might only be for this investigation. In time, when the Rouge Noir was no longer a threat, they might part, but the desire to hold on to him no matter what was too strong to ignore. She'd lost a great deal this morning, she would not lose this place in Bart's life, the only thing giving her existence meaning while everything else she loved was being torn from her. 'Please, Bart, time is passing and I have a tea to attend and a country to help you defend. Please, tell me I can continue to help you and how I should proceed with Lady Camberline.'

She stood still, despite wanting to throw her arms around him and bury her face in his neck until he relented. Even over the smell of the horses and smoke of the city, the spicy scent of him was unmistakable, as was the pressure of his fingers as he gripped her hand. In the heat of them permeating the kidskin of her gloves, she could feel him wavering. This was how he'd appeared the moment before he'd asked her to marry him, as if he were about to take more of a risk than with anything he'd ever done before. She silently urged him to agree. Without this holding them together, she might never see him again and it stung as painfully as being separated from little Nicholas.

'When you speak with Lady Camberline, do so as you would a friend. Encourage her confidence and ask leading but not overly obvious questions. She won't suspect what you're up to,' he said at last, letting go of her hand.

She allowed this subtle separation, determined not lose her head and make an already tense situation more difficult. He was going to allow her to continue assisting him. At the moment, this mattered the most.

'And if she doesn't confide anything in me?' Lady Camberline didn't seem like the kind of woman who extended confidences easily. 'Should I invite her to tea in return and try again?'

'No, there are two other things you must do. One is to establish some kind of solid connection between Lord Camberline and the

Comte de Troyen, perhaps where his valet is concerned.'

'His valet?'

He explained to her the connection between the Frenchman and Lord Camberline through the man.

'It will be difficult, as valets are not a subject ladies usually discuss, and I can't simply ask Lady Camberline to tell me about the affairs of her servants.'

'You're a clever woman. You'll find a way to broach the topic.'

'I appreciate your faith in me. I wish a few other people possessed as much of it.'

'If they can't see it then they are the ones at fault, not you.'

There were no veiled insults like with Aunt Agatha or lack of real thanks as with Freddy, but instead a genuine regard for her and she intended to be worthy of his unwavering faith. 'What's the second thing you wish me to do?'

'Tomorrow night, Lady Camberline is holding a dinner with a number of political men.'

'Political men? How odd, since the elder Lord Camberline's death, Lady Camberline hasn't troubled herself with politics and neither has her son.'

'Which makes this dinner all the more suspicious and your need to be there important.'

'Me?' Moira baulked. 'I can find a way to discuss valets, but I can't invite myself to Lady Camberline's private dinner.'

'You'll have to do it because I need someone there who's free to listen and ask questions, and move through the gathered guests. Talk up your connection to Prince Frederick or profess a desire to be involved in politics, whatever it takes to secure an invitation.'

'Even if I do, government men aren't likely to discuss anything nefarious in front of me.'

'You'd be surprised what men will discuss in front of ladies.'

'I'm sure I would be.' Moira didn't ask for details for she could imagine the secrets whispered across pillows. Many gentlemen thought too little of women's intelligence to believe they might comprehend or repeat what they'd heard.

Distant church bells rang the quarter-hour and Bart raised his head to listen to their deep chorus. 'You'd better set off. You won't work your way into Lady Camberline's good graces by being late for tea.'

Bart opened the carriage door and held out

his hand to help her in. She wanted to stay here with him, to walk in the park as she'd seen many soldiers and their young wives do, but they were not courting. With reluctance, she stepped inside and he closed the door behind her.

She perched one elbow on the window, putting off their parting a touch longer. 'How shall I send you news of my progress?'

'Meet me at the British Museum by the sarcophagus in the Egyptian display at five o'clock.'

'I'll be there.' She sat back in the carriage, out of sight of him, and the vehicle set off. As it rolled away from the curb to merge with the traffic, Moira did her best to concentrate on her coming visit to Lady Camberline and what she needed to accomplish instead of Bart, but it was difficult. His nearly removing her from the investigation had startled her more than when the pistol had gone off last night, but she'd changed his mind and for the moment all would be well. He hadn't been able to let her go and she was beginning to believe it was for more reasons than uncovering plots and traitors. It was an irresponsible thing to imagine, but it was as difficult to shake as her conviction to see this affair through. What the future might bring she couldn't say and with Lady Camberline's Mayfair house coming into view the time for considering it was over.

Bart watched Moira's carriage disappear into the maze of traffic before it turned a corner and drove out of view. He cursed his weakness where she was concerned. He'd been determined to remove her from this matter, but the moment she'd taken his hand he'd faltered. Her fortitude had been difficult to resist and he'd longed to stoke the fire burning inside her, not only for the chase but for him.

If only she'd demonstrated this much fortitude five years ago.

But it wasn't fair to hold her previous choices against her. She'd been young and naive, like he'd been in some ways about the ability to cross the imaginary lines separating him from the daughter of an earl. Since then, she'd tasted the frustration of isolation, disappointed hopes and a callous family while learning to better understand her own heart and mind. Instead of it forcing her deeper inside herself, it was forging her into a stronger, more determined woman. It boded well for her future, the one he was beginning to believe he wanted a larger role in.

He took out his pocket watch and checked the time as he laughed at the idea of having a woman in his service, especially one like Moira. She wasn't made for knives and pistols, but a home and children, and he wouldn't drag her any further into his world of brandy, plots, snitches and spies. Except it was clear by the mark on her lovely neck how much he'd already tarnished her with it. If only she could work on him the same effect he'd worked on her, to cleanse him of some of the dank and must of his life and make him a better man, one worthy of a woman like her. Maybe then there could be some way of being with her when this affair was over, but he'd learned a long time ago, after his first humiliating loss in court, not to plan the future until he'd achieved victory and not to allow emotion to cloud his judgement.

He slipped his watch back in his pocket and started off for Mr Flint's office. He and a contingent of men were to visit the pubs around the Surrey Docks that smugglers like Mr Dubois often frequented. They needed to find the Frenchman and force him to reveal whatever he knew about the Rouge Noir. Bart had never before allowed his personal life to interfere with business, not even as a captain in Austria when he'd sent men he cared about into dangerous duties. He couldn't allow it to happen with Moira. Theirs was a business relationship, not some odd way of courting, and when this was over, he'd return to his work as a barrister while she would return to whatever life still existed for her. They would part as friends and nothing more. During the entire walk to Mr Flint's office, this thought disturbed him more than the Rouge Noir.

Moira sat across from Lady Camberline, engaging with her in pleasant small talk about the weather and other mundane subjects. Moira worked to keep up with the conversation, her thoughts fixed on what Bart had asked her to accomplish. If he were here, she was sure he'd have no trouble steering the topic of discussion to the one he wanted. How in the world she would guide the conversation to the valet or secure an invitation to the dinner she didn't know, but she needed to think of something and soon. With the maid entering to clear away the tea service, Moira's time for action was running out. Bart had entrusted her with this important task and she wouldn't fail him.

Then, while the timid maid collected the tea cups, she fumbled one and almost sent it clattering to the floor before she caught it.

'Watch what you're doing, you clumsy girl,' Lady Camberline snapped, making the maid's hands shake even more than before.

'Sorry, my lady.' The maid set the cup on the tray with a rattle, picked up the heavy silver pots and china plates and made a hasty retreat back to the kitchen.

'My apologies for my poor-quality maid,' Lady Camberline apologised. 'But a number of illnesses and staff changes lately have left me scraping the bottom of the barrel for help.'

'I certainly understand,' Moira sympathised, seizing on the chance to broach the subject of the valet. 'We've had a number of staffing problems at our house, too. One of which is Freddy's valet. The man is hopeless when it comes to polishing boots or keeping coats properly brushed. Do you have the same troubles with your son's man?'

'He does well enough where Charles's wardrobe is concerned, but I'm not particularly enamoured of him. He comes and goes at the oddest times and is cagey when I ask him about it. I've tried broaching the subject with my son, but he's devoted to the man. It seems I have as little say in the matter of my son's servants as I do in so many other aspects of his life.' Her lips curled in displeasure, altering her graceful looks in an unpleasant manner.

Moira wondered if Lady Camberline would enjoy more influence over her son if she'd taken a greater hand in his upbringing instead of leaving it to paid people, but she didn't dare suggest it. Even Aunt Agatha had thought it strange for Moira to always take an interest in Nicholas instead of leaving the majority of his care to Miss Kent. Should Moira ever have children of her own, she would make sure they knew they were loved by their mother and father, not foisted off on servants who gave scant thought to their future. It was the love she'd enjoyed from her mother, and her grandmother, the love that had died with both of them along with her childhood. Moira put the thought aside. She was here for a reason and it wasn't to question the lady's parenting decisions.

'I understand you are quite active in Lord

Camberline's political ambitions.' Moira's mouth went dry with her nervousness as she began to venture near the subject of the dinner.

'Who told you such a thing?' Lady Camberline appeared taken aback at the suggestion and Moira faltered a touch before shoring up her resolve.

'Prince Frederick, at your ball, said you're holding a political dinner.' She hoped her blushes didn't betray her lies. She wasn't sure they didn't as Lady Camberline tilted her head in scrutiny at Moira.

'You're well acquainted with the Prince?'

'He knew my father. It'd been years since we've spoken, but he was quite amiable the other night.'

'Very interesting,' Lady Camberline mused, her usual poise returning. 'It's the rare person I hear regard him in such terms. He must like you.'

'I used to sit with him and my father and listen to them discussing politics and state business when I was younger. I very much enjoyed their conversations and the Prince was quite candid with his opinions.' Moira adjusted the thin necklace resting just below her wound to keep the metal from touching it.

Lady Camberline levelled one alabaster hand at her. 'What happened to your neck?'

Moira touched the ragged cut. 'I was playing with my young nephew in the garden when he took hold of a stick and swung it at me. I'm afraid I didn't move fast enough and he caught me with the edge of it.'

'Make sure to rub rose oil on it so there isn't a scar. We can't allow your lovely skin to be marred by such an awful mark,' Lady Camberline offered, but there was an edge to her helpful advice, one which made Moira still her hand against her throat. The possibility this woman suspected Moira's friendliness had other motives crossed her mind before she dismissed it. She'd given her no reason to suspect Moira's time here was anything other than a social call. More than likely, this titled woman who'd had so little hand in raising her own son didn't approve of a lady of Moira's rank playing in the garden with a little boy.

Whatever her feelings on the matter, Lady Camberline kept them to herself as she settled her hand in her lap once again. 'The dinner party I'm hosting isn't for my son's benefit, but for mine. Long ago, I used to host them with my husband and I find I miss the engaging talk and lively conversation. I'm also eager for more news on the war with Napoleon, things one cannot gleam by merely reading the papers.'

'They are so biased against him,' Moira offered, trying to draw out the woman's sympathies for the Emperor.

'Incredibly so.' Lady Camberline studied her once again and Moira resisted the urge to shift in her chair like a wayward child. The older woman's cold air was disturbing and even when she was doing her best to be friendly she still came off like a cat ready to pounce. 'Lady Allingford has had to bow out with her regrets and I find myself in need of one more person. I would very much like it if you'd attend in her place.'

Moira was careful not to show her enthusiasm or her surprise. She hadn't expected it to be this easy, nor did she wish to give herself away by rushing to accept the invitation. 'The dinner sounds lovely, but I have no idea what I'd contribute to the gathering.'

'Since you're acquainted with the Prince and not averse to discussing politics or Napoleon, I'm sure you'd be an excellent addition. Lord Lefevre and Lord Moreau will be there, too. I believe they were acquainted with your grandmother.'

'They were part of the French *émigré* circle of her time, yes.' And men her grandmother had held little respect for. Like so many others, they'd pined too much for a lost world instead of embracing their new life in England.

'Then I'm sure they'll enjoy the chance to speak with you. It would also be nice to have some pretty young blood in the group. I'm afraid everyone else on the guest list is much older than you.'

'Something I'm quite accustomed to after my time with my husband.' Moira struggled to hide her weariness at the thought of yet another evening surrounded by old men. She was young and wanted all the liveliness of life and love other ladies her age took for granted. She opened and closed her hand in her lap, picturing Bart as he'd stood across from her near Tyburn turnpike, his grip full of a force and energy she craved.

I never should have given him up.

'Then you'll attend?' Lady Camberline pressed with a touch more enthusiasm than she'd demonstrated either during her invitation to tea or the tea itself.

'I'd love to be there,' she accepted with feigned enthusiasm. 'It's been ages since I've enjoyed rousing company and debate.'

'Wonderful.' Lady Camberline rose to indicate the tea and the discussion were over.

Moira gathered up her reticule and fell into step beside Lady Camberline who escorted her to the door of the sitting room, ready to hand her off to the butler to see her out.

'Thank you for the interesting and enlightening tea.' Lady Camberline smiled, but it did nothing to soften her steely gaze, and something in her gratitude and her friendliness rang false.

Moira raised her hand to her necklace, the uneasy feeling she'd experienced when Lady Camberline had remarked on her wound coming over her again, and, not for the first time, she wondered if Lady Camberline was involved in the plot.

'Thank you for the invitation. I look forward to the dinner.' Moira forced herself to stand still and act gracious. She was eager to place some distance between her and Lady Camberline, and to meet Bart and tell him everything they'd discussed, and her increased suspicions.

Lady Camberline smiled again in a way to make Moira's skin crawl. 'I assure you, it will be an unforgettable evening.'

Chapter Eight

Bart leaned against the large sarcophagus lying on its back at the far end of the Egyptian exhibit, drumming his fingers on the hieroglyph-covered sandstone while he waited for Moira. During their time apart, he'd made little progress in finding Mr Dubois. The smuggler hadn't been at any of his usual haunts by the Surrey Docks, nor had he been seen frequenting them of late, leaving Bart's informants bereft of any helpful information. Even the smugglers Mr Flint had rounded up had only possessed vague information about the Rouge Noir with nothing more specific than whatever was going to happen would happen this week. What it was and who in the aristocracy were involved continued to remain obscure, except for the Camberlines.

Bart traced a cartouche with his fingers,

hoping Moira had discovered something. He needed some clue to lead him in the right direction and allow him to stop this plot.

The delicate click of a lady's boot heel over the stone floor caught Bart's attention and he straightened. He inhaled the faint hint of Moira's lilac perfume before he spied her approaching from around an obelisk. She was as beautiful as one of the Grecian statues lining the corridor, her dress fluttering behind her and against her legs the same way the togas did on the marble muses. It offered a heady hint of her thighs beneath the muslin, the beauty covered up by the many layers standing between him and her like the numerous rules of society keeping them apart.

She glowed with the sunlight coming in through the large windows along the top of the hall. Her beauty resonated through him as it did with the many priceless artefacts lining the room.

'I take it you had a successful tea?' Bart remarked when she came to stand across the sarcophagus from him, a self-satisfied smile gracing her lips.

'It was very successful.' They kept their voices low despite the lack of other visitors in the room. At this time of day, with most people at home preparing for the fashionable hour, they had the Egyptian gallery to themselves. 'I wasn't able to find out much about the valet, but I did receive an invitation to her dinner. She believes my presence will help charm Prince Frederick.'

'Well done.' Concern tinged his congratulations. The royal sons had a bad reputation for seducing ladies and the idea Prince Frederick might try to have his way with Moira disturbed him, but he didn't doubt she could hold her own. Yes, she might be going into a potential pit of vipers, but there would be many people about and she was clever enough to avoid danger. Also, one of Bart's men had secured a position as a footman inside Camberline House. Bart might not be present at the dinner to watch her, but one of his men would be. 'And the son? Any information on him?'

'No, she didn't discuss him much more than to complain about his lack of obedience. But there was something suspicious in her attitude.' She picked at a hieroglyph of a bee. 'I think we were right to suspect her involvement with the Rouge Noir.'

'It's possible. I chose you because people

rarely suspect a woman. The Rouge Noir may have recruited her for the same reason.'

'A dinner with influential men, especially ones who speak too much like Prince Frederick did the other night, would certainly be a good way to get information.'

'Which she then passes on to her son who instructs his valet to give it to the Comte de Troyen?'

'You still believe the Comte is involved?'

Bart tapped the sarcophagus. 'Given what I overheard at the ball, he and Lord Camberline are certainly embroiled in something secretive. Until I learn what it is, I can't dismiss him as a suspect.'

'Maybe there are other Frenchmen Lady Camberline is sending information to. She's good friends with Lord Lefevre and Lord Moreau. They were both at the gallery, and her ball, and they'll be at the dinner, too. I have no idea what their politics are in regards to Napoleon, but Grandmother never liked them and she was rarely wrong about people.'

'I'll inform Mr Flint and have him investigate the two lords. Given their proximity to Lady Camberline, they might be involved. In the meantime, while you're at the dinner, do your best to get into their good graces. You might be able to learn something much sooner than I can.' Bart clapped his hands together, the sound echoing through the long exhibit hall. 'Enough work for one day. Come with me and we'll have supper. There's a respectable place not far from here I'm sure you'll enjoy.'

'A widow dinning alone in public with a man of your reputation will set tongues wagging.' She joined him at the end of the sarcophagus, her warning only half-serious.

'I doubt anyone you know will be there. It isn't exactly a fashionable establishment.' He missed the protection of the stone between them. Being with her was more dangerous than almost any of the guns he'd faced in Austria. It threatened his promise to himself to keep every interaction with her above board. 'You walk away first, I'll follow behind. Once you're outside the gates, make for my carriage.'

With a saucy flick of her head, she turned and strode out of the gallery.

Bart followed at a discreet distance, admiring the swing of her hips beneath her dress, sure she exaggerated it for his benefit. He might be entirely professional when in her presence, but it didn't mean he couldn't admire the lush curve of her derrière. He'd have to be dead not to.

She strode out the front doors of the museum and descended the stairs at a leisurely pace, never once throwing a look back at him, confident he was following. He continued to watch her, but movement along the edge of his vision made him turn at the last moment. A man with a ragged scar on his cheek sprinted out of the shadows of a nearby alley and hurtled towards her, the long knife in his right hand glinting in the late afternoon sunlight. Bart jerked to the right and slammed into the attacker, sending him flying across the pavement. The knife clattered away from him and Bart snatched it up, facing the movement on his other side, ready to strike. He stopped when he saw it was Mr Smith, the man Joseph had assigned to follow Moira, taking her by the arms and pulling her to the safety of Bart's nearby carriage.

Bart turned his efforts on the attacker who, recovering from his shock, scrambled back to get out of Bart's reach. He failed and Bart grabbed him by his dirty lapels, hauled him to his feet and across the square and around the corner to a more isolated alley. He slammed him hard against a building.

'Mr Roth, what a pleasure to meet you.' Bart punched him in the stomach, making the man double over.

'Who the hell are you?' he coughed.

'Someone who doesn't like Mr Dubois sending cowards to stab countesses, especially ones who are friends of the Queen with powerful connections in the House of Lords,' Bart exaggerated, wanting to place enough fear in the man to make him talk. He jerked him up straight to face him. 'Do you know what they'll do to you for trying to kill her?'

'I didn't know she was a countess.' The man paled, making the pink of the scar on his cheek deepen. 'Mr Dubois said she'd double-crossed him in a deal. He didn't tell me who she really was.'

'But you were still low enough to try and murder a woman.' He'd confirmed Bart's suspicions without him having to pound it out of the scoundrel. The slight victory didn't ease the fury roiling inside Bart. 'Where is Mr Dubois? I think it's time I had a talk with him.'

Mr Roth shook his head. 'I don't know. He

hired me through one of his messengers, he always does, I've never met him.'

The same instincts Bart relied on when questioning witnesses in the stand told him Mr Roth was telling the truth. Scum like Mr Roth were willing to do anything for coin and didn't care how or why they were hired or by whom. Bart shoved Mr Roth at his man who'd come up beside him. 'Take him to Mr Flint for a statement and to see what else he can drag out of him. Here's his knife for evidence.'

'Yes, sir.' Bart's man pocketed the knife, took hold of Mr Roth and dragged him off to another carriage parked near Bart's. The man sitting next to the driver hopped down to help subdue a protesting Mr Roth. Mr Flint's men would question him, but Bart doubted they'd get much out of him beyond a confession naming Mr Dubois as a party to a crime. This was the second time the arms-procuring smuggler had been careless, or overly bold, as if he knew the plot was about to unfold at any moment and he didn't fear being caught. If Bart could find the smuggler, he could arrest him for attempted murder and use this charge to force him to reveal whatever he knew about the Rouge Noir. Finding Mr Dubois was the hard part. This failed attack was the closest Bart had come to the smuggler today and it'd been far too close to Moira.

Bart brushed the dirt off his hands and sprinted to his carriage, eager to see her. He gave instruction to the driver on where to take them, then pulled open the door and climbed inside. 'Are you all right?'

'Yes, I'm just startled, that's all.' Her voice shook, but her poise revealed the steely will hidden by her usually calm exterior. 'I could do with a bit of your brandy.'

Bart opened the secret compartment, removed the bottle and splashed a hearty measure of the aromatic liquor into one of the crystal glasses. He handed it to Moira who took it with both hands before downing the drink in one gulp. She winced, but the drink had the desired effect as her shoulders relaxed with her easing tension.

'More?' Bart raised the decanter.

'Please.' She held the glass to him with a much steadier grip. He obliged and she took another hearty sip before lowering the glass. 'Who was that man?'

'Someone paid by Mr Dubois to try and kill you.' His fingers tightened on the glass decanter. If the smuggler wasn't so pertinent to this investigation, Bart would kill the man when he found him for daring to try and harm Moira. Bart eased his grip on the decanter, determined to remain focused. Lashing out in rage would help no one. 'He must have recognised you last night and, through your connection to me, seen you as a threat.'

'Impossible, it was too dark and I never got a good look at him. I can't imagine he saw me.'

Each moment they were together, Moira began to sound more and more like Bart. It didn't make him happy, nor did how close she'd come to sharing Lady Fallworth's fate, and all because of him. 'Then it must have been in the gallery?'

'But he wasn't present when I was with you.' Moira touched her neck, her eyes widening with more horror than when Bart had told her why Mr Roth had tried to attack her. 'Lady Camberline remarked on my wound today.'

Their gazes locked across the carriage seat. Neither of them needed to say it aloud.

Moira held up the tumbler.

He refilled the glass and she clutched it to her chest, but didn't drink. Instead she stared at the floor of the carriage, their suspicions about Lady Camberline and her involvement in the plot growing larger in the silence. 'You were right. I shouldn't have gone to tea with her or continued on with this.'

Bart settled the stopper in the decanter and set it back in its compartment, not relishing being correct. 'I won't give them a chance to hurt you again. You'll stay with me until this is settled.'

'I can't stay with you.' She shoved the glass at him.

He took it, his fingers brushing hers across the smooth surface and making him pause before he set the glass in the compartment behind him. 'You can't stay at your house alone. Once Mr Dubois learns you're still alive, he'll try again.'

'And if society discovers I've been alone with you in your house, I'll never be able to show myself in London again.'

'My servants are as silent as gravestones and where I live doesn't attract a great deal of high society. Since your brother has returned to the country, most people will assume you've done the same.'

'Until I appear tomorrow night at Lady Camberline's dinner.'

'You're not going to Lady Camberline's dinner. I won't have what happened to Lady Fallworth happen to you.' He tightened his hand into a fist and banged it hard against his thigh. This wasn't the first time he'd watch someone he cared about face an attack. He'd seen friends in Austria rush into battle ahead of him, only to be struck down by bullets or bayonets. He'd done his best to protect them like he had Moira, but he hadn't, and the guilt he'd faced after each death continued to haunt him. None of the measures he'd taken to shield Freddy and his wife had saved her in the end. Despite his best efforts, he'd failed them both. He couldn't fail Moira or watch her belief in him turn to bitter blame the way it had with Freddy, his hard words as difficult to endure as Bart's father's insults.

Moira laid her hand on Bart's tight fist and squeezed it, trying to draw him back from wherever guilt and regret threatened to take him. He'd vowed to guard her and he'd almost been forced to break his word by nefarious forces. It'd shaken his confidence in his own abilities, but not her faith in him.

'You'll keep me safe. I'm sure of it.' She

slid up beside Bart and rested her head on his shoulder, revelling in the warmth and strength of him as he held her tight. In his embrace there existed a comfort and surety she hadn't experienced since before her mother's passing. Bart's world was full of uncertainties and yet he stood at the centre of it, the most certain thing of all.

'I don't deserve your faith in me.'

She looked up at him. The faint light from outside slipped through the crack between the curtains and cut across his face to highlight the light brown flecks in his dark eyes. 'Of course you do. You're the noblest man I know.'

'No, I'm flawed, more than you realise.' He slid one hand out from behind her to cup her cheek, his fingers firm upon her skin as he leaned down and touched his lips to hers.

She closed her eyes and savoured the heady taste of his tongue caressing hers and the whisper of his breath across her cheek. Moira wrapped her arms around his waist, her fingers brushing the hard butt of the pistol concealed by his jacket. Its presence marked the sharp difference between her life and his, and between her dreams and his reality. This clandestine intimacy was as dangerous today as it'd been on Lady Greenwood's dark portico, except there was so much more at stake this time. Yet Moira wasn't the petted and protected young lady Aunt Agatha believed her to be. She would stand beside Bart the way Helena had stood beside Freddy and face with him any challenge.

He had only to ask it of her.

She leaned deeper into him, waiting for him to guide them in this as he had in every aspect of her activities since she'd agreed to help him.

Then the carriage jolted to a halt, forcing them to break from the kiss. It shattered the spell between them and he let go of her, shifting back across the squabs, the passionate man who'd held her a moment ago replaced by the stoic barrister. 'I'm sorry, I shouldn't have done that.'

His riveting glance betrayed his words, but she feared his adoration would vanish if she pushed him for more. 'Don't be. I owe you more than a kiss for saving me today.'

'I was only doing my duty.'

She struggled to retain her smile as he lumped her in with his men as if the kiss had meant nothing or hadn't changed anything. Of course it didn't and she should be grateful for his honesty and for helping her to see reality instead of a misguided fantasy. He dealt in a shadowy world of London she was just becoming aware of, one, until this week, she'd only ever seen from the inside of a passing carriage. It forced her to concede he was right about not wanting a family and children for it would place them in the kind of danger she'd encountered today. She craved the safety and security of a home not under constant threat by rogue criminals who might either steal her life or Bart's away at any moment. She'd already watched one husband fade away. She couldn't imagine doing it again, yet the thought of giving up Bart when this was all over terrified her more. Except he wasn't hers to lose.

She moved aside the curtain to see the front of a building she didn't recognise in a part of town she was unfamiliar with, determined to be as nonchalant about what had happened between them as he was. 'Where are we?'

'At the home of a colleague.' He shifted past her and out of the carriage as if the small space had grown too close. 'He's an expert on pistols, cannons and gunpowder.'

He held out his hand for her to take and descend. She examined the lines of his palm,

hesitant to touch him and recall any hint of
the passion they'd just experienced, when they
were both doing their best to forget it had just
happened. Unable to sit inside the carriage all
day, she laid her hand in his, hopping down
fast so as to let go of him quickly. Her breath
caught in her throat when his fingers tightened
around hers, trapping her in his grip as he drew
her up the front path to the house.

While constantly surveying the street for
any hint of danger, he told her about the powder he'd found in Lady Camberline's house.
When they reached the door, he placed her
between him and the imposing wood while
they waited for the butler to open it. 'It's an
odd thing to find in a lady's salon, but given
your suspicions about the lady, it isn't so odd
any more.'

With his chest so close to her she could see
the facets in the ruby of his cravat pin, she
could barely concentrate on his words. His
presence projected power and strength, not
comfort and calm, and it resonated deep inside her, making the strain of their kiss and the
awkwardness between them afterwards even
more difficult to endure.

'Given the people she keeps company with,

maybe she thought to protect herself with a pistol.' She forced the words out through her tight chest, all the while resisting the urge to rest her palms on his shoulders and press up against him. She had to stop reacting to him like a silly girl in love with an actor. This was all part of his duty to her and nothing more, no matter how much her imagination prodded her to believe otherwise.

'This kind of powder isn't for musket balls.'

At last, the door behind her opened and Moira all but sprinted into the entryway and out from beneath Bart. He followed behind her, calm and collected as if their standing mere inches apart from one other, and the kiss, hadn't bothered him at all. It probably hadn't. Unlike her, he maintained excellent control of his emotions. It was a trick she needed to learn, and quickly.

'Good afternoon, Wilson. Is Mr Transom here?' Bart asked.

The butler, a sombre man of later years, nodded. 'He's in his study. I'll take you through.'

While they followed the butler, Moira took in the house to settle herself, surprised by the tidiness of it and the simple lines of the furniture and decorations adorning the few rooms off the main hallway. She wasn't sure what she'd expected from Bart's descriptions of a weapons expert, but numerous guns and knives lying about apparently wasn't involved.

The butler led them to a study near the back of the house. 'Mr Dyer to see you, sir.'

A young man with round spectacles and a bit of softness along the chin looked up from where he sat at the desk. Around him were piled all the small pistols and munitions she'd expected to see in the rest of the house. They were kept company by the numerous books and papers cluttering every surface. She touched none of them, afraid something might go off. Bart didn't hesitate, but approached his friend and reached across the desk to shake his hand.

'Mr Transom, it's good to see you.' Bart let go of his associate and waved Moira forward. 'Lady Rexford, may I introduce Mr Transom?'

Bart didn't offer an explanation about her presence and Mr Transom, apparently well versed in the ways of intrigue, didn't ask. Instead he offered her a little bow. 'A pleasure to meet you, Lady Rexford. Welcome to my home. I'm sorry it's such a mess, but I've had a great deal of enquiries lately into weapons and other such issues.'

'I understand and I don't mind at all.' Moira's graciousness brought a grin to the young man's thin lips.

'Have you had a chance to examine the gunpowder sample I sent you?' Bart's question ended the pleasantries.

'I was reviewing it again in anticipation of your visit.' Mr Transom came around his desk and went to the table by the window. He bent over it and stared through the magnifying glass affixed to one end of a brass arm. A whale-oil lamp burned near the magnifying glass, throwing light on a narrow slip of paper and the dark red powder on top of it. Mr Transom picked through the granules with long metallic tweezers.

'What do you think?' Barth stood beside him. Moira perched herself on the edge of a small stool at the end of the table to Mr Transom's left in order to watch.

'Definitely gunpowder, but a disturbing mixture,' Mr Transom declared. 'More potent than regular red powder.'

'Red powder?' Moira knew the ingredients for numerous cakes and pastries, but gunpowder was beyond her expertise.

'There are two kinds of gunpowder typically used,' Mr Transom explained. 'Weaker white powder for when a regiment wants to salute or make some other noise that's not intended to do damage. The other is red powder, for when you want to blow your opponent out of the water or off the field of battle. This concentration of red powder—' he waved a hand at the sample '—is so potent, a good quantity of it would sink three or four ships. I have no doubt if this small amount were to catch spark, it would kill us all and bring down most of the building. Whenever the Rouge Noir is planning to do with this, it will make the Gunpowder Plot look like a schoolboy blowing up toy soldiers in a field.'

Moira reached over and carefully slid the oil lamp away from the sample.

'Where did you find this?' Mr Transom asked Bart.

'At Lady Camberline's house.'

'Not something one usually finds in the house of a marchioness,' Mr Transom mused, giving further credence to Moira and Bart's growing suspicion of Lady Camberline's involvement.

'Who do you think prepared this?' Bart asked.

Mr Transom pushed his spectacles up over his head, drawing back the light brown hair against his temples. 'This is high-quality gunpowder, not the cheap stuff produced in America or other colonies. It's from our colonies in the West Indies. I can tell by the larger crystals that form due to the moister air out there and the way it hasn't decayed.'

'Decayed?' Moira asked.

'When gunpowder sits for too long, if it isn't a quality mixture, the ingredients can separate, making it useless. This sample came a long way and it's still holding together, indicating its quality and lethalness.'

'Is this something a smuggler might bring in?' Bart asked.

'Not likely given the blockade. This would have to come in on a Navy ship with free access and a number of guards. Something this potent isn't likely to be mixed with regular munitions or left unattended. My guess is it was stolen.'

'It isn't unheard of for men like Mr Dubois to skip the risks of loading up their own ships with contraband by stealing it from dock warehouses.'

'But a Navy warehouse? They'd be shot

dead before they got away with anything like this.'

'Unless Mr Dubois had help from someone with enough influence in the Navy to know about the transport, pay the guards a hefty amount to make them look the other way and give Mr Dubois and his men the time they needed to spirit this away.'

Mr Transom nodded. 'If high-ranking men are involved in the plot, it's possible one of them gave a smuggler access to a warehouse. I think it's important to know how much of this is out there and get some sense of the damage someone might do with it. Is there a way to find out if a great deal of this stuff has gone missing lately?'

Bart pressed his lips hard together, while Moira and Mr Transom waited for the answer.

'There is,' Bart offered with noted reluctance. 'My father is on the Navy Acquisition Board. If anything important has gone missing, he'd know about it.'

Bart stared at the uneven boards with their square nail heads beneath his feet. He'd been invited to the social evening at his parents' house tonight and he'd roundly rejected it. It seemed he no longer had a choice but to attend. How he would get his father alone and find a way to ask questions about the gunpowder without having to endure a barrage of insults seemed like a bigger challenge than sniffing out the Rouge Noir, or resisting the allure of Moira's kiss in the carriage.

He looked up to catch Moira watching him from across the room where she perched on the edge of a high stool near Mr Transom's desk. It took a great deal of effort for him to remain where he was and not stride up to stand beside her and experience the pressure of her fingers against his. When he'd kissed her, the connection between them had been as natural as breathing, and despite the warnings going off in the back of his mind, he'd only reluctantly let her go. He'd vowed not to do this to her again or to trifle with her. It was yet another pledge he'd been unable to uphold, and with this misstep torturing him, it appeared he had no choice but to face the disappointments of his father. It wasn't exactly how he wished to end this trying day, but with Moira beside him, his father's insults might sting a little less.

She smiled encouragingly at him and he offered her a half-smile in return. He'd held a great many prejudices against her in the years after their initial flirtation, but she was destroying every one of them. He could use her strength tonight and the advantage of her station for there was nothing his father loved more than titles and lineage, and Moira possessed both. If she was willing to help him again despite the foiled attack on her, he'd be willing to face an even greater danger than Mr Dubois and his assassins or the longing in Moira's lips drawing out the one in his heart.

He'd face his father.

Chapter Nine

'I hardly think I need a chaperon in my own home,' Moira protested when Bart followed her into her house. Once inside, with it being so quiet she was glad he was here. Freddy had put the house on minimal staff since his departure, meaning if she weren't going to stay with Bart then it would simply be her, the butler and the housekeeper here tonight. As she did not wish to be slain in her bed, Bart was the better option despite the risk of ruin. 'Wait here while I change and retrieve my things.'

She started up the stairs, surprised to hear the thud of his footsteps behind her. 'What are you doing?'

She whirled to face him, forcing him to stop short on the stair below hers. Despite the difference in their elevations, with his height he was more than even with her and so close to her she could lean forward and sweep her lips against his if she decided to. No, she'd done so once already and made a fool of herself. She wouldn't do it again. As thrilling as all this was, in a short while it would be over and she would have to return to her former life. It would not help her dreams of finding a new husband if she did so as a fallen woman.

'I'm not leaving you alone. If they've figured out you're working with me, then they've figured out where you live and possibly how to sneak in here and do what Mr Roth failed to accomplish.'

'It's bad enough the butler will see me leaving with you and a packed valise, but what will he or the housekeeper say if they catch you upstairs with me?'

'Hand them enough money and they'll keep silent.' His certainty indicated he had more experience with matters like this than she cared to consider.

'I hope so.' Thankfully the old butler was as near-sighted as he was hard of hearing, but the housekeeper wasn't so decrepit. They and the other servants had been discreet about the family's affairs in the past, but she wasn't certain they would be so tight lipped about her being reckless with her reputation. If Aunt Agatha learned she was alone in the house with Bart, the woman would collapse in an apoplectic fit and seal Moira's fate as a family outcast for good. 'Remind me to pay them before we leave.'

She turned and started up the stairs again. Thankfully, in London, she shared a lady's maid with Aunt Agatha and the woman was sure to have returned to the country with her aunt. It would make this brief visit home less expensive.

Bart followed her down the first-floor hall, but when she reached for the door to her room, he placed his hand over hers on the knob before she could twist it open. Their eyes met and Moira froze, aware of his steady pulse flickering against her skin.

'I'll go in first and make sure everything is safe.'

'You think bad men are hiding under my bed?' she challenged with a sly look, trying to ignore her racing heart.

His finger tightened on hers. 'One can never be too careful.'

'I believe you and I are being anything but careful.' He might pretend there was nothing more to their relationship than the investigation, but in the heat of his hand on hers, and the way he'd studied her at Mr Transom's, she knew there was more. Whether or not it was strong enough to overcome his reservations and her better sense remained to be seen. She withdrew her hand from beneath his, allowing him to open the door and step inside the room.

The curtains pulled over the window muted the already fading sunlight and deepened the shadows beside the wardrobe and bed. Bart checked everywhere in the room where anyone with vicious designs could hide. 'All safe.'

'I'm glad to hear it.' Even if she didn't entirely believe it.

She entered and he closed the door behind her. She tried not to focus on how alone they were, or the temptation of her bed and him while she removed a travelling case from beside the wardrobe and folded a few dresses inside for morning and walking. It was what to wear tonight that caused her to debate which gown to select next. She had no idea what the event was or who might be there besides his father and mother. She selected two gowns and held them up in front of her. 'Which do you think is more appropriate for meeting your parents tonight? The blue one or the red one?'

'The more conservative of the two.' Bart barely glanced at either of them as he pushed the curtain aside to study the street below. 'Change into it now and we'll go directly to my parents' house.'

She lowered the dresses. 'Are we invited to this event?'

Bart allowed the curtain to fall back into place. 'I am.'

'And what about me?' It wasn't like her to parade into homes to which she had not been invited.

'This will be the first time I've ever attended a family event with a lady. You'll most likely incite more curiosity than scorn.'

She returned the blue dress to the wardrobe. 'I hope so. I'd hate to be asked to leave.'

'My father is too enamoured of titles to risk insulting you,' Bart said with a half-smile Moira did not find reassuring.

'Then I'm glad I chose the red one.' The bodice on the red dress was cut much higher, but by current standards both were incredibly modest. Her entire wardrobe was less than appealing and, if she weren't embroiled in all this nastiness, she might consider at last visiting the modiste and ordering something fashionable and a touch more revealing.

She laid the dress across the bed and began to consider how to change out of her current one and into this one without asking Bart for help. There was no way for her to reach the buttons on the back without assistance. She glanced over her shoulder at him, her pulse pounding in her ears. 'Would you mind undoing my dress?'

He stared across the room at her, looking more shocked than he had after the attack on her earlier. Her confidence faltered a touch, but she held on tight to it. He probably hadn't expected her to be this daring, but Aunt Agatha was right, a little knowledge was a very alluring thing. She was no green girl unfamiliar with men and she would make sure he understood it. A thrill of power tripped through her and she wasn't sure what it was about him that made her bold, but at the moment she very much enjoyed it.

Without a word, he crossed to her, took hold of the buttons and began to undo them one by one. She didn't dare face him and tempt him more than she already had. With each subtle loosening of the bodice, her skin tightened, especially when his fingertips brushed the back of her shoulders. She held on tight to the front of the dress to keep it from sliding down when he reached the last button in the centre of her back. Despite wanting to let go of the fabric, to face him and have him show her all the pleasure she'd been denied for the last five years, she didn't move.

She peered over her shoulder again and twirled her finger at him. 'Turn around while I slip into the other gown.'

The pupils of his eyes were wide, darkening his gaze, and his chest rose and fell with each measured breath, making clear the effect the intimate moment had had on him. His human reaction offered a glimpse of the very real man beneath the controlled barrister she wished she could embrace. 'I'll stand outside if you insist.'

'You can remain. I don't want you to feel uneasy about my safety.'

He arched one surprised eyebrow at her before spinning slowly on his heel to give her the required privacy. With quick moves she slipped out of the dress. This teasing thrilled her, but it also put her on edge, for if she allowed things to continue any further she might compromise herself in a way she could never undo. She might not have had a baby with her husband, but it didn't mean she wasn't capable of having one with another man. She wanted children, but refused to taint them with the scorn of illegitimacy.

She flung the old dress across the bed, took up the new one and pulled it on. Thankfully the two buttons at the back were ones she could reach. She was both relieved and disappointed to not have to call on Bart's assistance again. They'd been weak while alone in the carriage, and even though they'd both resisted temptation here, there was no telling how it would be tonight when they were alone at his house with no interruptions or soirées to attend. Surely he had a housekeeper or maid who could help her dress and prevent any further temptation? She hoped the woman proved as discreet as Bart believed.

Without allowing him to turn around she went to her wardrobe to fetch appropriate shoes to match the dress, then fastened her diamond necklace and matching earrings in place. The set had been a wedding present from Walter and the only thing of value he'd given her. Then she gathered up the last few items she needed, put them all together in the valise and faced Bart. 'What do you think?'

His reaction to her in the dress made her blush. It wasn't mild appreciation, but a look of pure desire to quicken her pulse. She lifted her chin in pride and drank in the silent compliment, refusing to shy away from it or him. In his presence she felt beautiful and wanted for more than her assistance in catching criminals, but as a woman. She opened her arms and spun slowly before him.

'Will this be enough to charm your parents into forgiving me for my serious breach of etiquette?' she asked in all innocence, as if she hadn't noticed his reaction.

Bart took a deep breath, more cautious of his movements than the time in France when he and his men had backed out of a barn where an unexploded cannonball sat smoking in the ruins. Moira was like the ball, smouldering and dangerous to him, but instead of wanting to back away, he wanted to rush forward and lose himself in the fire of her eyes. It took every bit of control Bart had ever mas-

tered on the battlefield and in the courtroom
to resist going to her and claiming her as his.
They were alone, with all the troubles and
threats facing them outside the door. In her
arms he could forget the constant struggles
to keep evil from consuming England and innocent people, and him, but he wouldn't suc-
cumb. Circumstances had placed her under
his protection and he could not take advantage of it.

With her sparkling jewels enhanced by the
finery of her dress and her pale skin, he was
forced to face the reality of her situation and
his. There was a great difference between
them, one he wasn't certain they could bridge.
These were the things she wanted, things he
could not give her, and after years of her family
making her sacrifice everything she'd wanted
in life, he couldn't make her will subservient
to his. He was doing what was best for her by
not approaching her or giving into every single
emotion building between them.

Bending down, painfully close to where her
thighs were covered by the silk, he took hold of
her valise and then straightened. With a self-
control he felt slipping more than once, he rose
to stand over her. 'The dress is perfect.'

* * *

'Mr Bartholomew, I was told not to expect you this evening,' Tucker, the Denning family butler, greeted him, the wrinkles around the bottom of his eyes deepening when they went wide with his shock. This wasn't the first time Bart had confused the kind old servant who'd never been able to lie and cover for him the numerous times when Bart, as a boy, had been out late or up to no good, no matter how many pounds Bart had offered him for his silence.

'My plans changed, allowing me to come,' Bart explained.

Tucker's expression shifted from surprise to discomfort. If Bart's father had given the man orders to deny him entrance, Tucker would carry them out faithfully. It didn't appear he had as Tucker stepped aside and allowed them admittance.

'And who should I announce?' Tucker asked, ready to lead them through.

'The Dowager Countess of Rexford.'

Tucker offered what Bart imagined would be the first of the many amazed looks he'd receive tonight. Then, without anther word, he turned and made for the back sitting room.

'What kind of event is this?' Moira asked,

taking in the staid pictures of past Dennings from previous centuries lining the halls. The weight of ancestry and reputation settled on Bart as much as the possibility of facing his father and trying, for the first time since he was boy, and before he'd realised the effort was futile, to get on his father's good side.

'One of my father's regular political soirées for the men he serves with on the Navy Acquisition Board and their wives.'

'I know you said manners would keep your father from turning me away, but what about you?' she prodded with an impish smile.

'It's possible. As my father is fond of reminding me, I'm the commonest of commoners.' If his father knew of his work for the Alien Office he'd be proud. He certainly wasn't proud of Bart's accomplishments as a barrister as he made abundantly clear each Christmas when he complained about Bart having sacrificed a brilliant career in the military at a time when a man could really assert himself, and of wasting his father's connection with the War Office to defend widows from thieves.

Tucker stopped at a cheerfully lit sitting room where laughter and female voices hovered above the deeper tones of the men's conversation. Something inside Bart rebelled at being here. He'd endured these people enough while growing up, thinking to join their ranks until the day his father had unceremoniously made it clear Bart wasn't one of them.

'Brace yourself, the moment of reckoning is upon us,' Bart whispered, eliciting a smile of mischief from Moira as the butler stepped into the room and announced them.

'The Dowager Countess of Rexford and Mr Bartholomew Dyer.'

Bart and Moira stepped forward in unison, met by a stunned silence from Bart's family.

The rest of the guests paused in their conversation long enough to give them a perfunctory look before returning to their chosen topics, unaware of how astonishing it was for the youngest son to arrive home and with a woman of all people. He was the only brother not married, and even if his siblings took little more than a passing interest in his domestic arrangements, their wives and his mother were very keen on the subject.

His mother rose out her chair near the fireplace, her daughters-in-law falling into place behind her, all of them rushing forward to satisfy their curiosity.

'Bart, how wonderful to see you,' his mother effused, more focused on Moira than her son. 'We were told not to expect you.'

His sisters-in-law peered out from around Bart's mother, craning to hear every innocuous word.

'I have some business with Father I need to discuss tonight. It's very important.'

'Your father?' The colour drained from his mother's round face. 'You aren't here to cause trouble, are you?'

'Not at all. It's a matter of state.'

'State?'

'Trust me, all will be well and there'll be no trouble.' He leaned over and kissed his mother on the cheek. She was short and stocky, his and his brothers' height having come from their father, but her natural fullness could be seen in the solidity of her sons, none of whom shared their father's lankiness.

She viewed him out of the corner of her rich brown eyes, her worries somewhat eased but not entirely banished. Then she turned to Moira, waiting for the introduction.

'Lady Denning, may I introduce Lady Rexford,' Bart obliged, conscious of the whispers of amazement flying between the women behind his mother. The ladies were aware of Moira and Bart's brief engagement, as was his father who'd blamed him for it falling through, but none of them had met Moira before. Bart wasn't certain if their tittering was because of their knowledge of the past affair or their amazement at Bart being accompanied by a titled lady. Most of them had been present for the discussion between Bart and his father two Christmases ago when Bart had made his feelings about the aristocracy, and his father's ambitions among them, clear. It was not Bart's proudest moment and one of the few times he'd lost control of himself during a debate. His father could rattle him in a way that would be the envy of every opposing counsel.

'Lady Rexford, it's a pleasure to have you here tonight,' his mother greeted. 'Allow me to introduce you to my daughters-in-law.'

The noise of the introductions and the overly zealous welcomes from the ladies caught his father's attention. Lord Denning stood at the far side of the room, talking to a couple of men Bart vaguely remembered as having some connection to an arm of the Government. His father's eyes went wide at the sight of Bart and then narrowed, his mouth drawing down into his usual disapproving frown. He didn't so much as nod at Bart as he returned to his conversation, but it was clear from the tight grip on his claret glass that he was irked and it put Bart's teeth on edge. His father was unhappy when Bart didn't show up and unhappy when he did. He wished the man would bloody well make up his mind about what he wanted.

'Lady Rexford, you must come and sit with us. We're gossiping and we've run out of original stories to tell,' Richard's wife, Lucinda, encouraged, drawing Moira to the chairs where they'd been perched before Bart's arrival.

'I'm afraid I haven't been in London long enough to gather any stories to share,' Moira apologised, smiling with genuine delight at the ladies' welcome.

'Then it will give us a good reason to repeat our own,' Mary, his second-eldest brother Stephen's wife, laughed before they resumed their seats and began their tales.

Bart watched them, touched at how easily the ladies included Moira in their circle. If he were free to pursue any of the ideas she'd brought to his mind while she'd sat across from him in the carriage, as enticing then as the moment he'd turned to face her in her bedroom, then this would be a very welcome omen. Instead, it was another reminder of what they'd lost five years ago. If she'd been with him from the beginning, and they'd endured all the hardships and challenges of his life together, it would be a different thing altogether, but he couldn't chain her to it now.

Bart's brothers approached him, less interested in his companion than they were in what was occupying him of late. Bart described his last trial, and an upcoming case, unable to share with them his secret work. Despite having to hold back on the one subject, besides Moira, commanding his attention, the old rapport with his siblings was a heartening tonic against the scowls their father continued to lob at him. It'd been a long time since they'd been together like this, laughing and talking about old times. His brothers were men he admired and he missed the closeness they'd enjoyed as boys. With their father indifferent to everyone but Richard and Stephen, they'd banded together, loyal to their mother and each other. Time had pulled them apart, but not the bond which had once linked them. Bart missed it, and for this reason alone he considered coming here more often. He tugged on the cuffs of his shirt, aware of how he thought about this every time they were together, but never followed through on his pledge. His father's presence made it difficult for him to enjoy being here.

'Ignore him,' Andrew suggested, offering Bart a glass of port when he caught Bart giving another sidelong glance to their glowering father.

'I have been for years.'

'Have you? Or is everything you've done been to spite him?'

'Not everything.' He glanced at Moira, who laughed at something his mother said. 'But perhaps a good many things.'

'At least you have the courage to admit it.' His brother understood. He'd also refused a career in the clergy to pursue his interest in importing merchandise from abroad, but his quiet lifestyle as a well-to-do merchant whose name never appeared in the papers in connection with a notorious criminal or trial didn't gather his father's wrath like Bart's did. 'Not all of us do.'

He nodded at Stephen. Like Richard, he'd never experienced their father's disdain in quite the same way as his younger brothers had when they were growing up. His sudden fall from grace when his importance to the line had diminished after Richard's son was born was something he continued to wrestle with, often putting him at odds with his younger brothers.

A man waved for Andrew to join him and before he went he clapped Bart on the back. 'Don't give up. You still might garner his regard some day.'

'Have you?'

'Maybe not his regard, but a little more of his notice, and a little less of his churlishness.' Raising his glass to Bart, Andrew strolled off to join the man who'd summoned him.

Bart regretted seeing him go, along with his other brothers as various matters soon drew them away until one by one Bart was left alone.

'How am I doing?' Moira asked as Bart came to sit beside her on the sofa, the place having been abandoned by the ladies when they rushed to greet yet another newcomer.

'You've charmed them all.' He set his untouched port on the table beside him. 'But it isn't the women you need to win over. It's my father.'

She took in this stern man who continued to

stand with his friends, having made no move
to greet his son or his son's female guest. 'A
formidable task, but during my marriage to
Lord Rexford, I became adept at soothing over
a crotchety old man.'

The thought of a man old enough to be her
father with all the humourless joy of his own
touching her killed his good mood. She was
too young and pretty to have been sacrificed
to Lord Rexford simply because her father had
wished it. 'You never should have had to learn
a skill so intimately.'

'My father did what he thought best for me,'
she said quietly, studying her hands where she
rested them in her lap.

'Was it?'

'Fallworth Manor couldn't support me, my
aunt and Freddy and his family. My father was
dying and afraid for my future. He arranged
the match with Lord Rexford because he believed he was protecting me from a future of
straitened circumstances,' she explained with
a kindness to make Bart ashamed at having
railed against her father, and at one time her.
'He couldn't have known Walter would barely
outlive him, that there'd be no children and the
estate would go to his nephew, or that you'd

rise so well in your career after I broke things off with you.'

She traced her ring finger which was bereft of whatever wedding band she'd once worn.

'I'm sorry for being so callous. I never realised the situation you were in.' One of necessity and uncertainty in which she and her family had reached for what they'd viewed as the sure thing rather than taking a chance on a young man with no standing or fortune of his own.

His father had tried, in his own way, to do the same for Bart many years ago when he'd secured the curacy and a steady income. His father had been outraged the morning Bart, then sixteen, had refused his acceptance to Oxford and a career in the clergy by buying a commission. Instead of being proud, he'd railed at Bart for undermining his efforts to find him a good position and hoped he remembered the comfortable life he'd thrown away when he was dying in a ditch of typhoid fever in Germany. The hard bastard. His father hadn't appreciated Bart's desire to better himself and succeed through his own hard work, but had been furious he hadn't followed his dictates, and in doing so, had caused him some embarrassment. In the end, it always came back to his father and how he imagined Bart's actions reflected on him.

'Decisions aren't always easy to make, especially when things or situations are murky,' Moira lamented.

'Are they ever clear?' Bart longed to take her hand and still the restless encircling of her finger. He was glad to see her wedding ring gone even if it didn't mean a place for him in her life after this affair was over.

'No, I don't suppose they are,' she agreed with a winsomeness to tell him she understood the obstacles between them. Moira craved the calm of domesticity and he wasn't the man to offer it to her as the events of this afternoon had proven. 'And they're about to get a touch more difficult.'

She nodded across the room and Bart looked up to see his father approaching them.

'I hope you're ready to woo him.'

'I'll do my best.'

They rose to greet Lord Denning, who stopped before them, hands behind his back, less solicitous than the female members of his family.

'You said you weren't coming,' he barked at Bart.

'I changed my mind.'

'Without informing us and bringing an un-invited guest with you.' He eyed Moira as if she were an actress Bart had picked up after a Drury Lane performance.

He didn't blame his father for the assumption, since Bart had done exactly that a few years ago.

'And who may I ask is this? I couldn't hear her name over the noise in here.'

Moira didn't flinch under his hard scrutiny, but remained as serene as a painting of the Virgin Mary. The woman was an absolute saint for putting up with Bart and his father. 'Lady Rexford, may I introduce my father, Lord Denning.'

His father's prickliness lost its edge the moment he realised he was addressing a countess. He unclasped his hands and kept them stiff at his sides while he bowed to Moira. 'Lady Rexford, it's a pleasure to meet you. Please forgive my less-than-solicitous greeting, but my son failed to send word you would be joining us.'

'You're most eagerly forgiven.' Moira curtsied with all the graciousness Bart had come to expect from her, holding nothing against his father for his rude approach nor making him feel uneasy about his mistake.

'I had the pleasure of meeting your late husband once a number of years ago when he was in London. I was very sorry to hear of his passing,' his father offered.

'Thank you very much for your condolences. It would have meant a great deal to him.' She laid a reassuring hand on his arm to emphasise her lack of ill will. 'He was an admirer of your work with the Navy Acquisition Board. I used to read him the newspaper articles about your successes with the supply reforms when he was ill.'

'Did you, now?' His father's bushy eyebrows rose at this compliment.

'He was very impressed with your implementation of Lord Harding's suggestions. So was I, once he explained their significance. Perhaps you could tell me more about them?'

Bart had to stop himself from staring at Moira in amazement. Without him telling her, she'd immediately guessed the best way to gain his father's good graces. With a salubriousness Bart found shocking, his father offered Moira his arm. 'It would be my pleasure. Perhaps I can introduce you to some of the men who work with me?'

'I'd be delighted to meet them.' Moira took his proffered elbow and allowed him to lead her over to the gaggle of men gathered about the brandy table.

Bart, having received no invitation to join them, but in need of a chance to request a private interview with his father, and suspecting he'd get it if the old man were in a better mood, made a move to follow him. The soft voice of his mother stopped him.

'I'm glad you decided to come. I've seen so little of you lately.'

'I think you understand why.' Bart regretted neglecting her, but their meetings were always tainted by his father's insults. When this was all over he would make a point of coming to see her more often, perhaps while his father was at his government office. Like the promise to visit his brothers, he doubted his ability to keep it. He didn't want to risk running into his father and have their arguments give him more reasons to stay away. The thought of it deepened his disappointment in himself. He'd overcome a great many obstacles in his life from the horrors of war to forgers and traitors, but this was one situation he could not rout.

'I realise you and your father don't agree on very many things and in the past he's been incredibly hard on you, much more so than I've cared for, but he is who he is.' She glanced at her husband, defeat drawing her lips tight. Whatever influence she'd tried to exert over him, whatever expectations she'd once held about him as a husband and father, it was clear they hadn't been realised, making her failure as sharp as Bart's had been in not keeping Lady Fallworth alive. 'I've always encouraged him to be kinder and more loving to you and your brothers, but he so rarely heeds my advice. I suppose it's because of the way he was raised, a third son who never expected to inherit. He thought if he made you tough, you'd be better able to handle the rigours of the world and make something of yourselves since you wouldn't have the family lineage to rely on.'

'Then why is he so quick to criticise me for my success as a barrister?'

'Because, in some ways, you two are too much alike. You're proud of your work, just like he is, and you can both be very stubborn.'

Bart didn't reply, troubled at being compared to his father, especially by the one person, besides Moira, with real insight into him. It was a reflection of himself he didn't want to see.

'I'm very pleased you brought Lady Rexford with you,' his mother remarked, changing the subject as she observed Moira who stood with his father and some other gentlemen, laughing delightfully with them and flattering their egos.

Bart had never seen his father smile this much at a family-dominated event before.

'She's a lovely woman and quite charming, and I think she's perfect for you.'

Bart almost warned her not to get her hopes up about a new daughter-in-law, then decided against it. 'The lady isn't so enamoured of me.'

'Nonsense, I watched the way she looked at you. Don't let her get away this time. I know you think you can go through life by yourself, but you need a good woman beside you.' Genuine concern marked each of her words, making them difficult to dismiss. In many ways his mother was right. He'd seen old soldiers like Mr Flint who'd bypassed the happiness of home and hearth for their duties to the state. Their many years alone had fostered a certain stoniness in them, one he felt growing inside himself. A man could pay someone to make his dinner and keep his house, but the delights of conversation and the softness of a woman who genuinely cared about him did make a difference.

'I'll keep it in mind.' His solemnity brought a smile to her lips. 'Now if you'll excuse me I must join my guest. We have matters to discuss with Father.'

Bart strode across the room and joined the gentleman and Moira. They were kind in their greetings and their questions about his most recent trial. Their interest in Bart's work made his father's back stiffen and caused his smile to crack about the sides. Bart was sure if Moira hadn't been present, his father would've returned to his usual snide insults to belittle Bart's work and the notoriety it brought him, and by extension, the Denning name. There wasn't a newspaper article about Bart's trials that didn't fail to mention the connection, much to his father's chagrin.

At one point, while Moira was engaging the other gentlemen in conversation, Bart's father shifted around her to stand beside Bart.

'It appears you've done something right for

once in convincing this fine lady to give you a second chance,' his father complimented in his oh, so-backhanded way. 'Although why a countess, the daughter of an earl, would want to lower herself with a mere barrister I can't say, but if you're foolish enough to let her get away again, I'll disown you for good.'

Bart tried not to roll his eyes. His father would be sadly disappointed, and might possibly disown him for real this time when this was all over and Bart and Moira parted again. The idea made Bart's stomach tighten. These kinds of gatherings had never been easy for him, but with the many dangers facing the country, it made it even worse tonight. However, in the midst of his unease, with Moira beside him, something seemed very right with the world. His eagerness to leave didn't grip him like it had in the past, instead he wanted to remain here watching her flirt with his father, drawing the attentions of his brothers, and seeing his mother showing a bit of backbone he hadn't realised she possessed. It was the first time in a long time Bart had stood among them and not felt like an outcast, but instead as someone with a potential place here. It was an odd feeling because he hadn't expected it. He had done all he could to avoid his family, yet with Moira he wanted to recapture some of what he remembered as a boy when he and his younger brothers used to tear through the house wrestling and yelling at one another while ignoring their mother's entreaties to not break her vases. For all his complaints when he'd reached manhood, Bart couldn't give too many to his childhood. With his mother's love and his brothers' companionship it'd been a good one, despite his father's sternness and indifference. It was an innocence he'd lost a long time ago and for a brief moment he wondered what it would be like to have a pack of his own sons running through his house, livening up the dark wood panelling and the silent rooms with their laughter. He could guide them as a father should, while their mother gave them her unconditional love. It wasn't a thought he'd ever considered before, but the more time he spent around Moira, the more the idea drifted in and out of his consciousness, pushing aside all the ugliness of the world that soaked him.

The pretty image of a happy home life vanished when his father turned to him, leaving Moira to the other gentlemen. 'I'm surprised to see you here. Richard said you weren't coming, as usual. I told your mother we shouldn't have bothered to invite you, but she insisted.'

Honesty had never been a problem for his father. It was time for Bart to return the favour. 'I came to speak with you.'

'What do we possibly have to discuss?'

Bart leaned close to the man's ear, noting the fair bit of grey sprinkled in his dark hair. 'A certain special gunpowder imported by the Navy, some of which has gone missing.'

His father's jaw fell open. 'How do you know about that?'

'Escort me and Lady Rexford to your study and you'll find out.'

Minutes later, Moira and Bart stood together with his father in the book-filled study with the door closed. Lord Denning sat at his desk and waved for Bart to take his place in front of him. Not wanting to feel like a child, Bart stood before the desk while Moira hovered near the fireplace, all but forgotten by his father in light of this new development.

'Tell me exactly how it is you know about the missing gunpowder.' His father levelled a warning finger at him. 'And mind my words, if you're involved in anything smacking of treason or theft and think by coming to me you can get yourself out of it then you're wrong. I'll happily see you brought up on charges. All your fancy skills as a barrister won't help you then. I don't abide by traitors or thieves.'

'Thank you for your faith in me, but your threats aren't necessary,' Bart growled, bracing himself against yet another insult before a quick glance at Moira calmed him. He wasn't here to fight with his father, but to obtain information. He rolled his shoulders, shaking off the last of his tension as he always did before approaching the bench. When he spoke, he would do so calmly, with all the rational organisation he showed in the courtroom. His father threatened him because he had no knowledge of Bart's work for the Alien Office, but tonight he had to tell him. Whether or not this changed his father's impression of him was secondary to finding out about the gunpowder and how much was missing. 'I'm here on behalf of Mr Flint and the Alien Office in an attempt to halt an attack on our Government.'

In concise words he explained to his father his work, not as a barrister, but as a stipendiary magistrate. He told him about the Rouge Noir, sure his father would keep it a secret along with all the other government secrets he was privy to. His father might not care for Bart, but he adored his country and would do all he could to protect it. Love for England was, more than the stubbornness his mother had cited, the one thing Bart and his father shared.

'The Rouge Noir is planning to implement their plot in the next day or so and I'm running out of time to uncover their plans.' Bart noted the sharp intake of breath from Moira. He hadn't told her his fears the plot was now imminent, his suspicion based on Mr Dubois's brazen attack on her this afternoon and information he'd gleamed from the forger.

His father sat back in his chair, his face slack with horror and for the first time ever at a loss for words, good or bad, about Bart.

Out of the corner of his eyes, Bart noticed Moira at the table beside the window uncorking the decanter of brandy and pouring out a glass. With the quietness of a cat, she carried it to his father and handed it to him. 'I was as surprised as you are to hear about this, Lord Denning,' she offered in a soothing voice, easing him through his shock as if Bart had just told him his favourite retriever had died.

'I am.' With a compliance Bart had never

witnessed before, his father took the glass from Moira. He drained the drink, then stared at the empty crystal in his hand, appearing for the first time more like the grandfather he was than the stern authoritarian he'd been. 'Could I trouble you for another one?'

'Of course.' Moira took the glass, refilled it and returned it to him.

'Thank you, Lady Rexford. You're too kind.' He drained this one, too, then set it down on the desk.

'It's my pleasure.' She smiled with a sweetness to captivate the most hard-hearted of men, then took her place again in the chair by the fireplace.

Bart remained in front of the desk, not expecting a word of gratitude or apology to reach his ears, and he wasn't disappointed. For years his father had been ashamed of his work. He couldn't imagine he'd be proud of him now, but if he'd changed his mind, he decided not to tell Bart about it. His father also didn't pelt him with a barrage of disapproval for bringing Lady Rexford into this affair. Instead, with a touch of humility, he faced Bart. 'What do you need to know about the missing gunpowder?'

'How much is gone and the damage it can do.'

His father rubbed his fingers across the creases in his forehead. 'One hogshead full, enough to wipe out an entire street.'

'The mixture is that lethal?'

'Yes. We'd planned to test it in the new, sturdier cannons, to see if it makes them more powerful. If it does, it will give us the edge necessary to bring this war to an end and defeat the Emperor at last.' His father picked at a loose bit of leather on the blotter. 'There were ten hogsheads shipped here from the West Indies on a Navy frigate. They were unloaded at Greenwich in preparation for transport to the armoury. Ten went into the warehouse but only nine came out three days later. There was no evidence of a break in and none of the guards reported seeing anything or anyone unusual in the area before it went missing.'

'Then it could have been someone working at the warehouse, or one of the sailors involved in the transport.'

'They knew nothing about it, very few did. If they gave the casks any thought it was because they believed they held tobacco or some other such goods. We didn't exactly announce what we were doing in the papers.'

'An officer, then?'

His father slammed his fists on the desk, making the empty brandy glass jump. 'No, none of the men involved in this would turn traitor. Their superior lineages wouldn't allow it.'

'You investigated them all then, especially those with debts to make sure they couldn't be blackmailed or bribed?'

His father eased his tight fist and nodded. 'We did.'

'Then perhaps someone slipped up and mentioned it either on purpose or inadvertently.' He thought of Prince Frederick at the ball. He'd spoken in front of the Comte de Troyen about throwing the Government into chaos by killing a handful of ministers, and now there was a plot involving gunpowder. It was too much of a coincidence. 'Did Prince Frederick know about the shipment?'

His father jerked up straight. 'Are you suggesting a member of the royal household is a traitor to the Crown?'

'No, but I've spoken with him before and, as his past deeds have confirmed, he's careless with his position and the knowledge he holds.'

He related to his father the incident with the Comte de Troyen at Lady Camberline's ball.

'He didn't know about the shipment,' his father admitted with a sigh. Bart could see his father's pain at the thought that one of his own might have been at fault in this situation. He still believed in the nobility of the nobility. Bart knew better. 'He's been privy to very few Navy secrets since his resignation as Commander in Chief of the Army, despite his having been reinstated in the post. You aren't the only one to have noticed he can be indiscreet.'

'I'd like a list of everyone involved in the purchase and transfer of the powder. I'll pass it on to Mr Flint, who'll conduct a more thorough investigation of the men involved.' He expected his father to complain or protest, but with amazing compliancy, his father removed a piece of paper from the desk drawer, laid it on the blotter and began to write out a list of names.

'I'm familiar with Mr Flint's methods. I don't always agree with them, but they're far more effective than the Naval Office's. If anyone has any secrets we missed, he'll discover them.'

'Then why didn't you turn the matter over

to him sooner?' It might have cost them time they didn't have.

His father paused in his writing, the twitch near his eye indicating he didn't appreciate being questioned by his son. He seemed to recognise the merit in it this time for he didn't lash out, but resumed writing. 'We should have, but there were those above me determined to keep the matter a secret. I told them it was a mistake, but they outranked me.'

Bart's disgust for kowtowing to titled men seized him. He was about to say so and rail against the investigative time and opportunities lost because of it when Moira caught his eye. Her softness helped Bart to mediate his hardness and anger. He was making progress with his father and he didn't want his abrasiveness to affect his father's co-operation.

His father finished his list and handed it to Bart. 'The men with dots by their names are those who were out of London at the time of the theft or more distantly involved than the others. It should help you narrow your focus to the most important people while not overlooking any potential suspects.'

Bart folded the paper and tucked it into the pocket of his coat. 'Thank you.'

He waited for his father to concede to having spent too many years misreading Bart, but he didn't. Bart supposed he couldn't expect so large an about-face in one meeting.

His father rose and pressed his fingers into the blotter. 'I expect you to catch these men and bring them to justice, whatever that may be in your part of the Government.'

Bart faced him as he would a judge or one of his old superior officers, determined to give him the same courtesy. 'I will. Thank you very much for your assistance. I'll make sure Mr Flint is aware of it. Please send me any more information if you come across it.'

'I will. Good luck to you, Bart.' His father held out his hand. Bart shook it once, noting the new sense of respect in his father's eyes. He didn't expect they would always be this cordial with one another, but it was a start. Perhaps, some day, there could be peace and a better relationship between them than they'd enjoyed before.

Bart let go of his hand and his father came around the desk to Moira.

'I have to say, I'm a little surprised to see a lady involved in such matters, but I appreciate you and what you're doing for the nation as well.'

'Thank you, Lord Denning.' She smiled at him again and he visibly blossomed under her affection. Bart wondered if after all these years his father was finally mellowing. He hoped to see more of it in the future, it would make his desire to regain a larger role in his family's life easier.

Chapter Ten

'What do you make of the list?' Moira motioned to the paper.

Across the carriage, Bart studied the names, leaning forward, his arm perched on his knee, his fingers rubbing his chin as he did whenever he was contemplating evidence or their next course of action.

'Two people concern me the most right now. Lord Mandeville and Lord Carville.'

'I find it hard to believe Lord Mandeville is a traitor. His reputation has been sterling and Lord Carville is one of the most vocal opponents of Napoleon.'

'It's not them specifically I'm concerned with, but their connections. They're both good friends with the Comte de Troyen.'

'What about the Camberlines and Lord Lefevre and Lord Moreau?'

'The Comte is friends with them as well and they may be deep in this, but they still need a solid connection to France. Given the past evidence of the Comte, he could be the traitor. Like Lord Lefevre and Lord Moreau, he enjoys easy access to Lord Carville and Lord Mandeville and their houses. He could have either overheard things while drinking with them or slipped into their offices and perused their papers.'

'Or Mr Dubois overhead a sailor speaking about the gunpowder and where it was being stored and passed it on. Your father believes the Navy kept the transport secret, but I think we all know how easy it is for things to slip out.' Bart might believe Moira could conceal her time at his place from everyone, but she knew better. Even in the country, in almost near isolation with her husband, she'd heard London gossip at dinner parties or from her lady's maid. How long would it be until her tale of indiscretion made the rounds? 'Mr Dubois could be their French connection.'

'I've considered the possibility.' Bart folded the paper and ran his thumb and forefinger along the crease. 'Until we determine otherwise, we continue to investigate everyone, including Lady Camberline, Lord Lefevre and Lord Moreau.'

She liked how he included her in his plans, even if she shouldn't, but she didn't share Bart's faith in all being well when this was over. Not once in her twenty-five years had she placed herself so at odds with her family, and the very real possibility they wouldn't allow her back into their good graces continued to trouble her. The idea they might shun her, leaving her without their comfort, humour and love, chilled her. If her involvement with Bart also tainted her in society's eyes, it would make things even worse. She would lose not only her family, but any chance of gaining a husband and children of her own. Bart had made it clear there could be no future with him. He was against the things she'd set her heart on and, like trying to persuade her father against the marriage to Lord Rexford, she doubted her ability to change his mind. If she were as reckless as the many widows his sisters-in-law and mother had gossiped about, the ones who pursued their lovers without care and with only a fleeting nod to discretion, she might enjoy a relationship with him, but it would be temporary. She didn't want to be a mistress but a wife.

'You worked a miracle with my father to-night.' He tucked the paper in his coat pocket, then rested his hands on his thighs. 'He wouldn't have been half so generous with me if you hadn't wooed him with your title and your feminine charm.'

'He reminded me a little of my own father and the way he could be, especially towards the end when the pain made him as snappy as a wild dog.' She'd seen Lord Denning's reaction to Bart the moment they'd entered the sitting room and again when he'd approached them. He hadn't hesitated to lash out at his son until decorum had overtaken his irascibility. Then the change in him in the office, after Bart had told him about his work, had been remark-able. 'He was quite proud of you when you explained your duties to the Crown.'

'I thought for years my service in the Army, and my victories in court against fraudsters, would one day gain his grudging respect. It didn't. Instead it was the very thing I wasn't able to tell him.'

'Then perhaps the two of you can find more common ground now. Your mother would very much like to see you become closer to them. She told me so.'

He tapped his fingers against his knee. 'She believes you have influence with me.'

'Do I?'

'You do.' He peered up at her from beneath his brows, the look startling and tempting. 'When this is over, I'll do my best to try and be more involved with my family.'

This wasn't exactly the influence she'd hoped to exert over him. 'I'm glad to hear it. I hope mine is as welcoming of me when this is done.'

'Once this is over and you're safe, Freddy will come around.'

'We'll see,' she said quietly.

The carriage rolled to stop in front of Bart's Temple Bar town house. He handed her down and escorted her up to the front door. A solidly built butler greeted them, the square-chested man more like the ones who'd assisted Bart outside the British Museum than the many preened and pompous servants who'd shown her into fine residences over the years. She had no doubt this man would produce a knife or a pistol if the moment called for it. It helped ease her concerns about her physical safety, but not her moral safety. Even with these servants, she was a widow in a well-known barrister's bachelor household. She hoped Bart was right about his people being extremely discreet. Very few women could overcome a scandal like this.

'Welcome to my humble home.' Bart threw out his arms to the building before giving the butler instructions to see to Moira's valise.

Moira crossed the small entryway to one of the rooms flanking it. It was his office, with dark wood furniture of straight lines and sharp corners. Papers were spread across his desk, held down by a couple of open books. Thick tomes inscribed with gold-leaf titles concerning the law filled the short bookcase which was devoid of novels or other pleasurable reading. The messiness of it contrasted with the Bart she knew, but because of it, this room seemed more personal to him.

He came up beside her, hands clasped behind his back with what she thought might be a touch of embarrassment. It didn't seem possible for she was sure he was beyond ever being embarrassed. 'I apologise for the state of my residence. My office is usually more organised than this.'

'I don't mind. I enjoy seeing some of your flaws. I find them charming.'

'You're the only one who does.' The slight

tang of the brandy he'd indulged in at his parents' house flavoured each word. It mixed with the subtle scent of wood oil, leather and parchment permeating the air. It, more than all the brocade in any well-lit room of gilded furniture, appealed to something deep inside her. Despite the lack of decoration or softness, with him beside her, she was more at ease here than she'd been almost anywhere else in the last five years.

She wondered how long she could stay and what other secrets about him she might uncover during their time together. Except he was not her man to know, nor was his heart for her to capture. She was here because guarding her was part of his duty and nothing more. At least this was the lie he'd told himself and her.

'Allow me to show you the sitting room.'

He led her across the hall, past the narrow flight of stairs, to the other room at the front of the building. It was modest by aristocratic standards, but Bart's prosperity was evident in the fine finishing and furniture. Little ornamentation other than lamps and a few paintings adorned the room and the sedate furniture was arranged more for practicality than for entertaining guests. She wasn't sure if he brought clients here, but if he did, then these meetings were, judging by the decor, decidedly masculine affairs.

Above the fireplace, a painting of the ruins of Rome in the moonlight hung in a gilded frame. She approached it, reading the name of the painter scrawled in the corner and recognising it. 'My husband had a painting like this by the same artist.'

'I sent this home while serving with the Army, during a brief stint in northern Italy.'

'My husband purchased his on his grand tour, which was more years ago than I wish to contemplate.'

'Do you miss him?' Bart asked with a directness she imagined he used with witnesses in the docks, one daring her to answer with a lie.

'I miss what he represented and the opportunity he offered, especially for children.'

'And yet there weren't any.'

'There might have been in time, or there could be if I wed again.'

'I'm sure there will be, both children and another husband.' *But it won't be with me*, he might have well said for it was stated in his silence.

She touched her lips with her fingertips, not as quick to believe it tonight as she'd been at the gallery. He might insist the warmth of a home and wife had no place in his life, but his kiss this afternoon had said something different. Except, she couldn't be guided by what she thought she'd heard but by what he said. 'My marrying again is the single point on which you and Aunt Agatha both agree.'

He winked at her. 'Then it must be a cold night in hell.'

She studied the lines of his cheeks, and his broad forehead and straight nose beneath his dark hair, seeing again the man who'd first approached her at Lady Greenwood's. If she could hold on to this jovial Bart, they might recapture what they'd lost at the end of their engagement. It was as tantalising a challenge as when he'd first asked her to help him uncover the Rouge Noir and more risky. He'd fight harder than the traitors to maintain the protective walls he'd built around his heart to buffer himself from tragedy, the way she'd done during the awful year when both her husband and her sister-in-law had died. There was only so much grief a person could bear, and while some men like her brother allowed it to almost destroy them, Bart used it to grow stronger, but it isolated him, too. If she could overcome his barriers, then they might have a chance together or she'd suffer a more stinging defeat than when she'd broken from him to marry another.

The slap of shoes against the floor and a woman's voice interrupted them. 'Mr Dyer, it's a pleasure to see you home so early tonight.'

They turned to face a rotund woman with thick arms barely contained by the short sleeves of her dress.

'Lady Rexford, allow me to introduce my housekeeper, Mrs Roberts. Mrs Roberts, Lady Rexford will be staying here under my protection for the foreseeable future. Please assist her in whatever she requires. I'm sure, like me, she can expect your discretion.'

Mrs Roberts didn't blink at the pronouncement and Moira wondered how many other ladies of both reputable and perhaps not-so-reputable character he'd brought here to spend the night. She didn't wish to consider it.

'I haven't spilled one of your secrets yet, Mr Dyer. I'm not about to begin now,' Mrs Roberts assured them with a wave of her full hand. She flicked a glance at Moira, her happy smile drooping a bit about the corners. The house-keeper might not gossip, but it didn't mean she wouldn't judge, and this was something Moira wasn't accustomed to. She'd always followed the rules and never transgressed society or her family's expectations. She'd all but flaunted each and every one of them in the last few hours. 'The only room ready is the one next to yours. Will this do, Mr Dyer?'

'It will have to.'

'Come along then, Lady Rexford, and I'll take you up.'

With one last look at Bart, Moira followed the housekeeper upstairs to the hallway and the first door on the left.

'I changed the sheets yesterday so they're fresh. If you like, I can help you undress or have a plate of food sent up,' Mrs Roberts offered.

'No, I'm fine, thank you. I wish to rest for a while.'

'Of course. Call me if there's anything you need.' With a curtsy the housekeeper left, closing the door behind her.

It was the first time Moira had been alone since leaving Lady Camberline's tea. So much had happened since then, far more than she could contemplate. She wandered to the narrow bed in the centre of the room and settled down on the blue coverlet, the crisp cotton cool beneath her skin. This room, like those downstairs, was simple and without adornment, the furniture here for purpose instead of beauty. It was only welcoming because it was so close to Bart.

Bart's footsteps in the hallway, and the opening and closing of the door in his adjoining room, caught her attention. The clink of a porcelain pitcher meeting the side of a washstand, and the trickle of pouring water, drifted in through the door separating them. She closed her eyes, imagining him going about his toilette, his coat off, his arms firm as he raised the water to his face to allow it to run down his square chin. It was strangely intimate and yet disconnecting at the same time. They were together, but apart.

She longed to go to the door and join him, to help him off with his waistcoat and rub the weariness of the day from his shoulders. While she soothed his muscles, they could speak about the tangled evidence they'd gathered and enjoy the familiar pattern of a man and woman together at the end of the day preparing for rest.

Except it wasn't rest they were likely to indulge in if she entered his room, but something more ruinous, an act she'd never enjoyed before but felt certain she would with Bart.

She rolled on her side and watched the light under the door dim and then brighten when he passed between it and her. His body would be solid beneath her palms, his muscles taut against her fingertips, and every touch of his firm hands on her would be as light and tender as they'd been when he'd seen to her wound. If she went to him, she might at last discover the sensations and desires that could exist between a man and a woman beyond wishing for a child. They were the ones she'd heard in whispered conversations and seen alluded to in books but had never experienced.

The ones that could lead to a baby.

She turned on to her back and stared at the ceiling, frustrated and irritated. She was in an awkward enough situation without the scandal of an illegitimate child to make it worse.

Don't be silly, you're a grown woman who's perfectly capable of being with a man and not forgetting herself. And Bart is a respectful gentleman. Surely there can be no harm in the two of us just talking.

The allure of spending time alone with Bart proved more powerful than her reservations and she slid off the bed and went to the door. She raised her hand, hesitating a moment before she rapped her knuckles on the wood. She held her breath while she waited for him to open the door. When he did, she strode through it, refusing to be governed by worries and fears of what might happen. These things had led her into a marriage with Lord Rexford, kept her in the country when she should have been out living her life. She wouldn't allow them to hamper her any longer. She was tired of regrets, of giving up everything she wanted because of someone else's rules or needs or ideas. She would have her way, even if she wasn't sure exactly what her way might entail tonight.

'I thought you'd like to talk more about the case.' She stood in the middle of his room, waiting for him to respond. He left the door open, offering her the chance to leave. She was grateful for this small courtesy because for all her trying to appear at ease, she was shaking in her shoes.

'Let's not think about it for a while.' He removed the cravat from around his neck. His

coat was already off and draped over the back
of a wooden chair, leaving him in his fitted
waistcoat and shirt. 'Sometimes, talking about
other things gives the mind a chance to mull
over a problem and reach a solution.'

'Then what shall we discuss to take your
mind off the case?'

He caressed her with his gaze and she realised at once what kind of distraction he
would prefer. She would, too, but she wasn't
so bold, at least not yet. Discomfort settled on
her shoulders like a wrap and she cast about
for something to do to keep herself busy, and
to place some distance between them even if
she was the one who'd brought them together.
'Should we send down to your housekeeper
for some dinner before venturing on to more
weighty topics?'

'We should probably go down,' he said hus-
kily.

He was right. To stay up here alone together
meant inviting more censorious looks from
Mrs Roberts and who knew what other servants, but Moira didn't want to leave. She had
no idea how long this arrangement would last
before Bart decided to move her out of his
house and into safer quarters, or insisted she

leave for the country. She wouldn't go back. She couldn't return to the life of solitude, but in all her days she'd never imagined being in a room alone with a half-dressed gentleman who was not her husband.

She wasn't one to hop into the bed of a strange man, but Bart was no stranger. At one time, he'd been willing to make her his wife, but what she was thinking about now didn't involve matrimony. If she decided to cross the bounds of propriety with him, she must be completely aware there might be nothing more than this night, or whatever nights would come until his next case, or her family, or society, or whatever it was inside him that made him think he couldn't enjoy the contentment of a proper home rose up to separate them. She wasn't sure she could be so cavalier when it came to affection.

'I had enough of your mother's hors d'oeuvres to keep me going for the night. We needn't go down.' Her refusal meant they'd remain alone, with no interruptions and only their willpower to keep them apart. She hoped hers was strong enough and at the same time wished either it or his might fail.

'We'll stay here then.'

She waited for him to stride across the room and take her in his arms, sweep her half-open lips with his and she wouldn't reject him, but he didn't move. She should be glad he didn't accept the subtle invitation, but she wasn't. She wanted the heat of his hands upon her, to feel as alive and free with him as she had five years ago. In the slight tightening of his jaw, and the intensity of his eyes, she knew he wanted the same thing, but his self-control proved stronger than his desire or hers.

Disappointed, and eager to fill the uncertain quiet descending on them, she crossed to the sideboard where a small bottle of brandy and a crystal tumbler sat beside his wash bowl and shaving things. She poured out a drink as she had for his father and had done many times for her father, her husband and even Freddy. She offered the brandy to Bart and he took the glass from her, his fingers brushing hers and sending a jolt racing through her. She didn't pull back, but waited to see what might happen next. It was Bart who turned away, settling himself on the end of the short leather sofa situated before the fireplace.

'A man could get used to this treatment,' he

joked, but it didn't lessen the tension growing between them.

She sat down on the other end, but it wasn't very far from him. 'A woman could get used to performing these little deeds again, especially for someone truly grateful for them.'

'I'm grateful, but not worthy.'

'A man who fights as hard as you do for people who've been wronged deserves a little tender treatment now and again. After all, life isn't always about struggling and fighting. It's also about love and kindness, even to those who don't always show it to you.'

He tapped his fingers on the side of the glass. 'You mean my father?'

'I mean anyone, except of course hardened criminals.'

'Definitely not them.' He smiled, the stern set of his features easing to remind her of the Bart she'd first come to care for and not the experienced magistrate he'd become.

'Nor can you let those people define you,' she gently encouraged, 'to make you hard or lead you to believe all of life is one long struggle.'

'It's difficult not to fight when you've been doing it for so long. With four older brothers, it starts early. The stakes of the battles only increased when I grew older.' Bart swirled the brandy in the glass, making the amber liquid catch the light from the fire behind it. 'As for softness, too much of it leads to loss and I can't afford to lose. The futures of my clients and my country depend on me winning.'

'It doesn't mean there isn't room in your life for tenderness, and peace, or deeper accomplishments than those claimed in the courtroom.'

Moira shifted closer to Bart on the sofa, the muslin of her dress covering her legs brushing against his. They shouldn't be so close, but he couldn't push her away. There was an understanding and acceptance of him in what she'd said, which he'd never experienced with a woman before, even if this meant he didn't particularly like the man her perception revealed. It wasn't a face he wanted to show the world, or a lady like Moira, but she wasn't disgusted by what she saw. Through her, he might at last gain the more ephemeral things in life, which she almost made him believe were possible to achieve, especially with her.

'You're a saint, Moira.' One he couldn't ruin

with the ugliness of his situation, but still he couldn't tear himself away from the glitter of the firelight in her golden hair or the emerald green of her eyes. Five years ago he'd been struck by her beauty and the truth was nothing had changed except her willingness to defy a great deal in order to be with him.

'Hardly,' she scoffed, before pinning him with a sobering inflammatory look. 'I'm simply tired of fighting, and I think you are, too.'

'I can't give it up especially when my country needs me.' Circumstances had placed her here under his protection and he couldn't take advantage of them, or her.

'But you can refuse to let it consume everything.' She laid her warm hand on his cheek, the slight pressure of her fingertips against his skin igniting his insides like a cannon shot.

He should stand and pull away and not give in to the temptation in her touch. She wasn't a widow in search of a quick rendezvous, but a woman in need of a man who could offer her a respectable arrangement. It wasn't him.

'This isn't right, Moira,' he choked through a desire to hold her as powerful as his need to fight for his country.

'I don't care. I don't want to think about

plots and intrigues, regrets or how we should or shouldn't behave. I want to be with you and nothing else.' She leaned forward and touched her lips to his, snapping what remained of his self-control.

He wrapped his arms about her waist and pulled her against his body, barely aware of the crystal glass tumbling to the floor. She met his kisses with a passion to rival his, the two of them coming together like lovers parted by years of war and reunited at last. Battles had come between them, but they hadn't defeated them or their desire for one another. Even after everything her aunt had done to try and turn her against him, and each mistake he'd made while they'd been together, she embraced him with an eagerness to make him groan.

She brushed his short hair with her slender fingers and caressed the back of his neck, her light touch potent with her craving for him. He kept his hands around her waist while slowing the pace of his kisses, cautious of moving too fast. He longed to draw out this time with her before the world outside intruded to spoil it.

She brought her mouth close to his ear, her breath cool against his heated skin as she touched her lips to his temple. She moved her hands from around his neck to caress his shoulders and slid one finger inside the vee of his shirt to trace the muscles beneath with hesitant and curious circles. He reached behind her and began to undo her dress while her fingers worked the buttons of his waistcoat and tugged at the linen of his shirt. In short time, her dress came away and she sat before him in the white of her chemise and stays, her skin pink with the flush of her need, her eyes averted in the faint embarrassment of being so open and vulnerable to him. He wasn't shy in his admiration of her body as he traced the curve of her waist and pressed light kisses to the tops of her breasts. Sliding his hands around behind her, he worked free the laces of her stays until they came away.

Each subtle revealing of her body as he slid the chemise off her shoulders touched him as deeply as her caresses and told him of the depths of her trust in him. She didn't recoil from him in her nakedness, but helped him off with his shirt and timidly explored his chest and stomach. Her gentle, flawless hands were a contrast to the scars and bruises marking his flesh, each sweep of them against him increasing his need for her. He continued to hold back, determined to be as open and vulnerable with her as she was with him.

Then she shifted closer, her eyes bright with curiosity as she pressed her bare chest to his and wrapped her arms around his shoulders. She touched her lips to his neck and his resolve buckled under the gentlesweep of her tongue across his skin. He slid one arm around her waist and the other beneath her slender legs, clutching her around the thighs as he picked her up and carried her to the bed. She didn't protest, but rested her head against his chest, as confident in him with this as she was with everything else.

He laid her on the plain coverlet and settled down beside her. To hold her close, to be one with her was a victory like none he'd ever captured before. She was the light he'd craved in the darkness of his work and the forgive-ness he needed for his past mistakes and sins. In her arms, he could forget his struggles and the evils in life to revel in the beauty of her figure stretched out beside him, drawing him deeper into her than even the coming together of their bodies could achieve. She was beauty and life and the opposite of everything he'd become.

Moira lay languid in Bart's arms, following the ebb and flow of his movement as he led her deeper into the passion consuming them. She traced the lines of his sturdy body as he did the full curves of hers, marvelling at the firmness of his muscles beneath her palms. He was magnificent, like marble sculpted by a master, but gentle and easy with her, drawing from her surprising new feelings and sensations. The sweep of his tongue and the stroke of his fingertips revealed to her all the pleasures she'd been denied by marriage and widowhood. When her bare skin met his, she shivered, and when he pulled back again to admire her, she didn't try to cover herself or demand he look away. With him there was no hiding or uncertainty, no sense of duty, but only a passion to consume everything. She rushed into it, conscious of nothing but the weight of him above her as they became one, his embrace driving back the cold loneliness that had dominated her for so long. She clung to him as he guided her towards a bliss to rival the joy of being in his arms. He was finally hers and all the lonely years since they'd parted vanished as they reached their pleasure together, their hearts as close as their bodies.

* * *

Moira lay with her cheek on Bart's chest and ran her fingers lazily back and forth across his stomach. The fire had died down, but they hadn't summoned the maid to relight it, unwilling to disturb their solitude.

'What are you thinking?' Bart asked.

She shifted up to face him, breasts pressed against his chest. He rested with his hands behind his head against the pillow, more relaxed than at any other time since she'd been with him. She didn't entirely share his leisure and wondered if she should express the thoughts and concerns tripping through her mind. She wanted to lie with him for ever, never to leave this room, but it wasn't possible. They'd made no promises to one another, but she wasn't ready to ask for more and risk breaking the contentment of their lovemaking and this stolen time together. While they were here, she could pretend this wasn't all there might be between them. It was a fantasy, but it was hers to enjoy for however long it lasted. 'I was thinking how quickly things can change. The most I was considering two days ago was whether or not to order a new dress. Everything was calm and boring. It isn't any more.'

He brushed her hair off her forehead and tucked it behind her ear. 'It will be. I assure you, in a few days when this is all behind us, you'll miss the excitement.'

She would miss him, but she wasn't prepared to say it aloud. 'I won't miss people rushing at me with knives, but the excitement will be hard to leave. I see why it is you do it.'

'It can be more interesting than legal briefs and, at times, more rewarding.' He caressed her cheek with the back of his fingers and in his eyes something deeper than the mere pleasure or convenience of their time together flashed in their dark brown depths. It made her wonder if he would walk away from her when this was all over, or if he even could. 'You should get some sleep. You've had a long day.'

'Yes, I have.' She brushed his lips with hers, then settled down beside him, relishing the weight of his arm around her shoulders and the warmth of his chest beneath her cheek, while trying not to think about what the sunrise might bring.

Bart's peace slid into regret as Moira's breathing grew steady beside him. He adored her and it wasn't until they'd become close again during these last few days that he'd come to realise how much she'd never really left his heart. He might have privately railed against her after the end of their engagement, but with time he'd come to understand why she'd made the decision she'd made. Sadly, he also understood the world and society a little too well and what it meant for their future together. With the soft curve of her body against his, and when she'd been beneath him, he'd almost forgotten the realities of his situation or hers, but they couldn't be ignored for ever. In the morning, he would still be a barrister and stipendiary magistrate her family reviled and she a countess expected to marry a man of her own rank. Evil people would continue to stalk them and England would remain at risk. She'd shown great resolve in facing the trials of the last few days, all the while hanging on to her innocence. He shuddered to think of their time together changing her for the worse. He wanted her to remain above it all, a beautiful thing in the midst of the ugliness of London, but already he'd tarnished her by compromising her honour and reputation. How much more might he dull her brightness when years of stinking gaols, vicious traitors and conniving defendants made him a hard man like his father with no tenderness to spare for his wife and children?

It was easy in the quiet of his bedroom to vow he'd never become that kind of man, to live up to her challenge to not be defined by his work, but he'd also promised to protect Lady Fallworth and Moira, and he'd already failed at one and nearly failed at the other.

He stared down at her sleeping peacefully in his arms. He wouldn't see Moira's beautiful face marred by the same unfulfilled hope for her husband he'd seen in his mother's expression tonight, nor would he place her at risk of being attacked again from the shadows. She deserved a husband not mired in intrigue and lowlifes, someone who could provide her with a home filled with children. In the morning he would give her the chance to find such a man. It would be a victory for common sense, but a triumph for the ugliness in his life.

Chapter Eleven

A light knock at the bedroom door, so quiet Bart might have missed it if he hadn't already been awake, roused him from his thoughts. Moira slept soundly beside him. He'd spent the last two hours admiring her creamy skin in the increasing dawn light, her blonde hair draping her bare breasts and the curve of her hips where they rested beneath the white sheets.

A second, more urgent rap on the door forced him out of bed. Carefully shifting his arm from under Moira to keep from disturbing her, he rose, pulled on his breeches and went to the door. He cracked it open just enough to reveal Mrs Roberts. 'Yes?'

'This arrived for you, from Mr Flint. The messenger said it was important.' She slid a piece of paper though the crack.

'Thank you.' He closed the door and opened the note.

Important development. Meet me at my office at once.
Flint

Moira began to stir and Bart glanced over the top of the paper to where she lay. She opened her green eyes and raised her left arm above her head, making her breasts rise temptingly with her stretch. 'Good morning, Bart.'

'Good morning.' He tossed Mr Flint's note on the dressing table, plucked a clean shirt out of the wardrobe and slid it on. 'Mr Flint has summoned me, I have to go.'

She lowered her arm, her languidness evaporating as she frowned at him in concern. 'But that's not all that's wrong, is it?'

He draped a fresh cravat around his neck and began to tie it, hating himself for what he was about to say, but he couldn't allow this to continue. They'd made a mistake last night, the same one they'd made five years ago by being too impulsive and believing too much in the powerful emotions drawing them together instead of heeding the forces pushing them apart. As much as it killed him to give her up he must. 'We made a mistake last night, Moira.'

The concern in her eyes vanished and he wished he could take back the words, but he couldn't. He'd always been straight in his dealings with scoundrels, the courts and even women. It was something Moira deserved no matter how much it might wound her. It was better for her to hear this now than to allow her to continue under an illusion of happiness.

'You didn't seem to think it was a mistake last night.' She pushed herself up, her breasts as tempting as the subtle curve of her stomach and hips before she jerked up the sheet to cover them.

'I shouldn't have allowed our emotions to run away with us, but—'

'You saw an opportunity and decided to take it as opposed to walking away.' She stepped out of bed, grabbed her chemise and tugged it over her head. Then she gathered up her clothes with quick jerks, piling them in the crook of her elbow.

He went to her and gently grasped her by the upper arms, her skin smooth beneath his fingers. Part of him wanted to fall on his knees in apology and return them to the few seconds of peace they'd enjoyed before he'd opened his stupid mouth and ruined it. Instead, he spoke, further driving a wedge between them. 'I didn't make love to you last night because you were here.'

'Then why?' Tears glistened in her eyes, almost stopping him, but he had to go on, no matter how much it hurt them both.

'Because, like you, I was reaching for something I thought we could seize, but we can't. I'm not the right man for you, Moira, not only because of the difference in our stations, but because of the things you don't know about me.'

'You may not have told me everything, but I can guess. You visit gaols and see men forced to tell you what you need to know, and I'm sure it's ugly business, but it doesn't make you an ugly man.'

He took a deep breath, her continued belief in his goodness torturing him. If she railed at him or called him half the names the men he arrested did, it would make this easier. He could ignore the voice inside him demanding he stop and give a life with her a chance, except she deserved better than him. 'It isn't just me I have to think of, but you. Look at the risks you've faced these last few days simply for helping me. Imagine how much worse it might be if we wed. You'll become a target like Lady Fallworth and I could lose you like Freddy lost her.'

'I thought you were braver than this, Bart.' She twisted out of his grasp, anger flashing in her eyes. 'You talk about facing the dangers of thieves and scoundrels and yet the moment a little of it brushes past me you turn tail and run.'

He pressed his knuckles into his hips, his pride chafing at her accusation. 'You dismiss it now, but what happens when there are children? Will you be so cavalier when someone tries to kill one of them?'

She shifted the clothes in her arms, her resolve weakening in the face of reality. 'Of course not.'

'Even if none of the awful people I pursue ever threaten them or you, it doesn't mean they won't continue to come after me. One of these times they might get lucky and then what? You watched one husband die. Do you want to do it again?'

'If it means having a few years of happiness with you then I'll gladly take the risk. I want to be thrilled and excited, to know there's some kind of life both within marriage and with a man who loves me and whom I love.'

The word love silenced them both. It'd never been uttered between them before, not even when he'd proposed long ago, and he hadn't dared to explore it last night when she'd been one with him in spirit and body. Yes, he loved her and he was certain she loved him. It'd been in her trust and caresses, in her soft sighs in his ears, but love couldn't protect her from reality. 'You will find a man who loves you, Moira, but it won't be me.'

'You've never cared for me?' Her lip quivered with her barely concealed pain.

'I have, more than anyone else. I might have lost you five years ago, but it doesn't mean I ever forgot you. If I could take you to the altar today, I would, in spite of your aunt or any other obstacles, but too much has changed since then. I'm not the Bart who proposed to you, the one who might have made you happy.'

She swallowed back the few tears which hadn't slipped down her cheeks to drop on her cotton chemise, then tuned on her bare heel and stalked to the still-open door to her room. She paused at the threshold to face him, her back straight in her attempt to be brave. 'You say you never forgot me, but I never forgot you as well. Even when Aunt Agatha used to write to me about what you were up to with Freddy, and I thought I'd avoided making a disaster of a match, I always used to wonder if somehow she was wrong. The other day, you proved she was and that you were the honest, trustworthy and noble man I always believed you to be, until this moment.'

Bart didn't try to talk her out of her disgust. Let her think he was someone to be despised instead of admired, it would make it easier for her to forget him, freeing her heart for the man who would some day claim it, one who would be an excellent father and husband for her.

Answered only by his silence, Moira slipped inside her room and closed the door behind her.

Moira's hands shook as she tried to do up the buttons on her morning dress. She'd gone to sleep last night in a haze of bliss, naively be-lieving she and Bart could reclaim what they'd been denied five years ago. Clearly too much had changed—he'd changed, but she hadn't. She was still the woman desperate for affection and attention she'd been back then, except this time she should have known better. She had, but desperation had driven her to spin dreams out of nothing as easily as it'd driven her into Bart's arms.

She slumped down in a leather chair near the dark fireplace, the coals inside having burned out last night with no one coming in to relight them this morning. It left the room as cold as the hollow space inside her chest. She should've headed Aunt Agatha's warnings, taken Freddy's directive to not see Bart again. Instead she'd insisted on having her way and look where it'd got her. If she'd abandoned her family to marry him before, would a morning like this have happened after their wedding? It was difficult to imagine Bart being so callous after standing before a clergyman and swearing a vow, but after what he'd done, it was difficult to think charitably of him. He loved her, he always had and he'd possessed the courage to say it, but not even his love had been enough to overcome his reservations and allow them to greet the morning together. Instead, it'd pulled them, and her heart, apart.

This cut deeper than anything else he'd told her.

She reached back and at last slipped the

buttons through their holes, then did up her half-boots before looking over the room, at a loss for what to do next. She couldn't sit here shivering and starving while she licked her wounds, but she wasn't ready to go downstairs and face the servants or Bart.

She stared at the black and grey coals in the grate, Bart's words coming back to her again and again. Tears streamed down her cheeks, but the anger she'd hurled at him during their parting wasn't there. Everything he'd said was the truth and he hadn't spoken it to be cruel, but to force her to face what she'd ignored last night. He was a man who'd seen a great deal of both the good and bad of human nature and how it could affect people. He understood better than she did how life was not a fairy tale and things seldom worked out as people planned. One would think, after her failed marriage and shortened childhood, she wouldn't need to be reminded of that, but the girl inside of her had stubbornly held on to a few dreams.

They were all gone now.

'You summoned me?' Bart strode into Mr Flint's office and sat before the desk.

'I did. We interrogated Mr Roth last night.

He was difficult at first, but we brought him around. It seems he knows more about Mr Dubois than he'd first let on. He's heard the Rouge Noir is plotting to assassinate a number of government men tonight. Unfortunately, he didn't know where, or how.'

'I don't know where, but I know how they intend to do it.' He told Mr Flint about the missing gunpowder and his conversation with his father, then handed him the list with the names on it.

'Holy hell,' Mr Flint breathed. 'It'll be worse than if Guy Fawkes had succeeded.'

'What government meetings are taking place tonight?'

'I'll find out. In the meantime, I'll send men to investigate the buildings. If we can't find anything, I'll warn members off attending their meetings, but not until the last minute. We don't want the Rouge Noir getting wind of our plans and disappearing only to have them re-emerge in the future more deadly than before.'

'Did Mr Roth provide any names of the other people involved?'

'Not beyond Mr Dubois, but there's one more bit of evidence I've procured. It didn't make much sense to me until I heard the attempted murderer's confession. Take a look at this.' He laid a piece of paper on the desk in front of Bart.

It was a communication between the Comte de Troyen and Lord Camberline saying the details of their arrangement were at last in place and they would meet one final time this evening behind the Camberline Mausoleum in St Marylebone Burial Grounds to discuss the appropriate payment before they enacted their plan. Lord Camberline urged the Comte to act swiftly before they were discovered and stopped.

'I want you and your men to search the docks and find Mr Dubois, then be there tonight when the Comte and Lord Camberline meet, but be careful,' Mr Flint ordered. 'With men of their status you must be absolutely sure they're guilty before you move. Lord Camberline might be young, but he has a powerful name and an influential mother. He could be the ruin of you if you're wrong.'

'It must be nice to be able to hide guilt with a title,' Bart sneered, pushing back his anger, Moira's words about not allowing these villains to define him ringing in his mind. She was right, this job had made him hard and these kinds of things would only make it worse unless he stopped it now, before more damage was done. 'I've succeeded without the influence of great men and done my best to see the worst of the lot brought to justice. Let Lord Camberline or his mother strike at me if I'm wrong. I can handle the attack.'

'I don't doubt you can. It's why I assigned you to this duty.'

'And Lady Camberline?

'You think she's in on this?'

'Based on the information Lady Rexford has obtained, Lady Camberline is either involved or has a good knowledge of the plot. Lady Rexford is no longer attending the dinner tonight. I sent her regrets to Lady Camberline before I came here.' He explained about the attack outside the museum yesterday, doing his best to not think about what had happened afterwards, or this morning. She was no longer in harm's way and that was what mattered, along with his stopping these people and he would. By tomorrow this would be over along with all reason for a connection between them. The idea hit him as strongly as learning with certainty the plot was coming to fruition tonight had. 'I have a man inside the Camberline house who can gather information and possibly uncover who else is involved.'

'A bad blow at a time when we need Lady Rexford there, but I agree with removing her. In the meantime, gather your men and see what you find at the burial ground.'

'Yes, sir.' Bart left the room to assemble his men and at last crush the threat to England. There was no more time to think about Moira and what had happened between them this morning. Tomorrow, when the realm was safe, he'd mourn their parting. Today, he must help save England.

Moira paced back and forth across the small bedroom for what seemed like the hundredth time today, the only difference between now and an hour ago being the setting sun. She lit a reed in the grate and touched it to the wick of the candle beside her bed, allowing the light to fill the room, but it did nothing to warm her soul. Bart had been gone all day and he hadn't sent any word about where he was, what he was doing or when he might return. She should be glad he was gone, for it meant she didn't have to endure any awkward meetings or conversations, but she wasn't. She was bored and lonely.

After he'd left, she'd pulled herself together and ventured downstairs to eat and chat with Mrs Roberts. It'd been a tolerable enough hour, but the housekeeper's duties had summoned her, leaving Moira to poke around the bookshelf in Bart's office to try to find something other than a law book to read. She hadn't been successful, and the more she'd wandered around his house, the more isolated and upset she'd grown. There was nothing here to take her mind off Bart and what had happened between them, and it smacked of her time at Allwick Hall after she'd married Walter. The activity of the first weeks of learning about her new home and situation had quickly faded to endless hours of inactivity bleeding one into the other while she'd searched for some way to fill the long days. Walter had had his obsession with his health and his fossil collection to amuse him. Moira had had nothing except a desire to be useful, one Walter had blunted by limiting her duties to planning dinners and nothing else. It'd left her without any purpose in life, just like today.

Moira sat in the chair, frustrated, hurt and at

a loss for what to do. She could go to Fallworth Manor, tell Freddy he'd been right about Bart and ask to be accepted back into the family, but it galled her to go crawling back to them. They hadn't valued all she'd done for them and if she returned, they would merely take advantage of her again, all the while holding her mistake with Bart over her head. She couldn't go to her town house until Bart told her it was safe to return, but she didn't want to remain here, forgotten, and of no use to anyone once again.

She spied the red dress she'd worn last night draped over the arm of a chair where she'd discarded it this morning after changing into her morning dress. She picked it up and examined it in the fading sunlight. It was a touch wrinkled at the bottom from its time on the floor in Bart's room last night, but it was still clean and fresh. She could put it on and go out, perhaps to the theatre or even, if she dared, Lady Camberline's dinner.

She clutched the dress to her chest, afraid and emboldened by the thought. Bart had told her not to go, but after defying her family and risking her reputation to help him, to think all her efforts had been a waste was as irritating as this feeling of uselessness. At the dinner, she'd have a purpose. She could eavesdrop on Lady Camberline's guests and help England. If she learned anything pertinent, then it meant all her sacrifices wouldn't be in vain. Yes, it might place her at some risk, but she doubted Lady Camberline kept assassins hidden in her drawing room. There would be others present, and if she was careful to never be alone with anyone, and to remain aware of her surroundings, then it would minimise the danger.

If nothing else, being there tonight might offer her the opportunity to meet new people, maybe even a man who did want a wife and family, but who wasn't encumbered by plots and treason. It would dampen for a few hours the loneliness inside her and offer her the chance to at last obtain something of the new life she'd come to London to find, the one she'd believed she'd found with Bart until he'd pulled it away. Let him live in his filthy world of spies. She would and could at last claim a future of her own.

Chapter Twelve

Bart stood on the far side of the cemetery behind a large statue of a winged angel, her carved stone face pitted by time and the elements. Across the rows of tilted and weathered gravestones, Bart watched as the Comte de Troyen entered the cemetery and made for a tall mausoleum near the back wall. Into the quiet, the bells of a nearby church suddenly sounded out the evening hour. Lord Camberline had disappeared behind the mausoleum some time ago, obviously waiting for the Frenchman to arrive and join him. Neither man took any pains to conceal their identities, but Bart wasn't surprised. It was hubris and the mistaken belief they couldn't be caught combined with the ineptitude which usually brought plotters down. It would be Lord Camberline's and the Comte's downfall, too.

Around the cemetery, his men were positioned out of sight, waiting for his signal to pounce. Bart might have brushed off Mr Flint's warning about evidence, but he knew it was essential to seeing the aristocratic members of the Rouge Noir convicted in the House of Lords.

Bart, with the collar of his redingote tugged up high about his neck and his hat pulled down low over his eyes, moved quickly and quietly towards the Camberline Mausoleum while signalling his men to follow, but stay out of sight. Bart crept along the side of the stone memorial towards the back of it facing the high brick wall surrounding the burial grounds. The stone was cold against his shoulder as he pressed against it just near the edge where he could hear the two men speaking.

'Is everything in place?' the Comte demanded in his thick French accent. The languid man Bart had met the other night at the ball had been replaced by a hard-talking one and Bart could see at once the statesman Moira had described at the ball. If he was this duplicitous in his ability to present himself to the world, Bart could imagine how he might be involved in plots and assassinations.

'Yes,' Lord Camberline said, less confident

than the man he spoke with. 'I have a carriage prepared to take us to Scotland. By the time anyone realises what's happened, it'll be too late to stop us.'

'And the money? Were you able to raise it?' the Comte demanded.

'It was difficult to obtain such a sum without my mother noticing, but I managed it. Despite my majority she refuses to acknowledge I'm an adult capable of making my own decisions. She'll be sorry she didn't do it sooner. She's mistaken if she thinks she can control me any longer.'

'As long as you don't fail or you'll regret it. What time can I expect you?'

'The dinner is at eight tonight. I'll leave shortly after it starts. My slipping out should be easy once my mother is engaged with all her MPs and lords. I'll meet you at the entrance to Westminster Hall and we'll be done with this at last.'

Bart had heard enough. He stepped around the mausoleum and revealed his presence. 'Gentlemen, what a surprise to see you here. I hadn't expected to encounter such august men in these dour surroundings, but I suppose a cemetery is a fitting place to contrive plots.'

Lord Camberline, who'd been so full of confidence only a few seconds ago, wilted in the face of Bart's unexpected appearance. He shifted in his boots as if he intended to flee, but two of Bart's men stepped up on the other side of the mausoleum, blocking his exit. Bart heard the crunch of stones as Joshua and Mr Smith stepped up behind him, further penning in the two lords.

'Who are you?' Lord Camberline demanded, the two of them never having been introduced. 'Who sent you here?'

'He's Monsieur Dyer, the famous barrister,' the Comte answered, recognising Bart from their brief introduction at the ball. It gave Bart a grudging respect for the Frenchman. Bart thought the man had dismissed him, but like any true statesman he'd been observant of details, especially names and faces. 'To what do we owe the pleasure of your company?'

Bart was about to answer when Lord Camberline did first.

'My mother must have discovered our plan and sent him,' Lord Camberline whined to the Comte before turning on Bart and drawing on his lineage to shore up his backbone. 'Have you given up trying cases in order to chase after young lords at the insistence of their mothers? Whatever she's paying you to spy on me, I'll pay twice as much for you to forget about us.'

He spoke with all the contempt and arrogance of his station, but it had no effect on Bart. This wasn't the first time he'd faced a lord who, in the wrong and on the verge of a judgement against him, had tried to sneer down his nose at Bart or buy him off. 'I'm not here on behalf of your mother, but in search of traitors to the Crown about to commit treason.'

'Traitors?' The Comte laid a hand on his cravat, appearing genuinely surprised.

Lord Camberline's sneer dropped. 'We aren't involved in treason.'

'Then what are you doing in the back of the cemetery so late in the day discussing plans?' He didn't offer details, waiting for either of the men to clear or condemn themselves without Bart leading them too far into it.

Lord Camberline shot the Comte a worried look, but the Comte appeared more amused than alarmed. He pressed the tip of his walking stick into the ground and squared himself at Bart, not with condescension, but respect. 'I'd heard rumours about you, Monsieur Dyer,

after the Scottish Corresponding Society affair. Until this moment I hadn't realised they
were true. However, if it's traitors to the crown
you're searching for, you won't find them here.'

'Who was whispering in your ear about
me?' Bart asked, wary of the man's regard.

'I have one old contact in the Government.
Years ago, after I first came to England during the Peace of Amiens, I did my fair share of
shady work, not for Napoleon, but on behalf of
the English Crown. More than one man who'd
come across from Europe and into the French
community here had done so with nefarious
intentions. I used to find out who they were
and inform the proper people.'

'Then how come I haven't heard of your involvement before?' Mr Flint had never mentioned the Comte's old service during any of
their conversations about him.

'Because, at the time, only Mr Wickham
was aware of my work and he kept it a very
deep secret to protect me, especially when
I left his service after my wife died and my
daughter's care fell solely to me. As I'm sure
you're aware, there are certain unavoidable
dangers in this line of work.'

'I am.' Bart thought of Moira and the way

his heart had pounded when he'd rushed at Mr Roth, praying the entire time he would reach the assassin before the man reached her. However, for all the Comte's newfound camaraderie, questions still remained. 'If you were involved with working against Napoleon, then why did the Emperor restore your title and lands?'

'He believed he could bribe me into turning against my adopted country, but I refused. Where the Revolutionaries in France would've seen me executed because of my bloodline, England offered me and my family the chance to grow and thrive. It also offered my daughter a future she would not have had in France. It was her we were discussing. Her welfare forced me to meet Lord Camberline in an awful place like this.' He knocked his stick against the mausoleum.

'Your daughter?' The sense he and Moira had been wrong about Lord Camberline continued to grow.

'Marie and I are to be married in Scotland. We're journeying there tonight,' Lord Camberline explained with much more humility than the last time he'd addressed Bart. 'My mother is against it and she has been since the beginning, but circumstances of late mean we must be married, and soon.'

'She's carrying your child,' Bart surmised without delicacy. They were all men with no need to tread lightly around any subject.

'Yes.' Lord Camberline's face coloured with shame while the Comte's reddened with fatherly outrage.

'Lord Camberline was careless with Marie and I refuse to see her ruined because of it.'

'I wasn't careless. I love her, it's why I'm doing all I can to ensure we're together. I won't allow her to be ruined or for anyone to stop us from marrying.' Lord Camberline stepped up to Bart. 'I give you my word, everything we've told you is true. We aren't traitors.'

Above them the church bells rang out again, indicating more time had passed with him no closer to uncovering the plot or stopping it. Instead, he was wasting his efforts involving himself in young love, unless Lord Camberline knew more than he realised, especially about his mother. 'My apologies to you both for the intrusion, but in the absence of hard evidence, we were forced to follow all leads, including those connected to the both of you and Lady Camberline.'

Lord Camberline's jaw fell open. 'My mother isn't a traitor either.'

'Are you sure? She's a great admirer of Napoleon.'

'Many are, but it doesn't mean she's done anything wrong.'

'Then why did she speak with Mr Dubois, a notorious smuggler who's heavily involved with the traitors, at the gallery the other night?'

'I don't know, nor am I acquainted with the man,' Lord Camberline sputtered.

'I'm surprised given how easily he conversed with your mother.' Bart stepped up to Lord Camberline, forcing the young man to move back. 'If you are in any way connected to this man and hope to avoid being accused of treason, you'd better tell me all you know, including where I might find him.' None of his and his men's efforts to locate the smuggler today had been fruitful.

'I know where you can find Mr Dubois,' the Comte offered. 'As of late, he frequents the Town of Ramsgate pub near the Wapping Docks.'

'How do you know?' Wapping was far beyond where Mr Dubois usually operated, but

he must have figured Bart would come looking for him and gone there to hide.

'My driver came over from France right before the blockade, but his parents were trapped
in France. He often sends and receives letters
to them through Mr Dubois. Until this moment, I hadn't realised Mr Dubois was so nefarious. I simply assumed he was like all the
other smugglers eager to make money off a
bad situation.'

'And Lady Camberline?' Given the Comte's
involvement in the French community Bart
sensed he might have more insight into the
Dowager Marchioness than either he, Moira,
or even Lord Camberline could glean.

Lord Camberline turned to the Comte. 'You
don't think she's involved, do you?'

The Comte shot him a pitying look, then
turned to Bart. 'I can't say for I have no knowledge of any plots against the Crown, but given
what I know of her and her past, it wouldn't
surprise me if she was. I hope you find Mr
Dubois, Monsieur Dyer. I hate to think of
anything bad happening to this wonderful
country.'

The Comte's earnestness silenced any lingering doubts about him.

'Thank you for your help, Monsieur le Comte, and good luck to you both in your endeavours tonight.'

With a nod, Bart signalled to his men, and they dashed across the cemetery and out the far gate to where Bart's coach waited on the quiet side street. While they climbed inside, Tom hopped down from the seat and handed him a note.

'Mr Dyer, one of Mr Flint's messengers delivered this while you were in the graveyard.'

It wasn't on Mr Flint's usual stationary and, after telling the driver where to take them, Bart tore it open as he climbed in beside his men.

He practically jumped out of the carriage to order it to make for Mayfair when he read the contents. It was from Mrs Roberts, informing him Moira had decided to attend Lady Camberline's dinner after all.

'Damn.' He crushed the paper between his hands.

'Everything well, sir?' Joshua asked, the others falling silent at his outburst.

'Everything is fine.' Bart gave everyone instructions on what to do when they reached the Town of Ramsgate pub. They'd draw Mr

Dubois out and seize him, then find a way to make him talk.

When he was finished, the men returned to inspecting and preparing their weapons while the carriage hurried through the darkening streets.

Bart leaned over to Joseph. 'Lady Rexford has gone to Lady Camberline's dinner.'

There wasn't time to go there and, with them about to enter one of the seediest dock areas in London, he couldn't spare a man to visit Lady Camberline's or to make a scene by having him drag Moira away.

'I'm sure she'll be safe in company, sir. Don't forget that Mr Paulson is there as a footman and he'll keep an eye on her.'

Bart offered a terse nod, then set to checking the powder and ball in his pistol, frustrated more by Moira having defied him than the setback in the graveyard. Lord Camberline might have doubts about his mother, but Bart's concerns about the woman were growing. If he was right, then Moira might be walking into real trouble, except the woman wasn't likely to try anything with so many men of rank and influence seated around her dinner table or in her sitting room. It was as faint a comfort as the Marquess's doubts about his mother's involvement. If Lord Camberline was correct, and Lady Camberline was nothing more than a Francophile longing for a return to the glories of the Ancient Regime, then Moira would be fine, perhaps even safer than if she were at his house near Temple Bar, a potential target.

Besides, she was not his to command and he could do nothing but make requests of her. He'd surrendered any other rights to her life when he'd purposely destroyed any prospect of a future with her.

He shoved the pistol back in the holster beneath his coat and reached up to grab the leather strap over the door when the coach made a hard turn. Outside, the more polished streets of London gave way to the tightly packed buildings and cluttered streets near the docks. It was a bumpy and jolting reminder of why he'd had to disappoint Moira's hopes, and his. This was who he was and the life he'd chosen, and for a brief moment he wondered if he'd chosen wrongly. He'd never allowed anyone or anything to dictate his path in the past and yet he'd permitted his work to do just that this morning. She'd been willing to stand beside him and still he'd pushed her away, choosing the damp and mist of the docks and criminals over the charm of her voice and the tranquillity of her presence.

A regret as powerful as the one he carried over Lady Fallworth's death slammed into him. Then the carriage rolled to a stop across the street from the boisterous and rowdy tavern, leaving him no more time to consider the matter. If he didn't save England, there would be no future for anyone, least of all him and Moira.

Moira entered Lady Camberline's house with a sigh. From somewhere up the stairs, the low rumble of gentlemen's laughter punctuated by the higher tones of a woman's voice drifted down to her. Before the butler began to lead her up the massive Camberline staircase, she thought of slipping out the door and returning to Bart's house. Her heart wasn't into pretending to be charming, but she wasn't here for a social call, but for England.

'Lady Rexford, if you'll follow me,' the butler urged.

Instead of pleading a headache and leaving, Moira started up the stairs behind him.

This wouldn't be the first time she'd put on such a performance. In the past, she'd greeted overseers and callers while in the midst of mourning for her father or her husband. She'd even faced a cadre of guests on her wedding day while forcing herself to appear like the happy bride everyone expected. She'd have to feign indifference whenever she and Bart finally faced one another again and endure the awkwardness of their first meeting since this morning, so she might as well get some more practice in before that happened.

After tonight, she would pretend no more, not to herself, her family, not even society depending on how the events of last night ultimately played out. She touched her stomach as they reached the top of the hall and the butler led her to the sitting room. A small hope flared inside her. Maybe her misguided actions would at last give her the one thing she craved the most, but even this would be tainted. She wanted a child, but not one who would always be cursed by her foolishness. If there was a child, she was sure Bart would try to do right by her. No, she wouldn't marry for duty again, no matter what the consequences. She might not have much of an income, but she had something, and family standing and lineage. She wouldn't be compelled by any pressure, not her family's or society's or even Bart's, to marry where real love did not exist, no matter what the consequences.

But he did love me. Except it hadn't been strong enough to overcome his reservations and objections and ask her to marry him. *Good. It's time to forget him since it's clear he doesn't want me.*

The butler led her into the sitting room and announced her. The conversation died away as the other guests turned to take her in and she studied them, too. There wasn't one man here under fifty years old who wasn't involved in the Government in one way or another. Even Lord Liverpool, the Prime Minister, was present along with a number of other high-ranking men. Despite herself, Moira was impressed with Lady Camberline's ability to draw together such a worthy guest list. With so many influential government ministers, many of them smiling more widely now at the arrival of another young woman, she was sure to hear something of importance. Whether or not it would help Bart and England remained to be seen.

'Lady Rexford, I'm glad you were able to attend after all.' Lady Camberline approached Moira, elegant in her dark gown trimmed with white lace.

'Yes, my headache finally went away.' Mrs Roberts had told her this was the excuse Bart had sent the Marchioness this morning.

'Good, we can't have you ill,' Lady Camberline replied with a friendliness she hadn't displayed during their past two meetings.

Perhaps it was her pleasure in the success of the night rather than Moira making her so effusive, but the edge to her smile, the same one she'd flashed when she'd questioned Moira about her neck, lingered in the woman's greeting. Could this woman have really hired someone to kill her? Standing in the midst of her gilded sitting room it was difficult to imagine, but it reminded Moira to remain wary and observant. Bart wasn't here to protect her. 'You must come meet my other guests.'

Lady Camberline took her by the arm and led her deeper into the room, introducing her to one influential government man after another. Moira hadn't realised the depths of the Marchioness's connections. She thought her influence had died with her husband, but it appeared it hadn't. It didn't extend to her son who was not among the honoured gathering. 'Is Lord Camberline not here tonight?'

'I don't know where he is.' Irritation clouded her eyes before her gaze fell on two men standing together beneath a painting of Lady Camberline in her youth. 'Allow me to introduce you to Lord Lefevre and Lord Moreau. I'm sure they'd both enjoy the chance to speak to a fellow lover of France.'

She guided Moira to the two men and made the introduction. Moira's heart dropped in her chest while she worked to retain her smile. Entertaining old men who'd been contemporaries of her husband reminded her too much of the prison she'd lived in during her marriage, the one she thought she'd escaped. She hadn't. It sometimes seemed as if she was not meant to be around people her age, or to attract the attentions of men in their prime like Bart. Instead she must once again preen and smile for lords of many accomplishments and little youth.

'Lady Rexford, a pleasure to meet you. Allow me to introduce Madame Bernard. I was well acquainted with Lady Rexford's grandmother many years ago,' Lord Lefevre explained to his much younger companion. The woman was dressed more modestly tonight than she'd been at the Royal Academy, her gown a much brighter shade of red than Moira's and fashionably cut. The young woman clung to Lord Lefevre as if afraid Moira might snatch him away. Moira wondered where Monsieur Bernard was and why no one seemed to mind his wife's obvious regard for Lord Lefevre, but she could guess.

'Thank you, Lord Lefevre, my grandmother always spoke well of you,' Moira lied in perfect French, ignoring Madame Bernard's jealous looks. Lady Camberline left them to greet her other guests.

The sound of his native tongue widened Lord Lefevre's gapped-toothed smile. The two French lords had been part of the French *émigré* circle in London when she was a little girl. Unlike many others she'd met through her grandparents, she didn't remember these two being so warm and open with her back then. Instead, they'd stuck to themselves, never fully integrating as her grandparents had into the fabric of London life. Although their titles and wealth guaranteed them a place here, their unwillingness to truly embrace their new country continued to set them apart. Tonight, she pretended to be one of them by complaining with them about the English while listening to what they said about Napoleon. Unfortunately, they offered very little beyond a genuine dislike for England and a reverence similar to Lady Camberline's for Napoleon. If they or the Marchioness were involved with the Rouge Noir, they hid it well.

A short while later, Lady Camberline returned to the Frenchmen and Moira, standing on the edge of their conversation and attempting to appear at ease, but something in her manner reminded Moira of the impatient way Aunt Agatha often pounced into the middle of discussions when there was something bothering her. It turned Moira's attention from the men to her hostess, the air of irritated disquiet coming from Lady Camberline hinting at something serious.

'Lady Rexford, Madame Bernard, I must speak privately with Lord Lefevre and Lord Moreau. Madame Bernard, could I trouble you to go over and speak to Lady Waltenham?'

'It would be a pleasure.' The young woman didn't appear at all pleased as she grudgingly made off to join the aged widow.

'Lady Rexford, I'd be grateful if you'd join Prince Frederick? He was quite thrilled when I said you'd be here tonight.' She motioned to where the Prince stood by a gilded writing desk, frowning into his empty drinking glass and half-heartedly listening to the man at his elbow who punctuated his speech with exaggerated gestures. 'I'd hate to think of a member of the royal family bored at my dinner. You must charm him with your wit. You're so accomplished at charming people.'

The same unnerving smile she'd flashed Moira at tea yesterday when she'd extended the invitation graced her lips again and made Moira shiver.

'I'll do all I can to make him enjoy the evening,' Moira offered in all innocence, trying to concoct some reason to stay and listen to their conversation, but nothing came to her. She was sure their discussion would involve more than praising Napoleon, but she could think of no argument to make them let her stay. Whether or not it had something to do with the Rouge Noir she couldn't be certain. Perhaps it had something to do with Lord Camberline and why he was missing. There was no way for her to find out as Lady Camberline led her across the room to Prince Frederick.

She wished Bart were here to advise her on what to do, or at the very least allow his strong presence to calm the butterflies fluttering in her stomach. When he'd been with her at the Royal Academy she'd been so sure of herself and her ability to gain Lady Camberline's favour. She could use a good measure of his bravery now, except it wasn't hers to draw on any more as he'd informed her this morning. She would have to reach inside herself again for the courage necessary to find her way back to the two Frenchmen and try to learn something of their discussion with Lady Camberline. Her instincts told her it would be more valuable to her and Bart's efforts than anything she might gain from Prince Frederick.

Lady Camberline presented Moira to Prince Frederick who was as solicitous to Moira tonight as he'd been at the ball. Moira did her best to chat with him, but all she could think about was Bart. It was difficult not to, for he was the reason she was here, and the reason why she could offer no one, not even the Prince, a genuine smile.

Stop thinking of him!

She was in a room full of powerful men, all of whom were her equal or superior in breeding and rank. These were the men she should look to for companionship instead of a lowly barrister. Her spirits dropped further at the thought. She'd vowed to never be like Aunt Agatha and judge people on the merits of their lineage instead of their character. Except she'd tried to judge Bart by his character, and in almost every other way he'd been wonderful, except this morning when his shortcomings had made themselves painfully known. Part of her wanted to believe it was simply the stress of the investigation that had caused him to push her away, but after so many disappointments and heartaches in life, she couldn't be certain it wasn't some failing inside her which had driven him away.

Let him go.

She would hold out next time for an honourable offer before losing her better sense with any gentleman. Thankfully, it was Bart who'd taught her this difficult lesson. If she'd done so with some other man, he might not have been as discreet. Bart would be, for as much as she hated him, she could still recognise the honourable man who'd promised to protect her behind the mask of the one who'd callously cast her aside.

Bart and his men were out of the carriage before it even came to a stop in front of the painted blue entrance to the Town of Ramsgate pub. Drunken men, some with harlots hanging on their arms staggered out of the establishment, their rotten stench combined with the stink of the nearby Thames eye watering in its potency.

Bart and his men marched inside, stopping at the door to survey the raucous crowd of sailors and dockworkers spending their pay on ale and company. In the midst of this revelry sat Mr Dubois with a buxom strumpet on his lap. The smuggler dropped a handful of coins in the generous cleavage of the flaxen-haired woman, further tightening Bart's stomach. He was flush with cash and drink, marking him as a man who'd been paid handsomely for a finished job. His two men flanking him were also drunk on coin and women, flattering and cajoling the harlots draped across their laps and doing little to protect their employer.

'You two distract the henchmen. Joseph and

I will get Mr Dubois.' Bart had a score to settle with the man who'd tried to kill Moira. He'd see to it he never threatened her or anyone ever again.

His two men spread out on either side of the room, coming up behind the men and, with a few well-whispered words about the pistols and knives now at their backs, sobered them and forced them to be still. The women with them hopped off their laps with squeals of worry and sprinted away. Their cries were lost in the rowdy noise of the other drinkers.

Mr Dubois was not so easily distracted. Sensing a change in the air, he looked first to his white-faced men, then around the room until he spied Bart, Joseph and Mr Smith bearing down on him. He tipped the strumpet on to the floor and hustled towards the back of the pub. Ale made him slower and less sure footed than the night at the gallery. He was barely out the back of the pub when he tripped over a pile of stacked crates. The clatter of wood and Mr Dubois's curses echoed through the misty air.

Bart grabbed the smuggler and hauled him to his feet, then dragged him around the corner and into the narrow alley between the pub and the next building. Turning him around, Bart rammed his fist into the drunken Frenchman's stomach.

'That's for Lady Rexford.' Mr Dubois choked and doubled over. Bart hauled him up straight by his lapels and banged him hard against the wall, knocking whatever breath the smuggler had managed to scrape in back out of him. Bart slammed his fist into Mr Dubois's stomach again. 'That's for trying to ruin England.'

'You have no right to strike me. I've done nothing wrong,' the man wheezed as he dropped to his knees and clutched his middle, attempting to argue the law with Bart.

Bart pulled back his foot, ready to deliver a swift kick to the scoundrel's side. Mr Dubois cringed, waiting for the blow, but Bart stopped, disgusted by this rat, the dirty, stinking alley and himself. Mr Dubois deserved a beating, but the rage driving Bart to deliver it was loathsome. This wasn't who he wanted to be, a man so degraded by his work he wasn't worthy of Moira's love.

He dropped his foot and Mr Dubois unclenched.

Bart stood over him, pitying the smuggler as

much as himself. Life wasn't pretty and neat, but it didn't mean Bart's had to be filled with nothing but sharp edges. When this was all over, he'd do everything he could to win Moira back, to become a man worthy of her affection and the serenity she offered.

Until he could secure her heart again, there was the arms procurer to deal with and a plot to foil.

He clutched Mr Dubois's lapels tight and jerked the man up and so close he could smell the ale on his foul breath. 'You stole a lethal cask of gunpowder from the Navy and sold it to the Rouge Noir to be used in a plot to assassinate a number of government ministers. You'll hang for treason, if you live long enough, unless you tell me what's planned.'

'I had nothing to do with it,' Mr Dubois gasped.

Bart shook him hard as he spoke, jerking the man around to drive his words home.

'I have a great deal of evidence to the contrary, two of whom are sitting inside the tavern trying not to get knives through their backs. How long do you think it will take before they blame everything on you in an effort to save their own hides?' Mr Dubois's eyes widened in panic, not as brave as he'd been before. 'Tell me everything you know and I'll recommend you not be hanged and quartered, but transported instead.'

'That's the same as death,' Mr Dubois whined as if he expected sympathy.

'It's less certain than death and a man with your seafaring skills can make quite a life for himself there. You won't have as much success dangling at the end of a rope.'

Mr Dubois glanced back and forth between Bart and Joseph, contemplating his options of which there were few, and even those wouldn't be available to him for much longer. He sagged beneath Bart's grasp. 'It isn't a government building the Rouge Noir is going to destroy, but a private house.'

Panic began to curl deep in Bart stomach. 'Whose house?'

'Lady Camberline's.'

Bart went hollow inside.

'There's a dinner there tonight, with Prince Frederick, the Prime Minister, and many other notable men,' Mr Dubois continued. 'The gunpowder is in the basement and will be set off after dinner. I'm to take the conspirators to France afterwards.'

'Who are you taking? Who arranged this?'

'Lady Camberline, Lord Lefevre and Lord Moreau. Lord Moreau was the one who learned of the gunpowder and helped me to steal it. After the fuse is set, they're to meet me at my ship so I can take them through the blockade to France. They'll return with Napoleon and his army when he invades England.'

'He won't be invading.' Bart shoved Mr Dubois at Mr Smith. 'Take this scum to Mr Flint and tell him to gather his men and meet me at Lady Camberline's. Joseph, get everyone else and come with me. Be quick.'

Bart bolted towards his carriage, shouted instructions to the driver, then jumped inside, followed by Joseph and his men. As the carriage speeded back towards town, he perched on the edge of the squabs, silently willing the horses to run faster to Mayfair and praying Moira had changed her mind about attending the dinner. He refused to lose her again. He had no idea what their future held or if he even could win her heart after the way he'd treated her this morning, but he wanted the chance. He loved her, he always had and fate had given him what so many men never achieved, a second chance. He'd been a fool to throw it away this morning. He thought he'd lost her once to marriage and then he'd gained her back. He would never lose her again.

Chapter Thirteen

Moira sat through five courses and an ice while listening to the gentlemen around her. Government business dominated the conversation and most of it revolved around topics freely written about in the papers, but with far more details and debate. Moira wondered how much of what was being said was meant for open discussion and how much was the result of too much Madeira. Of all the men gathered, Lord Moreau listened the most intently while saying the least. Lord Lefevre and his favoured young lady barely spoke to anyone except each other.

She'd be sure to inform Bart, even if facing him again turned the ice in her mouth from sweet to sour. Last night in his arms, she'd felt cherished as more than a nursemaid but as a woman with thoughts, desires and dreams worthy of respect, or so she'd believed until this morning. She laid her spoon on the plate, finished with the overly sweet final course and trying her best to focus on the conversation around her. A footman leaned past her to remove her plate and she recognised him as one of the men who'd helped Bart outside the museum yesterday. She did nothing to indicate she knew him and he did the same, carrying on with his duties.

At the end of the table, Prince Frederick threw back his head and let out a hearty laugh. All but one person seated near him joined in the joviality. Lord Moreau, his face far more pinched than before, eyed the Prince with barely concealed disgust. Lord Lefevre also turned serious, his insincere smile betraying his distaste for the other guests and his impatience to be away. He glanced at Lady Camberline who sat at the head of the table, as if silently willing her to rise and lead the few ladies present away so the men could at last have their brandy. Both lords' reactions continued to play on Moira's instincts, making her certain they had something to do with the plot. It was Lady Camberline's involvement she found difficult to discern. Lady Camberline listened to her guests, directing the conversation while asking questions, some of which Moira thought were more pressing than they should have been regarding government business, but there'd been nothing specific Moira could point to, no hard evidence to prove the lady was anything more than genuinely interested in politics.

Maybe I'm wrong about the Marchioness.

Maybe she wasn't involved, but being exploited by the two Frenchmen who played on her and her love of France to encourage her to hold dinners like these so they could mingle with top men in the Government and listen and learn. She feared her desire to see good in people was blinding her once again to reality. Lady Camberline was a shrewd and intelligent woman and unlikely to be played upon by other men for their own gains. If she was holding this party it was for her own benefit and probably the Rouge Noir's.

What she needed was proof of Lady Camberline's involvement and she had yet to secure it.

Bart said he found the gunpowder in Lady Camberline's study.

Moira wondered what other incriminating evidence might still be in there. With so many guests and so much happening it wouldn't be difficult to slip down the hall and find out. She would have to be careful, but with these last few hours producing little other evidence, it was very necessary.

At last, Lady Camberline rose and asked the women to follow her through to the sitting room. Moira left the dining room with the other ladies, but fell back behind them as they filed down the wide hallway. She worried the entire time someone might call on her to hurry up and join them, but no one did. It was the first time her ability to be invisible to people had worked to her advantage. When the ladies went into the sitting room, Moira was so far behind them it was easy to dash off the other way without being seen.

She'd been in Lady Camberline's office a week ago with Aunt Agatha for a meeting of the patronesses of the Ladies' Lying-in Hospital. With any luck, it wouldn't be difficult for her to find it again, to search it and return to the sitting room before either the mistress of the house or any of the other guests noticed she was missing.

While Moira walked, she snapped off one of the pearl buttons holding her glove closed. If anyone came looking for her or wondered where she'd been she could simply say she'd gone in search of a maid to try to find someone to fix her glove. It was a flimsy excuse, but it would have to do.

Finding the study wasn't as easy as Moira had anticipated and she wandered down one plastered and gilded hallway dotted with past Camberlines and into two different rooms before she finally found it. Inside, a small fire burned in the grate, casting a soft light on the gilded trim work set in the light green walls. A painting of the late Lord Camberline hung above a narrow table decorated with vases and set between two doors. A writing table stood prominently in the centre of the room with a sofa before it.

Moira went straight to the desk. On top of it was a writing box with fine marquetry and a little lock. Moira tried to open it, but it was locked. She wished again Bart were with her. He would probably know how to open it without damaging either the metal lock or the fine wood around it.

Unable to get inside the box, she began to

search the two wide but shallow drawers set in the front of the desk. Inside the left one there was nothing but fine paper, quills and ink. In the right one she found correspondence, most of which was in French. She flipped through a few and read the contents, but didn't notice anything out of the ordinary except letters exchanged between Lady Camberline and French friends living in the north of England.

Then, one piece of paper at the bottom of the stack caught her attention. It wasn't a letter but a list of names, all of them French. At the top of the list were Lord Lefevre and Lord Moreau. Beneath them were five other gentlemen of French background. Moira recognised many of the names for they were the people her grandmother used to complain about, the ones who'd been quick to come to England, but reluctant to adopt their new country. Her hands began to shake as she realised this could be a list of the Rouge Noir members. She had to get it to Bart.

Moira put the other papers back in the drawer, then folded the list and slipped it in the bodice of her dress. While she straightened the lace along the hem, she accidentally dropped the button of her glove. It hit the wood floor with a plink before bouncing once and then rolling under the secretary against the wall behind the desk. She knelt to retrieve it and, in doing so, failed to hear the footsteps coming down the hall, or the click of the door opening until it was too late.

'Is there something in my office that interests you, Lady Rexford?'

Moira jumped to her feet to see Lady Camberline at the door, her regal features creased with displeasure. 'Yes. I lost the button to my glove which I dropped just now. I'd hoped to find a maid to sew it on for me.'

The words sounded false even to her ears, but she could hardly admit she'd been rifling through the lady's private papers. All she could do was continue her demure act and hope the most Lady Camberline did was insist Moira leave her house.

'And you thought to find a maid in here?' Lady Camberline closed the door with a quick flick of her hand.

'I thought I'd find one lighting the fire in here, but I was mistaken.' She approached the lady, hands clasped innocently in front of her and smiling as wide as she could. 'Shall we return to the others?'

'Let's not play games with one another, Lady Rexford. You think I didn't know you're working with Mr Dyer or who he is?'

Fear struck Moira, but she forced herself to remain calm. 'I don't know what you're talking about. Mr Dyer and I were acquainted once, but there is nothing else between us.'

'Don't lie to me,' the other woman snapped, her usually languid manners faltering under her anger. 'I know who he really works for and that he sent you to spy on me.'

'Then you are part of the Rouge Noir.' Moira didn't protest her innocence, thinking her honesty might lead the woman into saying more and revealing the plot. With it only being the two of them, Moira could still escape. Bart's man was in the house posing as a footman, she could find him and he would help her leave and deliver what she learned to Bart.

'I'm not just a part of it, but its leader. I'm the one who drew together the others, who contacted the Emperor and pledged my allegiance to him, the one who provided the money needed to set our plan in motion and bring about a glorious new future for England.' She spoke with a pride that made Moira feel sick. 'The English Government is weak, with no strong prime minister and a handful of useless men running things. The King is mad and his son a worthless buffoon. Wipe them out and it will bring this country to its knees. Napoleon can sweep in and restore order, the proper kind of order. The man is a visionary.'

'He's a ruthless mercenary who only wants his own glory no matter what it takes to achieve it, including ruining innocent lives,' Moira challenged, amazed at Lady Camberline's boldness.

'No one gathered here tonight is innocent and all of you will get what you deserve.'

Moira touched her throat. 'What do you mean?

'Haven't you figured it out yet?' The evil in Lady Camberline's eyes increased as the terrible realisation dawned on Moira.

'The gunpowder is here.'

'It is. And pretty soon all those useless men drinking my port and bragging about their accomplishments on the Continent will be dead and you will be, too. You will pay for betraying your lineage and me.'

Panic almost stole Moira's voice, but she forced the words through her tight throat. 'You're going to destroy your own house and your son's legacy just to see your sick plan enacted?'

'When the Grand Emperor marches into London, he'll reward me with a larger house and estates, perhaps even your family's.'

'You won't succeed.' Moira glanced at the door, waiting for the moment she could dash out and warn the others, including Bart's man. They had to get away from this house before this wicked woman brought it, and the Government of England, down around them.

Lady Camberline shifted to block the entrance. 'If you think you're going to warn them then you're mistaken. Bursting into my sitting room screaming about me destroying my own house will only make you look like a fool. They'll never believe me capable of such an outlandish thing and would view your ramblings as those of a madwoman related to a mad father and a mad brother.'

Moira sucked in a sharp breath. The secret about the family Aunt Agatha had feared escaping had finally done so and it now trapped Moira. 'How could you betray the country that saved you from the Reign of Terror?'

'Saved me?' Lady Camberline screeched. 'England ruined my life. My parents could have escaped from the Revolutionaries. My mother wrote to Queen Charlotte, a woman she was related to by marriage, begging for help, but she received nothing except silence. She wrote to every contact she had in England, including some of those very men sitting in the dining room, and not one of them dared to intercede on our behalf except Lady Elmsworth, and her only offer was to insist my parents send me to her, to rip me from their love and cast me on to her cold charity. I never saw my parents again. They died at the hands of Madame Guillotine and our entire fortune, legacy and estate were lost, centuries of tradition and lineage wiped away, and with it the only happiness I'd ever known.'

'All of England is not to blame for the mistakes of a few.'

'No one here cared about me. I was the poor French aristocrat everyone pitied and no one wanted to pay for. Lady Elmsworth bundled me into a marriage with an old man whose preference for young ladies made him overlook my lack of wealth. You don't know what I had to endure at Lord Camberline's hands. My son was the only good thing to come of it and even he has turned against me, courting Mademoiselle de Troyen behind my back. The only person who ever cared about me was Lady Lefevre, Lord Lefevre's mother. She used to sit with me as I cried my heart out in my misery. Then one day, she told me how I could have my revenge. She explained how I could steal my husband's papers and pass them to her to give to Napoleon.'

'But it wasn't enough for you, was it?'

'No. I didn't want to simply provide useless or old information, I wanted to act and do something and I will. I'll see this country destroyed, the royal family ripped apart just as my family was, and Napoleon crowned at Westminster Abbey. When it's done, he will return to me all the property stolen from my parents, all my childhood memories fouled by greedy peasants. My son will reign over his ancestral lands here and in France. He will be given one of Napoleon's nieces for a bride and become a member of the Emperor's family. I'll see it all done and I won't let anyone, not you or Mr Dyer, stop me.'

Lord Lefevre burst through the door, a slick sheen of sweat decorating his wide brow and moistening his cravat. Lord Moreau followed behind him, eyes wild with panic.

'Our plot has been discovered,' Lord Lefevre announced, slamming the door closed behind him and locking it.

Lady Camberline's wicked smile dropped. 'What are you talking about?'

'Mr Flint's men are coming up the drive. They'll surround the house and trap us. We must leave at once, reach Mr Dubois and slip away to France before they catch us.' Lord Moreau dashed to one of the windows leading to the garden and slid it open. A cool breeze rustled the curtains on either side while the shouts of men on the drive converging on the house silenced the night birds. Moira's heart leapt. Bart had uncovered the plot. He was here.

Lord Moreau crawled through the window and into the garden, not giving the other two a second thought as he bolted off into the darkness of the grounds.

Lord Lefevre stepped up beside Lady Camberline, more level headed than Lord Moreau. 'He's right. If we don't leave now, they'll hang us for treason. I've sent Madame Bernard for the carriage.'

Lady Camberline didn't even look at him,

but continued to sneer at Moira. 'No, I will have my revenge.'

Moira gaped at the woman. She was on the verge of losing everything, including perhaps her life, and still hate drove her on.

'If we're captured, it will help no one. If we escape, we can find another way to support Napoleon, to see our plans at last made real,' Lord Lefevre tempted, trying to coax her away.

'There will be no other way. We must set off the cask, finish our plan and do what we can to pave the way for the Emperor. We'll light the fuse, then we'll leave.'

'What about her?' Lord Lefevre nodded at Moira.

'Bring her with us. She can die like the rest of them.'

He baulked. 'She's a woman. It doesn't seem right.'

She turned on him. 'You knew all along what was involved in this. Don't become faint of heart now.'

'I'm not going anywhere with you.' Moira prayed Bart and his men would reach the house and her before these two could implement their plan, or kill her first. She didn't doubt Lady Camberline would strangle her with her elegant fingers if it suited her plans. Moira didn't want to die, not with Bart and freedom so close. He might have rebuffed her this morning, but he'd promised to protect her and she believed in the strength of his vow and his honour. He would save her.

'Yes, you are.' Lady Camberline snatched the dagger letter opener off the table beside her, grabbed Moira by the arm, and pressed the sharp end of the blade into Moira's side.

Moira sucked in a breath at the sting, shifting away to keep the dagger from slipping through her stays and deep into her lungs.

'Come along and don't think to cry out or I'll leave you to bleed to death in the passageway before I ignite the fuse.'

Lord Lefevre took one of the candles nestled in a brass holder off the mantel and lit it with a reed from the fireplace. He went to the door on the other side of the painting of old Lord Camberline and pulled it open, revealing a plaster-lined passageway used by servants to enter the room and light the fire without being seen by guests.

Lady Camberline, her fingers digging into Moira's upper arm, pulled her into the passageway and Lord Lefevre followed, closing the door behind him. The light from his candle danced in the breeze of his movements, twisting their shadows on the plain and rough walls.

He slid past them and led the way. The deeper they crept inside the building, the more Moira struggled to keep from panicking. There was no way Bart could find her in this maze of passageways leading to some strange place hidden within the house. At last, they reached a set of stairs leading down into a basement. The smell of onions and damp and mouldering wood permeated the air.

We must be near the kitchen cellar.

It gave Moira some hope. Perhaps a servant would see them, or in checking the building Bart and his men might find her. Moira considered calling out, but she didn't doubt Lady Camberline would kill her the second she did. The woman possessed no remorse, pity or goodness. She was driven only by her wickedness and a craving for revenge.

Down in the dank room, Moira caught the same acrid scent of gunpowder she'd smelled in the sample at Mr Transom's.

'The cask is in the corner. I'll light the wick and we'll run.' Lady Camberline shoved Moira and the knife at Lord Lefevre and took the candle from his hands.

'What about Lady Rexford?' Lord Lefevre asked, as unsure of the plan as Lady Camberline was determined.

'She stays here. Tie her to a post.' She yanked a yard of twine off a nail and handed it to him.

'It doesn't seem sporting to leave her to die like this,' Lord Lefevre protested, his grip on Moira's upper arm loosening.

Moira thought of wrenching free and running, but if he decided to chase her, he would catch her long before she reached the stairs, and then who knew what her fate would be.

Lady Camberline marched up hard on Lord Lefevre, causing him to step back and tug Moira with him. 'I said tie her to a post. No one gave my parents a sporting chance before they murdered them and who here in England cared when they did? Instead, they turned their backs on them, allowing them and thousands of others, including your father, to die. They deserve to feel the same pain.'

Lord Lefevre didn't argue, but took Moira's hands and placed them on either side of a pillar, then began to tie them together.

Moira glanced over her shoulder to where Lady Camberline stood beside the cask, her candle casting a flickering light over the deadly barrel. On the floor snaked a long white fuse.

'When I light this, we'll have only a few minutes to leave and they'll have no way of stopping it.' Lady Camberline picked up the end of the fuse. The diamonds at her ears sparkled in the candlelight, giving her a strange ephemeral air in the midst of the eerie darkness of the basement. 'This is a special fuse. Once it's lit, it can't be put out and Mr Dubois made sure it's well secured to the cask.'

'You won't escape,' Moira said. 'Bart will find you and everyone involved in your plot and you'll face the noose.'

'Neither he nor you will be alive to do so. When the powder catches, it will bring down the house and anyone near it.' She turned to her Lord Lefevre. 'Is she secure?'

'Yes.' Lord Lefevre loosely slipped the ends of the twine one over the other but he didn't tighten them. Instead, he left them to dangle by Moira's fingers. Lady Camberline, with Moira's back to her, couldn't see what he'd done. He looked at her and then the twine.

Moira nodded slightly, understanding he

was giving her a sporting chance to get away once the fuse was lit.

A spark and a flash lit up the room. Moira looked over her shoulder to see the end of the white string burning. Lady Camberline hurried up beside her. 'Now you'll feel the same panic my parents did when they faced the guillotine knowing there was nothing they could do to stop it. You and many others will suffer like they did.' She took Lord Lefevre's hand and pulled him to the stairs. 'Come, we only have five minutes until the cask explodes.'

Once their footsteps disappeared down the corridor, Moira untangled herself from the ropes. She rushed to the fuse and stomped on the flame, but it wouldn't go out. Casting about, she searched for anything sharp she could use to cut the burning end off, but there was nothing except root vegetables and old furniture. There wasn't even a bottle for her to break and pour over the spark or to use to saw through the fuse. She took hold of the fuse and tugged at it, but it wouldn't budge from the cask. She tried to snap it, but it held fast.

She dropped the wicked thing, realising there was nothing she could do except get out and warn as many people as she could of what was about to happen. She grabbed the candle from where Lady Camberline had left it and hurried up the stairs, coming to a stop at the top. The passageway split in two directions, each of them leading off into darkness and who knew where. She couldn't remember which one they'd come down and had no idea how to find her way back to any part of the house. From down in the basement the hiss of the burning fuse continued. She couldn't stand here, helpless, but had to make a choice. She bolted off to her right, thinking this was where they'd come from earlier. Even if it wasn't, it must lead to somewhere inside the house. She would find her way and get to Bart. She was certain, despite this morning, he was nearby. She held on to her belief in his honour as she stumbled down one passageway and then another, searching for a door or any way out, but finding nothing. The white plaster seemed to stretch on for ever and fear threatened to choke the breath out of her, but she beat it back. She would be strong and brave like Bart and escape. She would have her life and love and a future.

'Everyone out of the house. There's a cask of gunpowder in the basement prepared to blow this place to pieces,' Bart shouted as he and his men and Mr Flint's flooded into the Camberline sitting room. Behind him the rest of his men fanned out, a few of them rushing to collect the servants while the others searched the house for the gunpowder.

The gathered gentlemen and ladies stopped their card games and their chatter to stare at him, dumbfounded. Bart scanned their shocked faces, searching for Moira's, but she wasn't there. Neither were Lord Lefevre, Lord Moreau or Lady Camberline. He braced himself against the onslaught of guilt and worry, the same one which had seized him when he'd approached Lady Fallworth's carriage and seen the stricken face of her driver while he'd talked to Bart's men.

Prince Frederick, grasping the seriousness of the situation, was the first to move. 'You heard the man, out now, unless you all want to meet your maker.'

He hustled the ladies and the reluctant gentlemen along.

'Your Highness.' Bart rushed up to the Prince while his men led the bewildered guests through the halls towards the front door and the collection of carriages waiting on the drive to take them to safety. 'Where's Lady Rexford?'

'I don't know. She was with us at dinner, then went through with the ladies. I haven't seen her since.'

Bart darted back down the hallway towards the centre of the house, hoping he wasn't too late, that the fuse had not been lit and he and Moira were not now about to be in the midst of an explosion capable of bringing down the house. Thankfully, the house stood in the middle of an extensive garden, mitigating the possible damage to the streets, houses and people surrounding it.

'Moira! Moira!' he called as he ran, passing footmen and maids being ushered out of the house by his men. If he didn't find Moira, he'd see to it the people responsible for her death were drawn and quartered, their titles and privileges be damned. He wouldn't allow their rank to protect them this time.

He stopped and asked more than one guest if they'd seen Moira, but none had. Dread began to build in his chest, like the time he'd watched a regiment cut down by a French ambush during a battle. He and his soldiers had ridden as fast as they could to try to help them, but it'd been too late.

Then, through the throng of hurrying people, he spied Joseph.

'Have you seen Lady Rexford? Did she go out with the servants or another way?'

'No, I haven't seen her.'

'I have to find her.'

'This house is like a maze. If you get lost, and the fuse has been set, you may not make it out in time.'

'I won't leave her to die.' All chance of claiming the happiness he'd imagined in her arms last night, the one he'd tried to throw away this morning, would end if he didn't find her. He couldn't allow it to happen or for her to die thinking he didn't want to spend the rest of his life with her.

'Mr Dyer.' One of Mr Flint's men rushed up to him. 'We caught Lady Camberline and Lord Lefevre outside, along with Lord Moreau.'

'Was Lady Rexford with them?'

'There's a young lady with them, yes. Blonde and small, wearing a red dress.'

'Moira.' They must have taken her with them when they'd tried to flee, intending to use her as a hostage or some other guarantee against capture. It hadn't worked.

A group of servants flooded past him and out the front door, Mr Smith following behind them. 'That's the last of the servants, sir.'

'Then let's get out of here.' He ran from the house followed by his men. There were no more carriages, so they bolted across the wide grounds towards the wall at the far end, running fast to place as much distance as possible between them and the house.

They reached the large iron gate at the end of the drive and jogged through it. Their footsteps echoed down the street as they ran to where Mr Flint and the others from the Alien Office waited. They pushed back the crowd who watched the great house in the distance, waiting to see if the scare had been for nothing or if there was indeed a bomb inside that would detonate.

'Where are they? Where did they take the traitors?' he asked Mr Flint's man.

'To his carriage.' He pointed to the dark green carriage behind the crowd. In the flicker of the carriage lanterns, he caught site of Moira's blonde hair. She stood with her back to him near Lord Lefevre, Lord Moreau and Lady Camberline.

Bart pushed his way through the crowd to reach her, to hold her and kiss her lips. He didn't care who was watching or what they saw. He would be hers and he would give her everything she desired, a home, children, and his heart. He rushed up to her, took her by the arm and spun her around, letting go of the woman the moment she faced him.

'What are you doing?' Madame Bernard screeched, her eyes red from tears. 'Why is Lord Lefevre in shackles? He's innocent, we both are!'

'Where's Lady Rexford?' Bart demanded.

'She's in the house,' a female voice with a French accent hissed.

Bart turned to see Lady Camberline standing beside Mr Flint's carriage, two armed men flanking her. She didn't wear the shackles of her companions, her title and sex sparing her from the harsh treatment she deserved.

Bart strode up to her, vile hatred tingeing every step. 'What did you say?'

'She's in there, tied to a pillar in a cellar beside the cask, the one I lit to go off at any moment.'

Bart stared at her in horror and then at the house. He was about to rush back in and find

Moira, to tear the place apart with his bare hands in order to reach her, when a deafening roar and a ball of fire lit up the night. The screams of the gathered ladies were lost in the rush of wind roaring across the grounds and blunted by the high wall. They all ducked as bits of bricks and wood rained down around them. Flames shot up into the sky, lighting up the trees and the faces of everyone before dying down into a blaze to gut what remained of the house like the horror and grief did to Bart's heart.

He'd failed her.

It should have been me. I should have been the one to die, not her.

Moira had believed that Bart, deep down under the hard magistrate and the dedicated bachelor, was a good man worthy of her care and devotion. She'd been wrong. He hadn't been worthy of her and he'd lost her for good because of it. If he hadn't turned his back on her after they'd made love, but held her close, kept her in his house and away from these evil people, she might be alive and waiting for him to come home. Instead, he'd left her to die alone, believing he hadn't loved her enough to make her his wife.

Bart staggered on his feet while the wicked Marchioness laughed at his misery.

'Come on, you, get in the carriage,' Mr Flint commanded Lady Camberline. 'You'll tell us everyone who was working with you.'

'I won't, for they will rise up and complete what I didn't do.'

'Get in the carriage,' Mr Flint snapped.

The carriage door closed on her further protests and the shackles of the two French lords clanked while they were led away. Bart didn't care. All he could do was stare at the flames and everything he'd lost. He'd let her go too easily five years ago and again today. Tonight, when he'd fought for her at last, he'd been too late. There would be no more chances, no more listening to her charming voice or enjoying her tender presence. She was gone for ever and it was all his fault.

'I'm sorry, Moira,' he breathed, but his apology wasn't enough, it never would be for she would never hear it. Nor would she ever have the chance to obtain all the things she'd wanted, the happiness she'd deserved and he'd wanted to give to her.

'Mr Dyer?' Bart didn't turn to face Joseph. All he could do was stare at the house as an outer wall collapsed into the inferno. 'There's someone you should speak with.'

'I don't want to see anyone.' He wanted Joseph to go away and leave him to his grief and regrets. The plots, his assignment, accomplishments and determination to end the Rouge Noir meant nothing to him without Moira. In their time together, she'd given him something really worth fighting for and a reason to be a better man. He'd repaid her kindness with pain, sorrow and the end of her life.

'I think you will want to see this one,' Joseph insisted.

'Bart?' The voice of an angel drifted over him.

Bart whirled around to see Moira standing in the street behind him. The light of the fire flickered across her face and glinted in her blonde hair. It was the most cherished sight he could have imagined, more so than England after the horrors of war in Europe, or the end of a battle which he'd survived. 'You're alive.'

'I am.'

'I thought you were dead.' He rushed to close the distance between them, taking her in his arms and meeting her lips with a kiss from deep inside his soul. The despair of only a moment before was replaced by her. He hadn't lost her, not to his stupidity of this morning or the delays of tonight. She was here with him and he would never let her go again.

She met his kiss with a passion of her own before breaking from it to lean back in his arms. 'I assume this means you've changed your mind about us being together.'

He slid his hand to cup her cheek, marvelling at the softness of her skin and her presence. 'I was a fool to think I could live without you, or that my work is enough to keep me happy. It isn't. All my victories and everything I've ever strived for mean nothing if I don't have you to share them with. Marry me, Moira, please.'

Moira held her breath as she stared up at Bart. Rubble and dust whitened the shoulders of his coat and the light of the fire played in the darkness of his hair, but he didn't notice any of it, only her. Tears filled her eyes, driving away the stinging smoke hovering in the air and the last of her sadness and doubts. In the darkness of the passages, when she'd struggled to escape the house, she'd thought of Bart, drawing from inside her a memory of his courage to bolster hers. She'd never in those moments believed she would escape to find him holding her as if she was the most precious thing in the world. He wanted her to be his wife, to share his life with her. She'd caught the amazement in his eyes when he'd turned to see her, felt the relief which had swept through him when he'd taken her in his arms and kissed her. It told her more than any words could how much she meant to him and the true depths of his love. He'd held back from her this morning, but he didn't hold back from her now. She threw her arms around him, and whispered in his ear, 'Yes, I will be your wife.'

She brought her lips to his, offering him the same kiss of promise he offered her. He would be her husband and the father of her children and she would be his wife. Nothing, not his fears or hers or the expectations of family and society, would ever part them again.

A crash of bricks and wood made them turn to see the single remaining wall of Camberline House crumble into the flames. In their bright flicker, Moira studied Bart and the serious set of his jaw. 'The rest of the members of the Rouge Noir are still out there. They must be unmasked and found so they can never harm you or anyone else ever again.'

'I know who they are.' She tugged the list out of her bodice and held it up to him. 'I found this in Lady Camberline's study.'

He took the paper and read the names, a new determination entering his eyes.

'Come with me.' He grabbed her by the hand and pulled her to where Mr Flint stood taking to his men. Bart handed him the list. 'Sir, we believe these people are also members of the Rouge Noir and must be apprehended before they can flee.'

Mr Flint read the list in the light of the burning house. 'I agree. I'll see to it at once.'

'Sir?'

'You've done well, Dyer, and you deserve a rest. My men will see to it these traitors are caught.' Mr Flint clapped Bart on the shoulder, then nodded at Moira. 'You have other matters to attend to.'

His order given, he walked off to speak with his men.

'Are you disappointed you're not seeing it through to the end?' Moira asked, clutching Bart's hand tightly, not wanting to come between him and the work he loved.

'How could I be? I have you. It's all I need.'
He touched his lips to hers and everything
around them faded away.

Epilogue

'Guilty.'

'Guilty.'

'Guilty.'

Bart watched from where he stood beside Mr Steed in the audience behind the solicitor and barrister for the Crown prosecuting the case. As 'guilty' continued to ring through the House of Lords, Lady Camberline's face fell along with those of her barrister and solicitor. Bart smiled in satisfaction, then glanced up to the ladies' gallery where Moira watched the proceedings. She returned a subdued smile, as happy as he was to see justice done and this period of their lives finally at an end.

Lady Camberline was the last of the Rouge Noir to stand trial. Lord Lefevre, Lord Moreau and the others on the list provided by Moira had already faced their judgement and gone to meet their makers. Those further down the list had suffered less punishment, being stripped of their titles and estates. Bart and Moira had been called as witnesses in each of those trials making Mr and Mrs Dyer the most notorious married couple in England, especially when details of their involvement in what was now being called the Rouge Noir Plot became public.

At last it was Bart's father's turn to rise and call out his vote. 'Guilty.'

Before he sat down, he nodded his approval at Bart.

An hour later, with the verdicts read and the sentence of death passed, Bart waded through the many men praising him and Mr Flint outside the House of Lords' chamber to meet Moira.

She glowed as she watched him approach, the slight stoutness of her middle already beginning to show beneath her fitted pelisse. In a few months there would be something besides his trials to occupy Bart's time and he welcomed the coming distraction.

'Well done,' Moira congratulated when he reached her.

'I couldn't have done it without you.'

She laid her hand on her slightly swollen belly. 'I had to do it for everyone I love, including you.'

He took her hand and covered it with his. 'And how is my little one this morning?'

'Quite active. I imagine he or she will be just like his father.'

'If it's a boy, I hope so. If it's a girl, I want her to be like her mother.' He raised her hand to his lips and kissed it, then settled it in the crook of his arm and escorted her outside.

'It's hard to believe it's over at last.' She sighed as they left the shadow of the building for the sun of the street.

'For us, perhaps, but not for others. My mother would like us to join them and the rest of the family for dinner tonight. Since the case is settled and we're free to speak about it, I'm sure she and my sisters-in-law are planning to ply you for gossip.'

'I would hate to disappoint them. Speaking of gossip…' Moira removed two letters from her reticule and held them up '… I received a letter from Aunt Agatha this morning and one from Freddy.'

'I told you they'd come around.' Despite all of England, and even Bart's father, praising them, Freddy and Aunt Agatha had remained a stubborn pair, offering little in the way of reconciliation, even after Bart and Moira were married. The estrangement had weighed hard on Moira, but Bart had told her to be patient, sure his old friend would eventually forgive her.

'It seems I'm not the only Fallworth to create a scandal. Freddy and Miss Kent were married last week and very soon our child will have a new cousin to play with.'

'A little sin usually humbles a man enough to forgive others.'

'Indeed, and given Freddy's sin, Aunt Agatha feels she is at last able to forgive mine, though she curses being surrounded by nieces and nephews who insist on flouting convention.'

'I enjoy flouting convention.' With his thumb, Bart stroked the underside of her palm, offering a promise of what would pass between them tonight.

She winked at him with a wickedness to make him wish they were already home, but with men filing out of the House of Lords they would not have a moment's peace.

Mr Steed approached them, beaming like a street lamp. 'With this kind of notoriety, I imagine your career as a stipendiary magistrate is over.'

'It is, and good riddance to it. I have a wife and soon a child to think about.' He exchanged an affectionate smile with Moira, making his solicitor partner roll his eyes.

'I hope you don't intend to give up your work as a barrister. I've already had twenty different men make enquiries into retaining our services. By the time your notoriety wears off, assuming it ever does, you might be richer than most of these lords.'

'I already am.' He pressed his lips to Moira's, not caring where they stood or who saw them. Everything was as it should be, everyone safe, and their future as bright as the afternoon sun.

* * * * *

If you enjoyed this story, you won't want to miss these other great reads from Georgie Lee

A TOO CONVENIENT MARRIAGE
MISS MARIANNE'S DISGRACE
THE CINDERELLA GOVERNESS
THE SECRET MARRIAGE PACT

MILLS & BOON®

HISTORICAL

AWAKEN THE ROMANCE OF THE PAST

A sneak peek at next month's titles...

In stores from 2nd November 2017:

- **Regency Christmas Wishes** – Carla Kelly, Christine Merrill *and* Janice Preston
- **A Pregnant Courtesan for the Rake** – Diane Gaston
- **Lord Hunter's Cinderella Heiress** – Lara Temple
- **The Wallflower's Mistletoe Wedding** – Amanda McCabe
- **Her Christmas Knight** – Nicole Locke
- **The Hired Man** – Lynna Banning

Just can't wait?
Buy our books online before they hit the shops!
www.millsandboon.co.uk

Also available as eBooks.

1017/04

MILLS & BOON®

EXCLUSIVE EXTRACT

Unhappily betrothed to each other, Lord Hunter agrees to help Nell convince another man she's a worthy bride. But their lessons in flirtation inspire desire which has Hunter longing to keep Nell for himself...

Read on for a sneak preview of
LORD HUNTER'S CINDERELLA HEIRESS
the first book in Lara Temple's linked Regency series
WILD LORDS AND INNOCENT LADIES

'This most certainly isn't a waltz.' Nell laughed as he swung her out of the way of a portly couple who were clearly interpreting the music as a reel.

Her laugh collapsed into a gasp as her attempt to avoid stepping on his boot brought her sharply against him and somehow his leg slid between hers, straining her skirts against her thighs in a manner that definitely didn't happen in a waltz.

'I never said it was. No, don't pull back yet. Trust me.' His voice was as warm as the cider still tumbling through her and she didn't even manage to scoff at this outrageous demand, too stunned by the sensation of being held there in the middle of the chaos, just swaying gently against his thigh, his head bent next to hers.

She had ridden astride more times than she could count; she knew what it felt to have something firm and muscular between her thighs, the pull of fabric over that sensitive inner flesh. But not this. They continued to move, with no regard to the rhythm, his leg shifting between hers, hard and muscled, scraping and pressing in a way that should have been thoroughly uncomfortable and it was, it was, just not in any way that she wanted to stop. It made her skin heat and tingle and begin to shake and for one mad moment, still misted in the fumes of the cider, she thought it might be the return of that horrible fear, but that thought passed immediately. It wasn't that kind of shaking. It was… She was coming apart and reforming around a completely new heat at her centre, that burst of sun had sunk from her chest and stomach and settled between her legs, insistent and aggravating and in a dialogue with his body she could barely follow.

He bent his head, his mouth beside her ear as if talking to her, and perhaps he was, if talking was that gentle slide of breath over the curve of her ear and every now and then his lips brushed its tip and the heat between her legs would gather in and prepare to shoot up through her to capture that caress and out into the heavens.

Don't miss
LORD HUNTER'S CINDERELLA HEIRESS
By Lara Temple

Available November 2017
www.millsandboon.co.uk

Join Britain's BIGGEST Romance Book Club

50% OFF your first parcel

- **EXCLUSIVE offers** every month

- **FREE delivery direct** to your door

- **NEVER MISS a title**

- **EARN Bonus Book points**

MILLS & BOON®

Why shop at millsandboon.co.uk?

Each year, thousands of romance readers find their perfect read at millsandboon.co.uk. That's because we're passionate about bringing you the very best romantic fiction. Here are some of the advantages of shopping at www.millsandboon.co.uk:

* **Get new books first**—you'll be able to buy your favourite books one month before they hit the shops

* **Get exclusive discounts**—you'll also be able to buy our specially created monthly collections, with up to 50% off the RRP

* **Find your favourite authors**—latest news, interviews and new releases for all your favourite authors and series on our website, plus ideas for what to try next

* **Join in**—once you've bought your favourite books, don't forget to register with us to rate, review and join in the discussions

Visit **www.millsandboon.co.uk**
for all this and more today!